Detective Beavers cleared his throat. "I'll need to get fingerprint samples from each of you to eliminate some of those we took from the crime scene."

"What about our quilts?" Birdie asked.

"The three of you found Claire Terry's body. Then her quilt gets stolen and so do yours. I'm wondering what the connection is."

The longer I sat, the harder the chair became. "Coincidence?"

"I don't believe in coincidence."

"How was Claire killed?"

"OD."

"She did drugs? She didn't seem the type."

"Not recreational. Prescription."

"How do you know it wasn't an accident or suicide?"

"We believe she fought with her killer."

Beavers stood and handed us each another card. "If you have pictures of your quilts, make sure we get copies for identification purposes in case we ever find them."

"You don't sound very hopeful," I sighed.

"You never know. You ladies be careful. I don't want to alarm you, but a possible connection between the murder and the theft bothers me . . ."

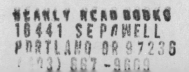

FORGET
ME KNOT

MARY MARKS

KENSINGTON PUBLISHING CORP.

http://www.kensingtonbooks.com

KENSINGTON BOOKS are published by

Kensington Publishing Corp.
119 West 40th Street
New York, NY 10018

All Kensington Titles, Imprints, and Distributed Lines are available at special quantity discounts for bulk purchases for sales promotions, premiums, fund-raising, and educational or institutional use. Special book excerpts or customized printings can also be created to fit specific needs. For details, write or phone the office of the Kensington special sales manager: Kensington Publishing Corp., 119 West 40th Street, New York, NY 10018, attn: Special Sales Department, Phone: 1-800-221-2647.

Kensington and the K logo Reg. U.S. Pat & TM Off.

ISBN-13: 978-0-7582-9205-6
ISBN-10: 0-7582-9205-8
First Kensington Mass Market Edition: January 2014

eISBN-13: 978-0-7582-9206-3
eISBN-10: 0-7582-9206-6
First Kensington Electronic Edition: January 2014

10 9 8 7 6 5 4 3 2 1

Printed in the United States of America

For Lisa, Justin, and Amanda,
my children over whom I kvell.
And for my beloved sister
Mici Marks
of blessed memory.

ACKNOWLEDGMENTS

This is the part of the book that sounds like an acceptance speech at an awards ceremony. (I should be so lucky.) Nevertheless, if not for the help and encouragement of so many people, this book would never have seen the light of day.

Top of the list: deepest thanks to my daughter Lisa Rojany Buccieri, who prodded me to take writing classes at the UCLA Extension Writers' Program. You were right, honey. I needed help. Your support has meant the world to me.

Eternal gratitude to my teachers and mentors Jerrilyn Farmer and Barbara Abercrombie for believing in me and pushing me and telling me (oh so gently) when my work was crap. You brought out the best.

Appreciation and affection go to my writing posse, who gave me such valuable encouragement and feedback over the years: Cheryl Jacobs, Rabbi Julie Pelc Adler, Tracy Tatta, and Barbara Lodge. Too bad we missed being on Oprah's Book Club by a couple of years. I am also indebted to my fellow workshop participants Cyndra Gernet and Lori Dillman for their perceptive feedback.

Special acknowledgment goes to a number of experts who generously shared their knowledge: Linda Greenberg Loper, Deputy DA (retired) Los Angeles County; Officer Rob Trulik, Senior Lead Officer LAPD; Barbara De Pol and Terry Hayes for their expertise in Catholic Church practices; and Hazel Wetts, who gives so generously of her time to the blind.

I am also grateful to my awesome agent and editor, Dawn Dowdle at Blue Ridge, for believing in my book and making me a better writer.

Finally, thanks to John Scognamiglio and all the wonderful folks at Kensington for helping me to put a check mark on my bucket list. You made my dream come true.

TUESDAY

TUESDAY

CHAPTER 1

For years, Tuesday mornings were sacred. No matter what, my friend Lucy, her neighbor Birdie, and I spent the day together working on our quilts. This particular Tuesday was supposed to be just another quilty morning, but that was before we found the body.

We headed toward another quilter's house, a potential fourth member of our little group. Lucy drove down Ventura Boulevard carefully, the way women over the age of sixty often did. If I were driving, we would have been there by now. At fifty-five I was the youngest and hadn't yet reached the age of hugging the right shoulder of the freeway at forty-five miles per hour. So I leaned back in the rear seat of Lucy Mondello's vintage 1960 Cadillac, sank into the luxurious creamy leather, and enjoyed the ride.

As we drove, I stared at the back of her head. It resembled the Santa Monica Mountains during a brush fire. Bright orange tufts of hair sprang up like burning chaparral from her scalp. "You've done something different to your hair, Lucy."

"Well, I decided to try a new color late last night. When I finally got to bed, Ray woke up and turned on the lamp. Then real quick he turned it off and rolled with his back to me. The bed started to shake, and I got scared. I said, 'Ray! We're having an earthquake.' Then he snorted and laughed out loud."

"He didn't." Birdie turned to look at Lucy.

"Oh yes he did. He told me, 'All you need are floppy shoes and a big red nose.'"

We all laughed. I could picture him stifling his laughter in the pillow to avoid hurting Lucy's feelings.

Lucy sighed. "He's lucky I love him so much or he'd be in bow-coo trouble today." Then she glanced at me in the rearview mirror. "Is it really so bad?"

What could I say to my best friend? Ray was right—you do look like Bozo? I just smiled and shrugged.

"I guess I'll have to cut this mess off."

Birdie clutched the grab bar above the passenger door with one hand while she nervously twirled the end of her long white braid with the other. Birdie Watson had been uneasy around cars ever since her driver's license was confiscated. While attempting to park her car a couple of years ago, she hit the accelerator instead of the brake and ran her car through the wall of our favorite quilt store. Because she was over seventy, the DMV made her go through a driving test, which she failed when she rammed a police car while attempting to parallel park.

"You could wear your hair like Jamie Lee Curtis or Dame Judi Dench. You'd look really good in short hair." Leave it to Birdie to try to smooth things over. She was the earth mother type, a magnet for the lonely and wounded. Clearly Birdie's kindness was the main reason Claire was drawn to our group. None of us really knew much about the woman we were visiting, so we all agreed—today would be a sort of trial. If we liked Claire Terry, she was in. If not, well, we hadn't thought that far yet.

We drove west on Ventura Boulevard, approaching Woodland Hills. The Google printout directed us to *drive south on Canoga Avenue.* "Claire's street should be about a mile up."

Lucy got into the left turn lane. "You know, I'm having second thoughts about this. As a matter of fact, I've had one of my funny feelings all morning."

I did a mental eye roll. Lucy often claimed she had a sixth sense about things, but I attributed her insights to natural intuition sharpened by raising five sons. "What are you channeling now?"

"Claire Terry is only in her early forties. Why would she want to hang out with a bunch of 'old broads' like us?" Lucy waggled her fingers in one of those air quotes she was so fond of.

"Speak for yourself. I'm not old yet. I'm still having hot flashes."

"Seriously, how much do we know about her anyway?"

Birdie looked at Lucy. "She's the best quilter in the guild. Always wins first prize in the shows. I always make a point to talk to her at the guild meetings, and when I suggested we get together, she seemed truly pleased. I think she's just shy."

Lucy smiled. "You're always befriending somebody. Let's hope she doesn't turn out to be a psycho like that other woman—what was her name? The one who voted for Bush and stole your antique scissors?"

"Eleanor Peavy."

I pointed my finger to the left. "Here she is." We were in an upscale neighborhood with Beamers and Mercedeses parked in the driveways. Lucy steered the huge old Caddy awkwardly onto Claire's circular drive, black fenders thrusting up in back like shark fins.

Claire's large Mediterranean-style house had a red tile roof and stucco the color of ripe cantaloupe. The front door was painted cobalt blue.

Birdie spoke first. "Will you look at this! I had no idea Claire lived in such a beautiful home."

Lucy turned off the motor. "Wow. What does her husband do for a living?"

I remembered hearing some stories at the board meetings about Claire Terry's divorce several years ago. I couldn't stand people who gossiped and I never repeated a confidence. However, telling stuff to my best friends wasn't gossiping, it was data sharing. "Messy divorce. Her money."

"Kids?"

"I don't think so."

Lucy was way taller than me and all elbows and angles. She seemed to unfold as she got out of the car like a large manila envelope refusing to stay closed. In addition to always wearing perfect makeup, Lucy was known for dressing with a theme. Once I'd seen no fewer than four Christmas sweaters hanging in her closet. Today's theme was gold. Her size ten slacks were honey colored and her blouse was a leopard print. She wore a hunk of amber the size of a hard-boiled egg on a gold chain around her neck.

I gathered my rather large fabric tote bag and dragged it across the seat. Inside was my latest quilt, made of blue and white fabrics in a pattern called Corn and Beans. Also inside was a wooden quilting hoop and a little plastic box full of quilting notions—special coated thread designed to slide easily through the fabric without tangling, small scissors to cut the thread, needles for quilting called "betweens," a metal thimble to push the needle through the fabric, a round circle of rubber to grab a needle stuck in the fabric, and an emergency package of M&M's.

I scooted out Birdie's side of the car and tugged

the hem of my white T-shirt down over my size sixteen Liz Claiborne stretch denim jeans. When you had a figure like mine, you used every trick in the book to camouflage the excess weight. Shirts stopping at midhip were the most flattering, but they did tend to ride up.

I opened Birdie's door to help her out of the car. When I bent over, my hair flopped in my face. Having curly hair is both a blessing and a curse. On the one hand, you don't have to blow-dry your hair, because it could become frizzy. On the other hand, your choice of hair styles is limited. My curly mop hasn't changed since I marched in antiwar demonstrations in the seventies. Well, almost. Now it's gray.

Birdie winced as she grabbed my hand and slowly got out of the car, putting her weight on her arthritic knees. Once she was vertical, she adjusted her signature denim overalls.

I suspected Birdie was a hippie back in the day. A while back she showed us a blue chambray work shirt she embroidered with brightly colored rainbows and peace signs in the 1960s for her husband, Russell. Somehow, I just couldn't picture prissy old Russell Watson wearing mutton chops and love beads.

I walked slowly with Birdie, who limped in her brown suede Birkenstocks. Lucy loped ahead of us with her long-legged, no nonsense stride. Anyone watching us would have seen three ordinary women of a certain age carrying large tote bags full of quilting stuff. Nobody would have taken a second look at us. Older women became invisible, especially in the culture of LA.

Lucy reached out and rang the doorbell. No one answered. After a minute, she rang the bell again. Still no answer.

"We're on time, aren't we?" Birdie whispered.

Lucy raised her eyebrows and gave us a meaningful look. "My bad feeling is getting worse."

I walked over to a front window, shoved my glasses back on my nose, and peered inside. The walls were painted a golden yellow. Wide hardwood planks covered the floors. A quilted masterpiece featuring appliquéd flowers and birds hung prominently on the wall behind a comfy-looking sofa.

There was something on the hallway floor. I squeezed closer to the window and put my hands around my face to cut out the glare.

A pair of red shoes . . .

Feet inside the shoes, and legs . . .

I couldn't see more because the wall was in the way.

"I think there's someone lying on the floor."

CHAPTER 2

"See if you can open the door." I stared at the body on the floor.

Lucy turned the knob, but the door was locked. She rushed over to the window. "Let me see."

Birdie came over, too, mashing her nose against the glass. "Good heavens. Is that Claire?"

I was about to pull my cell phone out of my bag to call 9-1-1 when a slender blonde in a red halter top and white shorts came out of the house next-door. She was carrying gardening shears. I hurried over to her yard and asked, "Do you know the woman who lives here? Claire Terry?"

"Of course. Why?"

"I think something has happened to her."

"Wha'?"

"Nobody answered the doorbell, so I peeked in the window. Someone is lying on the floor."

"Oh my God. I know where she keeps a spare key." She threw down the gardening shears and ran over to the corner of Claire's house, reached through a locked wrought iron gate, and took a key from somewhere on the side of the house. Then she sprinted like an athlete to the front door and opened the lock while I power walked right behind her.

She stuck her head inside the door. "Claire?" No answer.

"Over there." Birdie pointed to the red shoes.

We rushed forward and stopped suddenly at the sight of Claire Terry, lying on her back with a ring of dried yellow vomit around her mouth.

The blonde gasped. The whites of her eyes showed, and the skin of her face turned green. Her voice, small and high pitched, squeaked, "Is she dead?"

Claire lay on her back with one arm at her side and the other resting on her stomach. She wore a red cotton sundress and those red shoes. Faint freckles dotted her pale pretty face, turned slightly to the right, and her eyes stared vacantly at the wall. Her long dark hair spread out behind her head in a tangled fan. Under her right cheek her hair was crusted with vomit. She looked like a delicate porcelain doll discarded by a careless child.

I got on my knees and put my fingertips on her neck. Her flesh felt cold and wooden, and she smelled sour. I shuddered and felt light-headed. Tiny polka dots danced before my eyes and I thought I might faint. I blinked rapidly, took a deep breath, and quickly pulled my hand away. "No pulse."

Birdie clutched Lucy's arm. "Oh dear. What about CPR?"

The blonde looked at the vomit on Claire's face. "You don't mean mouth to mouth. . . ."

Lucy pointed. "Look at her eyes. People don't sleep with their eyes wide open unless they're dead."

She was right. This pretty young woman was gone. Pity squeezed my heart.

Birdie's voice hovered on the edge of hysteria. "Well, put a mirror under her nose. Does anyone have a mirror in their purse?"

I looked at Birdie and shook my head. "We're too late, Birdie. She's gone."

Lucy put her arm around Birdie's shoulders. "Come on, hon'. Let's go outside and wait while Martha calls nine-one-one."

I reached over and pushed her eyelids closed. Then I got on all fours, grunted, and stood up butt first; there was no other graceful way to do it. Being overweight was such a bummer.

I pulled my cell phone out of my tote bag and dialed 9-1-1. One recent TV muckraker reported the emergency lines in Los Angeles were often so busy a person could wait several minutes to get through. This must have been one of those times. *How long would Claire have lain there if we hadn't come along? Who would have been the first to discover her?* How awful to end your life alone.

I thought about how I wanted to die: in my own bed, surrounded by sobbing family and friends. My ex-husband, Aaron, would grab my hand and tell me tearfully, "I was so wrong to leave you. I was a total jerk. You were the best thing that ever happened to me. Can you ever forgive me?"

Tears stung my eyes as the poignant scene played out in my head. I'd look at him and whisper with my dying breath, "It's too late, moron."

Then a voice came on the line. "Nine-one-one Emergency."

"I want to report a death."

"What's the address?"

I turned to Claire's neighbor for the information. The dispatcher instructed us to go outside and wait for the police.

The blonde stood transfixed, staring at Claire's body. The way she ran, I thought she was much younger. I was envious of her slender thighs and the way her shorts didn't ride up at the crotch, like mine would if I owned a pair—which I didn't. I couldn't wear shorts because of my ample thighs. The skin of her cheeks was unnaturally tight and tugged a teensy bit at the corners of her mouth. I estimated she was closer to my age than Claire's.

I would bet my new microwave her perky boobs were one hundred percent saline. If I put my large breasts inside a halter top, they'd fall to my waist.

Los Angeles was full of women like Claire's neighbor—hovering around menopause and desperate to hang on to their lost youth. Women who still wanted to be seen.

"My name's Martha. Martha Rose." I touched her arm, attempting to snap her out of her trance.

She looked at me with tears rolling down her cheeks. "I'm Ingrid. Claire and I weren't just neighbors, we were friends. I can't believe she's dead."

"Come on." I took her arm and gently led her away. "Let's go outside with the others and wait for the police."

Ingrid sniffed and came with me.

Lucy patted Birdie's hand as they sat on a painted wooden bench outside the front door. Birdie dabbed her eyes with a tissue and kept muttering, "Poor, poor Claire."

I introduced Ingrid to my friends and she smiled politely. The muscles in her face barely moved.

"We have to wait for the police."

We sat on the porch steps. Ingrid put her forehead in her hands and cried softly. "What do you think happened?"

"Well, she could have had a seizure or a stroke or even a heart attack," I said.

Ingrid looked ready to puke.

I edged away a little. "Are you okay?"

She stood up. "I'm feeling woozy. I've gotta go home." She staggered back through her yard and disappeared inside her house.

Lucy sighed. "If I were a drinker, I'd be going for a stiff one right about now."

Birdie nodded. "I wouldn't blame you. I could use a nice stiff cup of tea myself."

A couple minutes later the sirens announced the arrival of the EMTs with an ambulance; right behind them were the police and a fire truck. Uniformed officers secured the house and told us to stay put.

Twenty minutes later a silver Camry arrived and parked on the street. A tall man got out, put on a gray suit jacket, and ducked under the yellow tape stretched across the driveway. A shorter man got out of the passenger side and followed behind him.

The tall one was about my age, only in much better shape. He had a shock of gray hair and a white mustache.

Be still my beating heart. There were two things in a man I was a sucker for: foreign accents and neat facial hair.

He stopped briefly and nodded at us. "Ladies." Then he disappeared inside the house with his much younger partner.

Ten minutes later they came back outside. "I'm Detective Arlo Beavers with the LAPD." The tall one handed each of us a business card. "I'd like to ask you some questions."

His dark eyes looked at me and I morphed into a silly, simpering bowl of vanilla pudding. Heck. I hated when that happened. I didn't feel out of control very often; I was a natural leader. Treasurer of our quilt guild. Retired UCLA administrator. Now my self-assurance slowly slipped away.

How did we know Claire? When did we arrive? How did we get in the house? Where did we go once we were in the house? Did we touch the body? Did we see anyone else? Where is the neighbor now? During the interview, he sent his partner to question Ingrid. I spilled my guts. By the end of the interview, Detective Beavers knew every single detail we knew about Claire. I even dished the dirt on the rumors surrounding her divorce. Rumors I had kept from my best friends. I had no shame.

When he was done, he smiled. "Thank you for your cooperation. You're free to go. If you think of anything else, call me."

Was it just my imagination, or was he looking at me again? All of a sudden, I had the pulse rate of a hummingbird and a hot flash was coming on.

Lucy drove away slowly from Claire's house, carefully steering the huge Caddy around the police cars parked on the street. She narrowly missed hitting the coroner's van coming toward us.

Once Lucy hit Canoga Avenue, she squeezed the steering wheel and sped up, exceeding the speed limit by a good ten miles per hour. "I *told* you I had a bad feeling."

Birdie clutched the grab bar. "I wonder how she died. All that vomit . . . Maybe she had a seizure. Do you know if she was epileptic?"

"What would account for the blood?" I wondered aloud.

"What blood?"

I glanced at Detective Beavers's card, still in my hand. The word *Homicide* jumped out at me. "You didn't see? Claire had blood on her hands."

That evening I called Quincy, my daughter who lived in Boston. She fell in love with the East Coast while attending Brown University and decided to settle there, working in the newsroom of WGBH Boston, a National Public Radio station.

"Hey, Mom, how are you?"

"Quincy honey. I had a terrible day. I found a dead body."

"Shut the front door!"

"Really, honey." I told her about Claire Terry.

"How awful. Are you okay? How about Aunt Lucy and Aunt Birdie? What did the police say? How did she die?" That was my Quincy. Always curious, always asking questions, ever the reporter.

I was proud of my daughter and missed her. Named after the father I never knew, she was my only child and the only good thing to come out of my marriage to Aaron Rose. I hoped she'd move back to California one day but kept those thoughts to myself. Quincy was fiercely independent, and if she suspected I was trying to push her into something, she'd go out of her way to do the opposite.

I answered her questions the best I could.

"Well, go get a glass of wine and relax, Mom. You

deserve it after such a shock. Wish I was there to give you a hug."

As I pushed the off button, I felt my neck muscles tighten, a familiar and unwanted response to stress that usually led to a migraine. If I didn't do something about it immediately, I knew from experience the pain would worsen until I had a full body migraine. Instead of a glass of wine, I took a Soma, a muscle relaxer that was my go-to medication for the fibromyalgia that plagued me.

SATURDAY

CHAPTER 3

Four days after finding Claire's body, we were back in Lucy's Caddy driving to the annual show of the West San Fernando Valley Quilt Guild. Lucy took her hand off the wheel to show us the bracelet she wore. "Look. My sweetie felt so bad about Tuesday he went out and bought this for me."

That was some serious bling. Diamonds mixed with something else. "What kind of stones are those?"

"Pink sapphires."

Ray's generosity didn't surprise me. At the birth of each of their sons, he gave Lucy a piece of good jewelry. The more successful his business grew, the bigger the gemstones. When Lucy wanted to remodel their house, he set up a separate bank account to cover expenses and never questioned her. What a guy.

"Lovely." Birdie's voice sounded wistful. Long ago she confided her husband, Russell, kept tax returns dating back to when they first married and still made her hand over the grocery receipts. I couldn't remember Birdie ever showing us anything Russell gave her.

Once she told us he tried to force her to stop buying fabric for her quilts. "There's enough material in this house to last a lifetime." Without saying a word, Birdie went into their bedroom with a pair of scissors and cut squares out of his best shirts. After that she bought fabric whenever she wanted to.

Lucy looked at me in the rearview mirror. "How're you doing, Martha?"

"Oh, I think I'm over the shock, but the whole thing still creeps me out."

I didn't have a husband at home to comfort me like they did. Aaron left me long ago for the wife of one of his psychiatrist colleagues. All I had now was Quincy and my elderly Uncle Isaac, and I didn't want to burden either of them. So, for the past few days, I'd turned to wasabi rice crackers with crumbled Gorgonzola cheese for consolation. Plus lots of chocolate. "I've been getting phone calls from guild members curious to know the gory details about finding Claire's body."

Lucy nodded. "Me too. You know Carlotta Hudson? The one who keeps trying to enter her quilts in Houston International and always gets rejected?"

"Sure. She once came to a board meeting and complained that having the same person always win first prize was unfair. She asked if there was some way the rest of the quilts could be judged apart from Claire's."

"Well, she had the nerve to ask me if I thought Claire suffered."

"Good heavens. What did you tell her?" Birdie asked.

"I told her she reminded me of a crow pecking at roadkill."

We laughed.

Birdie played with the end of her long braid. "Do you think they'll give Claire first prize again this year?"

"Are you kidding?" my voice rose. "She sold her last quilt for ten thousand dollars. During an emergency meeting two nights ago, the board decided to dedicate the show to her. I heard when the show opened yesterday, there was a huge line waiting to view her quilt."

Birdie looked surprised. "Can they give a prize to a dead person?"

"We're about to find out. The judges pinned the ribbons on the winning quilts last night after the show."

Lucy flipped on the turn signal. "Well, I hate to say this 'cause it really sounds awful, but if they give her a prize, this'll be the last time. From now on, Carlotta may have the chance she's been looking for."

I smiled. You had to love Lucy's honesty.

We pulled into the parking lot of the Woodland

Hills Marriott and found a space using Birdie's blue handicapped placard.

I got out of the car and snapped on my fanny pack with two quilt show essentials inside—my digital camera and my wallet. Dozens of vendors would be selling everything from sewing machines to antique buttons, and a quilter had to be prepared.

Then I bent down and helped Birdie out of the car. "I can't wait to find out if your wall hanging won. It's your best quilt yet."

Lucy locked the car. "Who were the judges this year?" She slung her pink bag over her shoulder and adjusted her pink pantsuit. You had to admire her. Lucy's outfit matched her new bracelet.

"The usual. The group of ladies from Glendale."

Our guild traded judging duties every year with the Glendale guild. In an effort to keep the procedure honest and impersonal, the judges weren't allowed to know the names of the quilters until the process was over.

In deference to Birdie's knees, we maneuvered our way slowly through the hotel lobby toward the grand ballroom where the quilts were displayed. A hundred other quilters were trying to do the same thing. Vendor tables lining the walls created a bottleneck as women stopped to browse.

As we progressed, I sometimes glimpsed women quickly turning their heads away and whispering to each other. Was it my imagination or were they talking about us?

Carlotta Hudson made a beeline toward us with a smirk. My heart sank. Any conversation with Carlotta usually began with a complaint and ended in a thinly veiled insult.

Carlotta was tall, but not as tall as Lucy. Her short mousy brown hair was streaked with gray and her bangs hung in her face in limp strings. A red exhibitor ribbon was pinned on the collar of a blouse she'd sewn from a lavender and yellow floral fabric.

Carlotta looked smug. Not a good sign. "Well, well," She peered at us through glasses with lavender plastic frames. "The three amigas. Be sure to check out the winning quilts at the back of the ballroom." She put a look of mock sympathy on her face and turned to Lucy. "I'm afraid, however, yours isn't among them."

What a witch. We had never been able to figure out what Carlotta had against Lucy.

Then she turned to look at Birdie. "I received a third-place ribbon today. It's the fourth ribbon I've gotten in the last five years."

Like anybody cared.

Lucy's eyes flickered. She shifted position, forcing Carlotta to look at her. "I don't quilt for recognition. I quilt for family." Then Lucy turned to Birdie. "How many times have you applied to the International Quilt Show in Houston? You know, the one where the *best quilters* from all over the world get to show their quilts?"

"Two times."

"How many times have you been accepted?"

"Twice."

Carlotta glared at Lucy, red creeping up her cheeks. She picked angrily at a gauze bandage wrapped around her arm.

"Did you win any ribbons?"

"Once." Birdie picked up her braid and looked nervously at the now-livid Carlotta.

Lucy turned back to Carlotta. "Congratulations on winning another *third place*, Carlotta. Maybe we'll see you in Houston one of these years."

Carlotta stormed away.

Lucy smiled and shook her head slowly. "That was way too easy."

We continued to make our way past hundreds of people to the winning quilts at the back of the ballroom. Claire's latest wall hanging was certain to be there, and we all hoped Birdie's would be right beside hers.

CHAPTER 4

We arrived at the platform where the winning quilts hung from black plastic tarp clips along their top edges. Birdie gasped and rushed forward, beaming and lightly touching the white ribbon pinned to the corner of her wall hanging. "I won second place in the appliqué category."

Her quilt featured fabric images of plants from her garden plus her signature bird's nest with eggs. I especially loved the egg made out of blue fabric with tiny brown polka dots. Birdie's real name was Hazel Elizabeth Nightingale. The nurse presented her to her mother after she was born and with a smile said, "Here's your baby birdie, Mrs. Nightingale." The name stuck.

Like many quilters, Birdie gave her quilts names and wrote them on labels she sewed to the back. The sign next to her quilt read, BIRDIE'S BOTANICALS. HAND APPLIQUÉD AND HAND QUILTED BY HAZEL ELIZABETH NIGHTINGALE WATSON.

I was shocked to see a blue ribbon pinned on the top corner of my Double Sawtooth Star quilt. "Oh. My. God." I put my hand over my gaping mouth. "I got first place in the pieced category." The sign next to my quilt read, CIVIL WAR REPRODUCTION BED QUILT. MACHINE PIECED AND HAND QUILTED BY MARTHA ROSE.

I served as judge once for the Glendale show and knew how picky the criteria could be. Quilts were divided into two categories for judging: pieced and appliquéd. The pieced quilts were made of blocks with geometric designs joined together in an overall repeating pattern. These traditional quilts were my favorite, but this was the first time ever a quilt of mine garnered a ribbon.

Appliquéd quilts like Birdie's and Claire's featured images sewn together in the same way a painter created a picture. Small pieces of fabric were applied with hidden stitches to a background fabric. The fabric image was built up layer by layer, much like the brushstrokes on a canvas. Innovative appliqué artists like Claire and Birdie created true works of art.

Lucy clapped her hands. "I'm really happy for you both. I know how hard you worked on those quilts. You both deserve those prizes."

Birdie put her hand on Lucy's arm. "I'm sorry you didn't win a ribbon, Lucy dear. Your baby quilt is so sweet."

Lucy waved her hand dismissively. "Oh, I don't

care. My family's too big and I have too many quilts to make. I know you put hundreds of hours into making a single exquisite quilt, but I can't afford to give that much time to each one of mine. I don't expect to win prizes. By the way, which one belongs to Carlotta the crow?"

"That one." I pointed to the quilt with the appliquéd Rose of Sharon block. Each block featured a stylized rosette, a circle with scalloped edges. Radiating from the rosette were four straight green stems, each with two leaves and a one-piece rosebud at the end.

The Rose of Sharon was an old design that I thought lacked creativity. Still, I knew looks could be deceiving. Carlotta had probably spent months finishing this quilt. Effort alone had earned her third place.

The sign next to the quilt read: ROSE OF SHARON. THIS TRADITIONAL BLOCK IS ALSO KNOWN BY THE NAMES OF WHIG ROSE, COLONIAL ROSE, KENTUCKY ROSE, AND MEXICAN ROSE. HAND APPLIQUÉD AND HAND QUILTED BY CARLOTTA MARIE HUDSON. Quilt block designs frequently got renamed as they traveled from region to region. You could trace the journey of this block by its various names.

"You have to admit this is a pleasing quilt."

Birdie peered at it closely. "Yes, but if you look carefully, you can see some of the stitches around the edges of the appliqué. Also, her quilting stitches aren't even. She'd do better to take fewer stitches per inch and try to make them more uniform."

I walked over to Claire Terry's quilt, hanging in the place of honor. Two ribbons were pinned at the top: First-Place Appliqué and Best of Show.

The quilt featured a background of light gray fabric. Scattered on top of this background were appliquéd hearts and roses in pinks, reds, and purples. Each rose was composed of petals individually sewn and layered. In between the roses and hearts, hundreds of little scarlet bumps of knotted embroidery thread called French knots created texture and interest.

The sign next to the quilt read simply, ASCENDING. HAND PIECED, HAND APPLIQUÉD, AND HAND QUILTED BY CLAIRE TERRY. The design of hearts and flowers reminded me of Valentine's Day and I thought of a joyful heart ascending with love. Then a picture of Claire lying alone on the floor flashed through my mind and I shuddered.

Birdie must have felt it, too. "Poor Claire." Her eyes teared up.

Lucy reached out and gave Birdie's shoulder a little squeeze.

I took out my digital camera and shot pictures of the winning quilts: full-length shots as well as close-ups of the wonderful red knots that gave such interest to the background. "Come on. Let's find Lucy's quilt."

We roamed up and down aisles created by row

upon colorful row of hanging quilts. People of all ages enjoyed the show. A few women had actually dragged their husbands along.

One particularly bored man in a Dodgers baseball cap turned backward stopped suddenly at a pink and white quilt with a repetitive pattern. Each of the twelve-inch blocks making up this bed-sized quilt featured an outline of a square with a triangle outside each corner. He turned to the petite redhead next to him. "Here's your blanket, Peaches."

The sign next to this quilt disclosed some of the many names for this common block: Churn Dash, Monkey Wrench, Hole in the Barn Door, and Shoo Fly. Peaches handed her husband a camera and stood in front of the quilt. "Take my picture."

He snapped a couple of shots. "Well, it sure looks good, Peachie. Uh, now that we've seen it, can we go? I don't want to miss the game."

Peaches gave him a withering look and walked over to the next quilt. "Turn on your iPad."

Women wearing white gloves and white bibbed aprons patrolled the aisles. They were there to turn a quilt over if someone wanted to see the reverse side. However, the White Gloves, as they were called, were mostly on the lookout for anyone daring to ignore the dozens of signs warning Do Not Touch the Quilts.

Some quilts really begged to be touched, especially if they had a lot of texture from heavy quilting or surface texture like the French knots on Claire's quilts. The only problem was hundreds of caressing hands left oil and dirt deposits and spoiled a quilt. One vigilant White Glove discovered a woman yesterday who more than once fondled Claire's quilt with both hands. She had to be told several times to stop.

I closed my eyes for a moment and listened to the chatter of hundreds of women. They sounded like the rushing waters of a mountain river in the spring.

I opened my eyes when there was a loud crashing sound from the back of the ballroom. The room suddenly became quiet. Then someone screamed, "Stop him! Stop him!"

The noise rose again, and the news started to flow up the aisles in a torrent. Words like "stolen" and "back door" and "Claire's quilt" bubbled and eddied through the crowd.

I looked at Lucy and Birdie. "Claire's quilt was stolen?"

Lucy headed for the back. "Let's find out."

Women started to surge toward the entrance in a kind of controlled panic. We struggled to swim against the current, like salmon going to spawn, and made our way to the back of the ballroom.

The exhibit of winning quilts was a shambles with display racks overturned. A door next to the podium stood wide open.

A woman lay on the floor near the door and

moaned while a knot of her friends tried to comfort her. "Don't worry, Selma dear. The paramedics are on their way."

I rushed over to them. "What happened?"

Selma's friend scowled at me until she saw the badge pinned to my shirt identifying me as a board member. "A man yanked down some quilts and escaped out that door. Poor Selma was standing in his way, and he pushed her down. I think she's broken something."

A dozen years ago, this couldn't have happened. Every quilt had a sleeve sewn on the back to accommodate a hanging rod. The rod was fitted onto support poles, and the quilt hung down like a curtain. A snatch and grab would have been impossible. Nowadays, quilts were hung by clips, much like those from an old-fashioned clothesline. Just one hard tug and the whole thing could come loose, especially the wall hangings that were smaller and lighter than bed quilts.

"What did he look like?"

"Not too tall. Stout. He wore a stocking mask, so I really didn't get a good look, but there was something really odd about his eyes. Selma probably saw more than any of us."

I peered through the open door and down a hallway leading to a parking lot at the end. The thief was probably long gone.

I made my way back to Birdie and Lucy, who stood next to the podium. Birdie wept softly.

"What?" I looked at Lucy.

"They're gone, Martha. Yours, Birdie's, and Claire's quilts. They're gone."

I stood in shock, trying to figure out what to do next, when someone in a blue blazer with the hotel logo on the pocket walked over to the microphone next to the podium.

"Ladies and gentlemen, the police are on their way. If you witnessed anything suspicious, you're asked to remain and give a statement. The rest of you may go. We sincerely apologize for the inconvenience."

My stomach churned. This was the second time in less than a week we'd been mixed up in a police investigation involving Claire Terry. That woman was turning out to be a terrible jinx.

CHAPTER 5

We found three chairs near a vendor table selling thread in more colors than I'd ever seen in one place. The rainbow displays were beautiful enough to hang as wall art. The next table sold stencils cut out of thin acrylic sheets for marking stitching designs on quilt tops: cables, fans, grids, feathers, clamshells, and Bishop's Fan were the most popular.

I estimated we'd been there for at least an hour, because Birdie had already gotten up to go to the bathroom twice. Clusters of women spoke to each other in hushed tones. An electronic tapping sounded through the speaker system in the grand ballroom.

"Testing," a voice boomed. All conversation stopped. The announcer's mouth was too close to the microphone, so she made little explosive sounds with the letter *p*. "Will the following people please report to the podium: Martha Rose and Birdie Watson."

As I helped Birdie get out of her seat, Lucy got up, too. "I'm coming with you."

The podium had been taped off and someone in a white jumpsuit with a toolbox dusted the over-turned quilt display stands for fingerprints.

Lucy snorted. "Look."

I followed her finger to a heap on the floor. The thief left Carlotta's Rose of Sharon quilt behind.

A policewoman in a blue shirt and pants waited for us. Her name badge said Salazar.

"I'm Martha Rose, this is Birdie Watson, and this is our friend Lucy Mondello."

"Right. Please come with me." The leather hol-ster holding Officer Salazar's gun squeaked slightly against her right hip as she moved in front of us down the hallway. A radio was clipped to her belt over her left hip. A baton and handcuffs hung off loops in the back.

The hotel restaurant had been commandeered as a temporary interview room. Two police officers sat at linen-covered tables taking statements from groups of women. Salazar led us to a table in the back.

The man at the table stood up as we ap-proached. Oh my God. Could this be? I'd recog-nize his mustache anywhere. I straightened the hem of my T-shirt and shoved my glasses back on my nose, regretting my casual attire. I really wished

I'd chosen something more attractive to wear that day.

Detective Arlo Beavers sat down again. "We meet again, ladies."

I tried to make my voice sound jaunty. "I thought your business card said you were a homicide detective."

"Robbery *and* homicide."

"Do you manage to show up at every crime scene in the Valley?"

"Do you?"

Touché. "I'm beginning to wonder. This time, though, we're not witnesses; we're the injured parties."

"You and a couple of others. Three quilts stolen and one elderly lady injured in the escape. As soon as I arrived, they handed me a list of victims and I recognized both your names. Tell me what happened."

Birdie's eyes filled with tears. "We were too far away to see anything. Why would anyone do such a thing?"

Beavers shrugged. "Why do you think someone would steal them? How much could a couple of blankets be worth?"

I bristled and squared my shoulders. "For your information, those quilts are legitimate works of art. Only the artists didn't use paint, they used fabric."

He put up his hand. "I stand corrected. How much are these works of art worth?"

"Claire sold her last quilt for ten thousand dollars. Birdie is an unknown artist, so I'm not sure anyone would pay that much money for hers." I quickly looked at my friend. "Sorry, Birdie. Your quilt was every bit as beautiful as Claire's."

Birdie nodded. "I know what you mean."

"As for my quilt, well, only a Civil War buff would be interested. It's historically accurate, but hardly worth a lot of money."

Birdie's normally gentle voice cut sharply through the air. "Well, money isn't the point!"

Whoa. The last time I heard that tone was when she discovered Eleanor Peavy had stolen the hundred-year-old embroidery scissors that belonged to Birdie's great-grandmother.

"I worked over a year on my quilt. Hundreds of hours. Now it's gone." Her voice quavered.

Lucy opened her pink purse, handed Birdie a tissue, and looked at Beavers. "What are the chances of your finding the quilts?"

"The eyewitnesses are working with a sketch artist. The preliminary description identifies the thief as 'stout' and wearing a knit ski mask. Does that ring a bell?" We shook our heads.

"I didn't think so. We'll try to do some kind of composite drawing and have you take a look. Meanwhile"—he pointed to a nearby table—"you can file a formal complaint with the officer over there."

I felt a surge of disappointment. "So you're not investigating the theft?"

"Right now, I'm more interested in solving Claire Terry's murder."

Birdie gasped. "Murder?"

My stomach churned again.

Lucy's face turned white. "Oh my God. Do you remember I kept saying I had a bad feeling?"

"Yes."

Lucy raised her eyebrows. "Do you think I'm becoming psychic? Like Allison DuBois or something?"

Beavers cleared his throat. "I'll need to get fingerprint samples from each of you to eliminate some of those we took from the crime scene. You can go to the West Valley station when you're finished here."

"What about our quilts?" asked Birdie.

"The three of you found Claire Terry's body. Then her quilt gets stolen and so do yours. I'm wondering what the connection is."

The longer I sat, the harder the chair became. "Coincidence?"

"I don't believe in coincidence."

"How was Claire killed?"

"OD."

"Wait. She did drugs? She didn't seem the type."

"Not recreational. Prescription."

"How do you know it wasn't an accident or suicide?"

"We believe she fought with her killer."

I felt like I was in an elevator descending too fast. I'd forgotten about the blood on Claire's hands.

Birdie put her hand over her mouth. "Dear God."

Lucy whispered, "Look. Carlotta's watching us. Over there."

I turned. Carlotta Hudson sat at a nearby table filling out a form with a cheap Bic pen. She looked up at us with an expression on her face I couldn't quite figure out. *How many cards are missing from her deck?*

"What's up with her?" I whispered.

Lucy snickered. "Probably mad because nobody wanted to steal her quilt."

Beavers stood and handed us each another card. "If you have pictures of your quilts, make sure we get copies for identification purposes in case we ever find them."

"You don't sound very hopeful." I sighed.

"You never know. You ladies be careful. I don't want to alarm you, but a possible connection between the murder and the theft bothers me. Call me if you think of anything that might help."

"Shall I call you if I get another bad feeling?" asked Lucy.

"Why not." Beavers looked at me and turned up the corner of his mouth in an affable smile that made his brown eyes crinkle. "Sorry about your work of art."

My heart skipped a little. I didn't even care he initially referred to my first-place Civil War reproduction bed-sized quilt as a blanket.

On the drive home, I watched from the backseat as Birdie wrung her hands and sighed. "Poor Claire. Murdered. Can you believe it?"

Lucy switched on the turn signal and slid into the right turn lane. "I find this all hard to comprehend."

"Also very scary. Why would anyone want to kill her?"

Lucy waited for the oncoming traffic to thin out so she could make the turn. "My money's on Carlotta Hudson."

"Whatever for?" asked Birdie.

"She's so outclassed. The only way for her to ever get to Houston would be if she killed off the competition."

I laughed. "Well then, you'd better be careful, Lucy. You really pissed her off today."

Lucy made her turn onto Vanowen Boulevard. "Don't worry about me. I'm from Wyoming, remember? I can take care of myself."

Birdie worked furiously on her braid. "We know Claire's hands were caked with blood, probably from fighting with her killer. Did you notice Carlotta had a bandage wound around her arm?

What if Lucy's right? What if she's out to kill the competition?

"Claire got the first-place ribbon, I got second, and Carlotta got third. Do you think she'll be coming after me next? Do you think she's behind the quilt thefts?"

"Oh, hon', I'm sorry if I scared you." Lucy's voice softened with sympathy. "I was just trying to be funny. I'm sure you don't have anything to worry about."

"They'll find our quilts." I tried to sound convincing.

"Yeah, I have a good feeling about this."

"So what are you now," I asked, "the Ghost Whisperer?"

Lucy looked at me in the rearview mirror and scowled. "Go ahead and laugh, but I've always had really powerful intuitions."

"Like when you agreed with Birdie we should invite Eleanor Peavy to join our group?"

"How was I supposed to know she was a klepto?"

"Intuition?"

As we parked outside the West Valley Police Station to have our fingerprints scanned with a modern digital reader—no ink—Birdie smiled for the first time in hours. "Oh, Lord. What more could possibly happen?"

CHAPTER 6

When I got home I went straight to the refrigerator, the place I always visited when I was upset. I was angry about my missing quilt. I'd spent months searching for and buying just the right reproduction fabrics because I wanted my Civil War quilt to be authentic. Now it was missing. Possibly in the hands of the person who murdered Claire Terry.

I cracked open a diet cola and drank straight from the can. Why would anyone want to steal my quilt? Claire's I could understand; hers sold for thousands of dollars. Maybe the thief thought he could also sell Birdie's beautiful quilt for the same price. However, why bother with a traditional one like mine? Another quilter or a Civil War collector might appreciate the authenticity, but it was hardly in the same class as the other two.

I pulled out the freezer drawer and rummaged around for the frozen cheese tamales. They were under the Angus burger patties from the super-market. The phone rang, and I slammed the freezer shut. What now?

"Hi, Martha. It's Barbara North from the guild. I'm so sorry about your quilt."

Barbara was the board president. She ran the guild meetings like a drill sergeant, but I didn't really blame her. The feminist in me hated to admit this, but three hundred chatty women in the same room could be hard to control. Barbara was all about control, a trait I understood and admired.

After my divorce from my manipulative husband, I took charge of my life and vowed never again to allow anyone else to tell me how to feel, think, or live. The only exception I'd ever made had been for my Uncle Isaac, who practically raised me, and my daughter, Quincy. Her needs had always deter-mined my priorities.

"Thanks, Barbara. I just got home from Birdie's. We were all pretty upset."

"That's why I hate to ask you this." She took a deep breath and her words tumbled out as if she were running a race with them. "Martha, since you're on the board, and since you had a connec-tion to Claire Terry, and since your quilt was stolen, too, I thought you'd be the logical person to make an official condolence call to the family." Finish line.

Oh no. The last thing I wanted was to face Claire's family. What if they asked about finding Claire's body? What would I tell them?

"Oh really, Barbara, I think as president you'd be the best person to call them."

"Well, I would, but Hal and I are leaving in about ten minutes, and we won't be back for two weeks. I can't trust anyone else on the board. You know how they are. I really need someone sensible to handle this."

Darn it! She was right. I gritted my teeth and reached for a pencil and notepad. "Okay, give me the info. It's spelled *how*?"

I hated things hanging over my head and decided to make the call right away. I deserved an extra tamale for my trouble, so I put two of them in the microwave and dialed the phone number Barbara gave me.

"May I speak to Siobhan Terry?" I pronounced her name "ShaVAHN," the way Barbara pronounced it.

"May I say who's callin'?" The woman spoke with a thick Irish brogue.

"This is Martha Rose calling from the West Valley Quilt Guild."

"May I tell her what this is regardin'?"

Who talks like that anymore? "This is a condolence call."

"One moment, please."

I watched the digital countdown on the microwave. Four minutes and thirty-nine seconds to go. At three minutes to go, the same voice returned to the phone. "Mrs. Terry will speak to ya now."

There was a click and then a faint voice. "Siobhan Terry."

"Mrs. Terry? My name is Martha Rose. I'm calling on behalf of the quilt guild to offer our deepest sympathy on the death of your daughter, Claire."

"Martha Rose did you say?"

"Yes. I just wanted to tell you how sorry—"

"The same Martha Rose who found my daughter?"

"Yes. I'm so sorry."

"Miss Rose, I wonder if you'd be kind enough to pay me a visit."

She was going to ask me about finding Claire. I just knew it. How could I say no? The poor woman just lost her daughter. I resigned myself to the inevitable. "Of course. How about tomorrow?"

"I'd be most grateful. Let me give you my address. Just announce yourself at the gate. Say at two? I'll have tea waiting."

I wrote down the information as the microwave dinged. Announce myself at the gate? Not unusual for her million-dollar neck of the woods.

I took out the steaming tamales, peeled off the cornhusks, and plopped them on a plate. My mouth watered at the smell of hot cheese, masa, and peppers. I pulled out a plastic container of guacamole with one more day until the expiration date and plopped about two tablespoons on top of each tamale. No use wasting good guac.

One of the best things about living alone was I didn't have to worry about cooking for anyone else anymore. Aaron and I'd been divorced for years, and our daughter, Quincy, had her own life working on the East Coast.

I savored the tamales. There was something very comforting about spicy hot food in the stomach. Food didn't make up for the theft of my Civil War quilt, but eating always made painful things more bearable. *That's why I have size sixteen hips,* I thought with just a tinge of self-justification.

I reflected again about my Civil War quilt and why so few of the old ones survived. Army supplies were sometimes so scarce soldiers on both sides had to come up with their own provisions. Most families sent their quilts with their fighting men to keep them warm during the bitter winters. Also, groups of women, such as those in the Ladies' Sanitary Society in the North, got together to make quilts for the Union soldiers.

Those quilts got hard use as bedrolls when the soldiers slept on the ground. Historians estimated that up to seven hundred thousand people died in that war, many of them buried wrapped in their quilts as shrouds.

As I finished the last bite, the phone rang again. It was Lucy.

"Just thought I'd call and see how you're doing."

"Lousy!" I told her about the condolence call and the invitation from Siobhan Terry.

"What are you going to tell her?"

"God help me, I don't know."

SUNDAY

CHAPTER 7

The next day I wound through the very pricey hills of Beverly Hills, pulled up to an iron gate blocking a long driveway, and double checked the address on my Google printout: 248 Benedict Canyon. I rolled down the window and pressed a button next to a speaker on a pole.

A few seconds later a voice asked, "Yes?"

"Martha Rose."

There was a buzzing sound and the gate swung inward. I looked up into a security camera pointed at my face. At the end of a long driveway stood a very large, white, colonial, two-story mansion with eight columns in front divided by a porte cochere. Holy crap. *Bring out the mint juleps, Hattie. I think I've landed at Tara.*

My knock was answered by a red-haired maid dressed in a black dress with a starched white apron. "Please do come in, Miss Rose." She had the same lilting accent I heard on the phone yesterday. "Mrs. Terry's expecting ya."

Who has Irish servant girls these days? I stepped inside a foyer the size of my entire living room and easily two stories high. The creamy walls were washed with natural light from a window high above the porte cochere. A red silk Tabriz carpet lay in the middle of the white marble floor. Directly ahead was a graceful curving staircase of dark, polished mahogany. To the left was a set of closed double doors and to the right a wide entrance leading into a living room.

I was glad I wore my good pearls with a silk blouse and my Anne Klein skirt. I followed the maid to the right and tried to ignore the slight swishing sound my panty hose made as my thighs rubbed together. I'd been blessed with a Jewish figure: large bosoms and a smallish waist with abundant thighs and rear end.

Siobhan Terry sat like a small bird in an armchair generously upholstered in blue damask. Her long hair was arranged on top of her head creating a white halo around her face. I guessed she was Birdie's age, but aside from the hair, the similarity ended.

Aquamarines sparkled in her ears, and her gray cashmere sweater hugged her tiny figure. She looked at me with eyes the color of her earrings and extended her right hand but did not rise.

I wrapped both of my hands around the older woman's. Her fingers were bony and dry. A huge diamond ring pressed sharply into my palm. "Mrs. Terry, I'm Martha Rose."

"So good of you to come. Please, sit here." She indicated a matching chair near hers.

I sat and looked around the room. The blue silk drapes pooled extravagantly on the creamy wool carpeting. Crystals hanging from a massive chandelier deflected shards of light around the room. A seventeenth-century oil painting of fruit and flowers on a dark brown background hung over a massive fireplace. Didn't I once see this very painting at the Getty Museum? If so, it was worth a gazillion dollars.

The maid wheeled in an old-fashioned tea cart with a silver tea service, Belleek china, platters of finger sandwiches, and fancy small cakes.

Siobhan picked up the teapot with both hands. "What do you take in your tea, Ms. Rose?"

"I prefer milk or cream, and please call me Martha."

The older woman sighed. "The only way to enjoy it, I think. You must call me Siobhan."

The maid placed a small plate, fork, and linen napkin on the small table next to my chair and brought the platters of food over.

I felt like a schoolgirl taking an important test I hadn't studied for. What if I spilled something on the pristine furniture or, God forbid, on the creamy wool carpeting? I looked longingly at the chocolate petit fours but chose instead a small cucumber sandwich and a vanilla cookie because if I dropped either of them, the damage would be invisible.

When the maid left the room, Siobhan put down her tea and looked at me with tears in her eyes.

I braced myself.

"Please tell me about my daughter."

I felt a rush of empathy for this grieving mother. God forbid anything should happen to Quincy. My own tears would never stop.

I pretended I didn't know where this conversation was headed. "Well, I didn't know her very well. . . ."

"I mean tell me how you found her. What did she look like?"

Rats! "Siobhan, I don't think—"

"Please. I want to know. Did she suffer?"

"I really can't answer that. When we got there, she was already gone. She was lying on the floor like she just went to sleep." I was not going to tell Claire's mother about the vomit around Claire's mouth and in her hair, or the blood on her hands.

"So you don't think she suffered?"

"She didn't look that way to me," I lied.

"You know"—I hoped to deflect further questions—"Claire was widely admired. She was the best quilter in the guild. My friends and I were so pleased she invited us to quilt with her."

"I was upset when they told me yesterday a thief stole her quilt."

"I know how you feel. My quilt and my friend Birdie's quilt were also stolen."

"Yes, Detective Beavers told me. Claire had no children, so her quilts are all I have left of her. I think this last one is the best she'd ever done. I'd very much like to get it back."

"Yes, but I don't think the police are very optimistic about our chances. They're more interested in . . ." I stopped myself.

"In who killed her?"

"I'm sorry. Yes. In who killed her."

The older woman looked somewhere over my shoulder. The blue in her eyes turned to ice and her face hardened. Parchment skin stretched over the white bones of her knuckles as she clenched her fists. "Whoever killed her will pay."

I didn't know what to say in the face of her grief and anger. I decided this was one of those times when it was better to just say nothing.

After a minute, Siobhan relaxed a little and looked at me. "How did you get involved in quilting?"

"Well, my grandmother was a quilter. I have fond memories of her cutting out pieces of colorful old clothing and sewing them together to make beautiful patterns. I made my first quilt for my daughter's crib. That was thirty years and over one hundred quilts ago."

"I'm afraid I would never have the patience required to sit and sew like that."

"That's a common assumption people make. Quilting has nothing to do with patience. Working with your hands can be a form of meditation. It can bring great peace." I looked at the other woman's well-manicured hands and doubted they'd ever done a day of work.

"Would you say you know a lot about quilts after thirty years?"

"Actually, yes. I've studied technique, textiles, and quilt history extensively."

"In that case, you may be just the person I'm looking for. Claire once told me her quilts were her journals. When I asked her what she meant, she said they each have a story to tell about her life. Because you know so much about quilts, maybe you can figure out what those stories were."

"Well, there is such a thing as a Story Quilt. Those depict everyday scenes from the life of the quilt maker. Each block is appliquéd or embroidered to make a scene of some significant event in the quilter's life. The pictures are usually quite obvious and simple, like planting corn or sweeping the house. The overall effect is primitive but quite charming. Did Claire ever make one of those?"

"No, but I keep thinking maybe she left some kind of message in her quilts."

"You mean like a note sewn inside each one?"

Siobhan looked up earnestly. "I don't know. That's what I'm hoping you can figure out."

"Why don't you tell all this to the police?"

"I tried talking to that young detective, but I don't think he took me seriously."

"Detective Kaplan, Beavers's partner?"

"Yes, I think that's the one." Siobhan fixed me with a pleading look. "Martha, I want you to look at her quilts. Most are privately owned now, but a few are at Claire's. Go back to her place. There's a key on the side of the house. You can let yourself in."

I remembered Claire's neighbor, Ingrid, reaching around the corner of Claire's house to get the key. "Her neighbor took the key to open the door last Tuesday, when we were there."

"I know. She called. I asked her to put it back. Take the key and keep it for now. See what you can find, and please hurry."

We stood.

Siobhan appeared diminutive and breakable, but her gaze was firm. "Maybe the clue to my daughter's death is in her quilts, especially the last one. I keep thinking that whoever stole Claire's quilt may also have killed her."

I bent down to hug the older woman, something I wouldn't have dreamed possible when I first walked into this imposing house. Bird bones hid under her soft cashmere sweater. "I'll do what I can," I said, mother to mother. "I promise."

CHAPTER 8

I drove back to my house in Encino to change clothes. Peeling off my panty hose was like opening a bag of compressed marshmallows. Instant release. I stepped into a pair of jeans and comfortable shoes, grabbed a blueberry muffin the size of my head and a cold Coke Zero from the refrigerator. You had to draw the calorie line somewhere.

The yellow tape was gone from Claire's circular driveway, so I parked my white Corolla near the front door. A horn honked briefly somewhere down the street, stabbing the Sunday afternoon quiet. I walked over to the side of the house where the neighbor had removed the key. My way was blocked by an iron gate secured by a heavy steel padlock. I tried to look around a large oleander bush, but the branches were in the way.

I closed my eyes and snaked my arm through the bush and the iron bars of the gate, feeling blindly along the smooth, melon-colored stucco of the side wall. My fingers brushed against something hard that felt like a miniature aluminum awning. I knew what this was: the vent cover for the clothes dryer, just like mine at home.

I hesitated to put my fingers inside a hole I couldn't see. God forbid there should be a spider lurking there. I held my breath, squeezed my eyelids, and felt around the edges of the vent cover until I found the bottom. I pushed at the little piece of aluminum hanging down like a tiny swinging door and walked my fingertips inside the hole. The key rested on a bed of soft lint and felt cool to the touch. I grabbed it and quickly withdrew my hand.

When I let out my breath and opened my eyes, there sat a fat brown garden spider on a web in the oleander leaves about three inches away from my face. All of its eyes looked straight at me.

"Ewww," I yelled, jumping away and brushing imaginary spiders out of my hair and clothes. "Ewww. Ewww." I did the spider dance all the way to the front door.

Still shuddering, I turned the key in the lock but hesitated before opening the door. Did Claire have an alarm? Siobhan hadn't mentioned anything. I took a deep breath and slowly pushed the heavy blue door open. Silence. Okay, good.

The air in the house smelled faintly like the men's restroom in a bus station. I didn't remember any noxious odors five days ago when we found Claire's body.

The inside of the house was pretty much as I remembered—yellow walls, hardwood floors, generously upholstered white sofa with an appliqué quilt hanging behind. Claire must have loved yellow, because the dining room was painted a mustard color. Beyond that was a kitchen with white cabinets and black granite countertops.

I looked at the litter on the floor from the EMTs. I pushed at some of the paper wrappings and empty plastic bags with the toe of my blue Crocs. Were they allowed to just leave a mess like this?

A faint whine suddenly came from the other room. I froze in place. Another whine, a little louder now. *Oh my God, there's someone else here.* I looked around desperately for something to defend myself with and picked up a ceramic table lamp. Then I saw an orange tabby cat padding cautiously around the corner. He looked at me and whined again.

I put the lamp back down on the table. "Gosh, you scared me." I bent to pet the cat. "You must be Claire's kitty, you poor thing. Did everyone forget about you? Are you starved?" I went to the kitchen. The smell grew much stronger. I looked around and found two empty cat bowls sitting on the laundry room floor along with an overflowing litter box. "Yuchh." I looked over the cat. He slowly closed his eyes and regally disavowed any responsibility for the mess.

I found some cat food and filled one bowl with

kibble and one with water. The cat made up for lost time while I cleaned the litter box and poured in some fresh sand. Then I went back to the hallway and picked up the debris on the floor where Claire's body had lain.

Spots of blood were smeared on the wall, probably when they were swabbed for evidence. A gray, powdery film appeared in smudges here and there. Dusting for prints?

I put the debris and used cat litter in the trash barrel outside, came back inside and washed my hands. "Okay, kitty, time to look at quilts." The cat was too busy crunching little star-shaped pellets to care.

I went back to the living room and over to the quilt hanging from a wooden board with clips behind Claire's sofa. I remembered seeing this work of art on the cover of *Pieces* quilting magazine a couple of years ago.

The flowers, herbs, and birds resembled a painting of a garden. When I got close enough, the subtle layering of different fabrics created the illusion of brushstrokes. The light tan background was heavily dotted with Claire's trademark French knots in dark brown embroidery thread. They reminded me of a pointillist painting. Not wild and generous like van Gogh. More controlled—like Seurat.

I took off my shoes and stood on the sofa, sinking unsteadily into the soft cushion. Reaching up to the wooden quilt hanger, I pulled the wall hanging out of the clips and sat down, sinking again into the downy cushion. The quilt was about three feet by four feet. The label on the back read, Secret Garden.

Secret Garden won a first-place ribbon two years ago and appeared shortly afterward in the magazine. What a privilege it was to be holding this exquisite piece of art in my lap.

I rubbed the quilt between my fingers, searching for a note Claire might have sewn inside. Cotton fabric was soft and pliable. A piece of paper inside the layers would feel stiff to the touch. Maybe I could even hear it crinkle. I started methodically in the top left corner, feeling through the layers inch by inch.

I closed my eyes in concentration as my fingers explored. There was something very sensual and comforting about a finished quilt. Sewing through the three layers of the top, batting, and lining produced a bumpy texture—a real testimony to the hundreds of hours spent sewing. A quilter left her very essence in the texture of her quilts.

I reached the bottom right corner without detecting anything. If there was a message to be found, it wasn't on paper. I decided to look for the other quilts Siobhan had said were in the house. If there weren't actual notes sewn inside, maybe I could decipher some sort of hidden relationship between the different designs or maybe there'd be a clue in the names of the quilts.

Once again I approached the spot in the hallway

where Claire's body had been found. I looked at the space where she'd fallen. What a terrible waste of a young life and a fine artistic talent. A picture of my daughter flashed in my head, and I shuddered. Even though Quincy was grown and living on her own, I still worried about her every day. Eternal worry was a mother's curse.

A picture of my mother flashed by. She was the exception to that rule. My mother wasn't very functional and needed to be taken care of herself. She was the reason we lived with my uncle Isaac and my *bubbie*, my grandmother. They told me my mother was devastated by the death of my father. Had she always been that way—remote and dreamy and disconnected from life? Every time I asked, they changed the subject.

Walking down Claire's hallway, I passed two bedrooms with an adjoining bath. A quick search revealed no quilts in either room. A third door was shut, and at the end of the hallway was the master suite. I opened the third door to find a well-appointed sewing studio.

The wall facing the backyard was all windows, flooding the space with natural light. No wonder Claire chose this room as a studio. Fabric colors were truest in natural light. An old wooden sewing table sat under the windows next to an upholstered chaise longue, the perfect spot for sitting and quilting.

White floor to ceiling shelves and cabinets lined

two of the walls. The third wall was painted white and featured a white quartz counter spanning the entire length. The counter was empty except for two sewing machines, a CD player, and a green cutting mat with one-inch yellow grid lines. The drawers beneath contained every gadget and notion a quilter could possibly want.

There were several things a serious quilter needed besides fabric, needles, and thread: a reliable sewing machine, a rotary cutter, a cutting mat, an acrylic ruler, sharp scissors, a good thimble, a steam iron, and a wooden hoop. Claire's sewing room was a warehouse of quilting supplies.

On the shelves were books about quilting and a large collection of audio books. I quickly scanned the titles and discovered Claire preferred mysteries, memoirs, and biographies. Like Claire, I also listened to stories while quilting. Were there other things we might've had in common? If she'd lived, would we have become friends?

I didn't like the idea of prying into the life of someone who was defenseless to stop me. With a mental apology to Claire for the intrusion, I started opening the cabinets. Piles and piles of neatly folded fabrics sorted by color sat on shelves. Clear plastic storage boxes held smaller pieces of fabric and were labeled according to color or theme. In this we couldn't have been more opposite. I didn't own a label maker, and fabric was strewn over every surface of my sewing room, resembling the Gulf Coast during hurricane season.

I mentally drooled when I saw the plastic Rubbermaid container labeled Vintage Fabric. Collecting old fabric was a particular passion of mine. Vintage fabrics weren't easy to find. They usually became available when somebody died and their heirs cleaned out the attic or sewing room. Then the fabric might occasionally find its way to a quilt store or antique shop, but you really had to look hard. I was dying to see what was hidden in Claire's stash.

Carefully lifting the layers of fabric, I discovered a piece of sky blue cotton printed with little cowboys dressed in tan and red. Suddenly I was back in the fifties in elementary school when my cousin Barry once spent Passover night with us. I was sure his pajamas had been made out of this same material.

I carefully put the cowboys back, closed the container, and continued my search. I came to a locked cupboard and guessed this was where Claire stored her quilts. Something tickled my ankle. Oh God, I thought in a panic, a spider!

The cat meowed. "That makes twice in one day you've scared me." I bent down and scratched him under the chin. "Are the quilts in this cupboard? Did your mommy tell you where the key was?" The cat blinked twice and started to purr. I swore he smiled.

I opened every drawer in the room and didn't

find a key to the cupboard, so I moved on to the master suite. Luxurious pink silk drapes hung like ball gowns in front of the tall windows. A matching silk duvet and lots of puffy pillows covered in silks, brocade, and lace adorned the queen-sized bed. Decorative bone china plates hung in a grouping on one wall and a real Mary Cassatt painting of a mother and child hung on another wall. This room was a luxurious feminine retreat.

The key to the cabinet wasn't in the bedroom, so I moved to the room-sized closet. Claire's clothes hung precisely like soldiers in a military parade: blouses all together, size six slacks neatly pressed, a row of designer dresses in pink garment bags, and dozens of shoes in plastic containers that weren't only labeled but identified with snapshots of the actual shoes glued onto the outside of the boxes.

Really? What would compel someone to be such a compulsive neat freak? What was the driving need behind all of this organization?

I opened the top drawer of a built-in dresser and found neat little piles of scanty underwear. I lifted out a lacy black thong no larger than the palm of my hand.

Maybe if I lost about fifty pounds.

Well, well. What had we here? Next to the underwear was a half-empty box of condoms. So Claire had a boyfriend. Did they have a fight? Did he kill her?

I replaced the tiny piece of black lace and the

box of condoms and came out of the closet feeling a lot fatter than when I went in.

At the back of the bedroom was a door leading to an office. A polished walnut desk sat under a large window facing the backyard. A laptop and a telephone sat on the uncluttered desk. No mess here. No surprise.

I sat and opened the top desk drawer. A red and white Altoid tin rattled when I picked it up. A faint peppermint smell lingered inside along with unmarked keys of various sizes.

I took the tin full of keys back to the sewing room and unlocked the cupboard on the third try. Inside were only three quilts. I unfolded the first one.

This quilt was a brilliantly designed appliqué about four feet square. Mother's Asleep featured a naked woman with her arms over her head. She floated with her eyes closed on white clouds discretely covering her private parts. French knots made of gray thread covered the clouds like thousands of silver seeds. Clear teardrop-shaped beads dripped from the bottom of the clouds.

I felt for a note inside the quilt. Nothing. Claire's message must be in the design itself. Silver seeds. Water. Clouds. All of those elements suggested rainmaking, but what did that have to do with the title, Mother's Asleep?

I took out my cell phone and punched in Siobhan's number. The maid put me through to the familiar soft voice.

"Yes?"

"Siobhan, this is Martha. I'm at Claire's and have found three of her quilts. Four if you count the one in the living room. Is that all of them?"

"I'm sure there are more. She kept a record somewhere of all the quilts she made. Maybe you could look for it."

"I think you're right about the messages in the quilts, but it's going to take a while to figure out what they are. Do I have your permission to take them home where I can study them more at length?"

"Yes. Just give me a list of the ones you've taken. And, Martha, I'm afraid whoever stole Claire's quilt might try to come after the others."

"Why?"

"Well, they're valuable, you know. So let's keep their location secret for now. It's safer that way."

I snapped the cell phone shut and looked outside. It was past six and the sun was going down. Siobhan warned me the thief might strike again. If so, I didn't want to be alone in Claire's house after dark.

I locked the empty quilt cabinet and put the Altoid box of keys in my shoulder bag. If someone was going to come after Claire's quilts, I wasn't going to make this easy. If he figured out Claire locked her quilts in the cabinet, he'd have to look for the key just like I did. He wouldn't find it, so he'd be forced to jimmy open the door. Not only would he not find the quilts there, he might actually leave fingerprints for the police.

I smiled at my cleverness. I'd never played chess, but if I had, I thought it would feel exactly like this.

When I opened the door to the linen closet, the fragrance of lavender and gardenias floated out in a pleasant cloud. I closed my eyes and took a deep breath. Then I pulled out a couple of crisp pillow-cases and put the quilts into them. I locked the front door and put the bundles in the trunk of my car.

On the drive home I remembered the cat. I decided to leave him there for now. He had plenty of food and water and a clean litter box. Anyway, I'd be back soon to look for a record of Claire's quilts.

CHAPTER 9

I lived in a midcentury house on a street lined with towering liquidambar trees providing dappled shade in the summer. Their roots had broken the sidewalks, raising the concrete like so many playing cards. Our street was on the list for sidewalk repair, but in this economy, work wasn't scheduled to begin for another fifty years.

I pulled into my driveway and a wave of fatigue washed over me. I took the quilts into the house and dumped them on the ivory chenille sofa in my living room. Beyond the living room was an open plan kitchen and dining area that made the house feel more spacious. I plopped down on the sofa and closed my eyes. It was only seven o'clock, but felt like midnight, and my emotional fuse was about to blow.

I opened my eyes. The living area soothed me with its neutral colors ranging from cream to taupe. I loved the way the white gauzy curtains dressed the windows. Watercolor paintings of blue and orange beach scenes added spots of color, as did the blue and orange pillows and area rug. This was a cozy space where a person could put up her feet—totally the opposite of Siobhan Terry's vast and formal living room.

I hadn't lied to Siobhan. Claire really had looked like she'd just fallen asleep on the floor. You'd think a murder scene would look a lot messier. Then there was the matter of the blood on her hands. How could someone who was drugged end up with blood on her hands?

I touched a pillowcase, curious to see the other quilts, but decided to wait until after I ate something. I nuked some macaroni and cheese and sliced some Persian cucumbers and sprinkled them with rice vinegar, salt, and pepper. Just five hours ago I'd eaten cucumber sandwiches with Claire Terry's mother.

I ran my hand appreciatively over the new apricot-colored marble counters. They looked as pristine as the day they were installed a year ago, and the stainless steel oven was still shiny inside. Only the microwave seemed to get a daily workout. I really needed to get my act together and cook healthier meals. I used to be a fabulous cook for my daughter and husband. That was then. Now, cooking for one hardly seemed worth the effort.

As I ate, I was intrigued by the idea of hidden messages. The thought of the thief coming after the quilts, however, was scary. Especially if the thief was Claire's murderer.

Cleaning up after this meal meant putting a few utensils in the dishwasher and the plastic container in the recycle bin. I dried my hands on a towel and the phone rang.

"Miss Rose?" The voice was urbane and male. "This is Will Terry, Claire's father. I want to thank you for visiting my wife today. I'm sorry I wasn't at home to greet you."

"Oh, Mr. Terry, I'm so sorry about your daughter. Her death is a real tragedy."

"Yes. A parent should never outlive a child." He cleared his throat. "I understand my wife has involved you in a wild goose chase."

"What do you mean?"

"Siobhan believes our daughter left some mysterious messages in her quilts. My wife is desperately trying to make some sense out of Claire's death. When she finds out there are no messages in the quilts, she might go off the deep end. She's already hinting about organizing a séance."

"Well, I'm not so sure, Mr. Terry. Your wife may be right about those messages."

"I doubt it. You see, my wife is so fragile now, I'm afraid if you can't come up with what she wants, she might have a complete breakdown."

"What if there *are* messages, Mr. Terry? Wouldn't you want to know?"

"Of course I would. What we have here is a

double-edged sword, Miss Rose. As long as you have the quilts—and they are in your possession?"

"Yes."

"As long as you have them, my wife is going to harbor great expectations. On the other hand, the higher her hopes, the harder she'll fall in the end if you find nothing. I've already lost my only child. I don't want to lose my wife, too."

"Yes, I see what you mean. Nevertheless, she seems to really be counting on me, and I'd like to try. For her sake."

"I'm a very rich man, Miss Rose, but I didn't start out that way. I was a penniless Irish boy from Chicago who came to California and made good. I didn't get to where I am by chasing rainbows. I started to fill my pot of gold in the movie industry and parlayed that into a global communications business."

Okay, okay, I'm impressed.

"However, for my wife's sake I'll give you three days, after which you'll have to return the quilts. We plan to display them during the wake on Thursday evening and after the funeral on Friday."

"What a wonderful tribute, Mr. Terry. It's a privilege to be able to study such important quilts. Your daughter was a gifted artist."

The tone in his voice softened. "Thank you for understanding. I'll call you on Wednesday to arrange for someone to pick up the quilts."

Will Terry was pushy, a man who was used to

telling people what to do. He also seemed genuinely concerned about Siobhan. I felt sorry for both of them.

I poured myself some Ruffino Chianti Classico in my favorite Moroccan tea glass painted on the outside with red and gold curlicues. I appreciated the solid reliability of the flat-bottomed tea glass because stemware tipped over too easily. I took a sip of the fruity, deep red Chianti and lamented that Will only gave me three days to crack the code of the quilts before they had to be returned. Tomorrow was Monday. I hoped Lucy and Birdie were free to help me.

The phone rang again.

"This is Detective Beavers. Could I come over and show you the composite drawing the eye witnesses came up with?"

"Now?"

"Actually, I'm nearby. I can be there in five minutes if that's convenient."

"Well, I suppose so." I looked at the clock in the kitchen. The time was eight and *The Closer* was on. Thank God for the DVR. I never missed an episode, not even the reruns.

I hurried to the bathroom and checked myself in the mirror, smoothing my clothes over what I fondly referred to as my ample but honest curves. Maybe the extra weight in my face ironed out the wrinkles, but my skin was still tight. I wore my fifty-five years well. I put on some lipstick and ran a wide-tooth comb through my curls. What was I doing this for? I reached for a bottle of Marc Jacobs and then put it back. Too obvious.

The doorbell rang. I tugged the hem of my pink T-shirt down over the hips of my Liz Claiborne jeans and headed for the door, sucking in my stomach. So what if he smiled at me yesterday at the quilt show. *I'm an idiot.*

The dark circles under Beavers's eyes were evidence of a long working day. Still, he was the kind of man who always appeared neat. His white shirt was still crisp, his blue necktie hung straight, and his gray pin-striped suit was unwrinkled. I caught the very faint scent of a woodsy cologne. "Come in, Detective. Would you like some water? Tea?"

Beavers shook his head. "No thanks." I could have sworn he took in my geography as he casually looked at the floor. When he looked up again, my cheeks warmed.

I led him toward the kitchen. "The light is better in here." I stretched up to sit on a stool at the island, but Beavers looped a long, easy leg around his and slid smoothly onto the seat.

He pulled the sketch out of his pocket. "Look at all familiar?"

I adjusted my glasses and studied the drawing, glad for a reason to hide my still burning cheeks. The drawing was of a stocky figure with a ski mask. The only thing showing on his face was a pair of small eyes.

"This looks like my cousin Barry."

Beavers took out a pad and clicked the top of a pen, preparing to write.

"No, no, don't get excited." I held up the palm of my hand. "Barry lives in Tel Aviv and is much older than this man seems to be. I haven't a clue who this is."

"I'll leave a copy with you anyway. Something might come to you later."

"So, are you investigating the theft after all?"

"Both. I'm still not convinced the theft was a random act apart from the murder. I'm looking for a connection."

"I agree." I told him about my visit to Siobhan and what Claire said about her quilts being her journals and how Siobhan wanted me to figure out the hidden messages in them. "I've only examined two, but I think Mrs. Terry may be right. I just have to figure out what the messages are."

"Do you mean she left notes in them?"

"That's what I thought at first, but there were no hidden written notes. I want you to see something." I went to one of the pillowcases and pulled out Mother's Asleep. I showed him the silver knots on the clouds and the teardrop beads. "This is symbolic for rainmaking."

Beavers looked skeptical. "How is that relevant?"

"Well, if you seed clouds with silver something-or-other, they start to rain."

Beavers looked impressed. "Silver iodide. So, what's the message?"

"If I can solve that one, maybe I can work out who the thief is."

"How?"

"I'm thinking maybe the thief stole Claire's quilt because he didn't want anyone to figure out what it could reveal."

Beavers ran his fingers through his gray hair. He looked tired.

I studied the wrinkles around his dark eyes and the way the skin of his eyelids drooped. Definitely the right age range. I snuck a look at his left hand. No ring.

"Sounds a little far-fetched to me."

"Your partner, Kaplan, definitely thought so, too. When Mrs. Terry tried to tell him about the messages, he blew her off."

"He never mentioned anything to me. I'm sure he didn't think it was worth pursuing."

"Neither does Will Terry. He doesn't want me to research this because he thinks his wife won't be able to stand the disappointment if I come up empty handed. Still, I don't think Siobhan Terry is deluded. If there are hidden stories in Claire's quilts, I'm determined to find them."

"Finding hidden messages is a long shot, but if what you say is true, you may be getting in over your head."

"Oh?"

"If the thief finds out you're poking around, you could be in danger." Beavers shifted, leaned forward, and looked me hard in the eyes. "This would be a good time to back away, Ms. Rose, and let the police handle this investigation."

I hated ultimatums, even from sexy brown eyes. This was the second one thrown at me tonight by a man in charge. How many of these did I have to suffer in one day? "How many quilters do you have on the police force?"

"Huh?"

"Exactly. You don't have anyone who can do what I can. I know quilts, Detective."

"And I know thieves and murderers, Ms. Rose."

I was getting pissed. "Well, if I run into any, I'll give you a call."

Beavers stood and looked at me. "Let's hope it won't be too late by then."

I thought I saw him looking at my bosom again. I hated when that happened. I stood and crossed my arms. Beavers towered over me by about ten inches so I craned my neck to look at him. "Detective! Were you just looking at my chest?"

He smiled. "No, but if I were, you couldn't blame me for admiring a flower in full bloom, *Ms. Rose*."

I desperately searched for a comeback. "I—I have thorns."

Beavers chuckled as he closed the door behind him.

I slumped against the door. *Oh God, I'm an idiot. Thorns?*

A bank of fog settled over my brain. I hit the familiar wall of fatigue and pain that happened so often when stressed. I wanted to look at the quilts, but my mind was beyond processing any more data. The clock read nine-thirty, and I headed toward bed. As excited as I was to have these wonderful quilts to study, they would just have to wait until morning.

I stepped into a steamy shower and let the jets of hot water coax my neck, shoulders, and back to relax a little, but my overall pain index was still high. In my grandmother's day, my condition might have been called rheumatism. Nowadays it was called fibromyalgia. My body was so sensitive, I could predict a rainstorm three days before, and the weather didn't have to be local. I could tell when it drizzled in Fresno two hundred miles away.

I toweled off, put on a clean pair of cotton jersey pajamas, and took a Soma. I nuked a long fabric tube filled with raw grains of rice and lavender buds in the microwave. Then I wrapped it around my neck and shoulders, breathing in the waves of lavender fragrance. The heat penetrated my muscles like honey on a waffle. I crawled into bed with my rice bag collar and almost immediately fell asleep.

MONDAY

CHAPTER 10

The persistent ringing of the phone woke me out
of a deep sleep. The sun was up and the clock read
eight. I'd slept almost eleven hours and felt much
better. Most of the achiness was gone. I reached for
the phone.

"So, tell me what happened."

"What?" I cleared my throat.

"With Claire's mother. What happened? I kept
waiting for your call yesterday. I couldn't wait any
longer. Did I wake you?"

"No problem." I yawned. "Listen, Lucy, I know
it's only Monday, but are you free today? Can you
get Birdie and come over? There's a lot to tell you,
and I have some of Claire's quilts here."

"No way!"

"Just come over and I'll tell you everything."

An hour later we were eating pastries out of a
pink box from Bea's Bakery and sipping fresh
coffee in my living room. I told them Claire said

her quilts were her journals and Siobhan asked me to search for the messages. I explained I'd searched Claire's house and found four quilts and Will Terry told me I could only keep them until Wednesday.

"Will you help me?"

"Does a chicken have lips?" Lucy joked. "I'm dying to see them."

"There's one more thing. Detective Beavers came over last night to show me the composite drawing of the thief, but I didn't recognize him."

Birdie sat up straighter. "Yes, he came over to my house yesterday afternoon. I didn't recognize him either."

"Neither did I." Lucy shook her head.

"I also told the detective about the possible messages in the quilts. At first he was skeptical and then he warned me to back off and leave the investigating to the police. Said poking around could be dangerous."

Lucy peered at me through narrowed eyes. "You know, he's a good-looking man, and I didn't see a ring on his finger."

"I didn't notice," I lied. If Lucy knew I was the tiniest bit attracted to a man, she'd go out of her way to push us together. Lucy and Birdie worried about my being single, but I was perfectly happy living alone. Besides, I hadn't been particularly successful with romantic relationships in the past. My daughter, my uncle, my quilting, and my friends were my life. Why would I want more?

I picked up the pillowcases and walked over to the dining room table situated at the end of the living room near the kitchen. "So, let's open these up and make a list of what we've got."

All of these quilts were meant to be used as wall hangings and none were larger than four feet by four feet. I showed them Mother's Asleep and pointed out the silver seeds in the clouds and the water drop beads below. "Doesn't this remind you of rainmaking?"

Lucy bent over the table to get a closer look. "Yes, but I don't recall seeing this quilt. Did Claire ever show it?"

Birdie picked up a corner of the quilt. "I don't think so. I'm pretty sure we'd remember a quilt as odd as this one."

I reached in a pillowcase and pulled out the quilt I removed from Claire's living room wall. "Here's Secret Garden."

Lucy reached out and gently touched it. "Ooh, I remember this from the show two years ago. Wasn't it featured in *Pieces* magazine?"

"Yeah. Can you make anything out of the design?"

Birdie shook her head. "Just looks like a painting of a tranquil garden."

Lucy nodded in agreement.

"Let's look at the next one then."

We looked at the label on the back of a quilt measuring about three feet by four feet. We didn't feel any notes sewn inside, and the only writing was on the label: Jamey I Hardly Knew Ye. The traditional pieced blocks on the front were composed of squares and triangles within triangles. The whole thing was also embellished with French knots.

"I remember this quilt." Birdie smiled. "Jamey was in our show a few years ago. This block design looks like something I once did called Cat's Cradle."

"Well, let's look in BlockBase to make sure of the name." I booted up my laptop and opened the software program containing a database for thousands of traditional block designs. I typed in Cat's Cradle in the search box, and up popped a picture of Claire's block.

"Look how many names this block has. Cat's Cradle, Double Pyramids, Dove at the Window, Flying Birds, and Wandering Lover."

Lucy pointed her finger. "You know, the title of this quilt contains a man's name—Jamey. What if he was Claire's 'wandering lover'?"

Birdie patted Lucy on the back. "Brilliant! Do we know if she had a lover?"

"Well, when I searched for the key to Claire's quilt cupboard, I discovered a half-full box of condoms in her panty drawer."

Lucy nodded. "There you go. Now, if the condoms were in her sewing room, I'd say she could have been using them as grips to pull a stuck needle out of a quilt. Since they were in with her panties, we have to assume they were being used as God intended."

"That's pretty funny coming from a Catholic girl, but you're right. Aside from those little rubber circles you can buy in the quilt store, I've seen quilters use finger cots and even pieces of balloons to grip on to a stubborn needle—but never a condom."

"What kind of panties?" asked Lucy. "You can sometimes tell a lot about a person by their underwear."

"Black lacy thongs, about the size of the palm of my hand."

"Bingo. Those are 'do me' panties." She wiggled her fingers in air quotes. "Claire could've been having an affair with someone named Jamey. Maybe he was the wandering lover. They could have fought and he killed her."

"So why steal her new quilt and not this one?"

Lucy shrugged. "You said this quilt was in a locked cupboard, right? Maybe he didn't know about this one."

Birdie smoothed her hand over the quilt. "Just look at all these French knots. They remind me of an odd kind of painting they did. What was it called?"

"Pointillism?"

"Yes, that's it."

"You know what else they remind me of?" asked Lucy. "The funny pictures in old-timey newspapers.

Do you remember when you were a kid looking really close at the Sunday funnies and discovering the colors weren't solid but made out of hundreds of tiny dots of ink?"

"Well, if there's a picture in these knots I don't see it."

The next quilt was an appliqué Claire named Night Flower. Stunningly detailed red roses were appliquéd over a field of navy blue. Each flower was created by layering the petals one at a time. The petals of the roses were attached with great skill, using invisible stitches around the edges. Claire arranged the roses in the middle of the quilt in the shape of a *T*.

Small four-leaf clovers nestled randomly around the edges of the quilt created a border of green. Claire had used a great deal of skill to appliqué those small inside curves without visible stitches. Did she use silk thread? Silk was thin and slinky and tended to sink into the weave of the fabric where it couldn't be seen. Sewn in among the clovers were the same clear beads in Claire's other quilts and, of course, the ubiquitous French knots in the background.

"I don't remember Claire ever entering this in a show. Do you?"

Both Birdie and Lucy shook their heads.

"Look at this. Here are those beads again. They

must mean something if she has them sewn in so many quilts."

Birdie fingered one of the beads. "Well, look at the pear shape. Maybe they don't just symbolize water drops. Maybe they're tears."

Lucy reached out to finger the beads. "If they represent tears, she must've lived one really sad life. Many of her quilts seem to have those beads. Whoa . . . Look! Do you see this? The quilting stitches are so close to the roses, I almost missed them."

I adjusted my glasses to get a closer look.

Lucy pointed to the visible, even quilting stitches. Unlike appliqué stitches, quilting stitches are meant to be seen. They're the things holding the three layers of a quilt together. They're usually sewn in a regular pattern yielding a secondary geometric design of intersecting straight lines, regular curves, or stippling. These stitches were different.

I could hardly believe my eyes. "There's an outline of a woman who appears to be lying behind the roses. She's almost hidden under the flowers. See? There's just an outline, but her legs are slightly spread to either side and her arms outstretched. You can see her head peeking out from behind the top of the *T* and sort of hanging down on the side. Like a crucifixion, only the body is under the cross, not on top of it."

Birdie's eyes widened. "This is just like finding

an image of the Virgin Mary in a grilled cheese sandwich."

"Better. I'm going to write this all down in my notepad."

I looked at what I had so far. Rainmaking. Crucifixion. Tears. Lovers. I was convinced we were on to something but couldn't quite figure out how to find the story. Clearly no paper notes lurked in any of Claire's quilts. Siobhan said Claire kept a list of all her quilts. I needed more data to connect the dots. I needed to see Claire's other quilts, and that meant going back to the house to look for the list.

"I'm starved." Lucy put her hand on her stomach.

"I'll fix us something to eat. What do you feel like?"

"How about grilled cheese sandwiches?"

CHAPTER 11

I took out my black cast iron skillet. I preferred cast iron over any other kind of cookware. A well-seasoned pan had a natural nonstick quality and cast iron distributed the heat evenly. My bubbie was the best cook I'd ever known, and she always used cast iron pans, one set for meat and one for dairy. The weight of those pans made the wooden shelves in the pantry sag over time. My uncle Isaac still lived in our old house, still cooked with those pans, and the shelves still sagged. I totally got why he didn't fix them; doing so would be like erasing decades of family history.

I put slices of sharp cheddar cheese on pieces of challah and sprinkled each with a hint of powdered garlic. I slapped a second piece of bread on top of each one and buttered the outside of the sandwiches. When the pan was hot enough, I cooked the sandwiches a couple minutes on each side. The bread turned a golden brown and the yellow cheese dripped luxuriously down the crust of the bread. I garnished each plate with a handful of baby carrots and fresh apple quarters. You had to draw the calorie line somewhere.

Since the dining table was covered with quilts, we sat at the kitchen island. The island served as a divider between the cooking area and the living area and also served as an informal eating surface. We climbed on the high stools, and Lucy's were the only feet resting on the floor. Birdie and I dangled like children at the grown-ups' table. Birdie picked up her sandwich and turned it over. "Does anybody see an image in their grilled cheese?"

I munched on an apple quarter and studied my plate. "I think I see a picture of Elvis Presley."

Lucy perked up and reached for my plate. "For real? His image could bring hundreds on eBay. Let me see."

Birdie started to giggle.

"Dang it, Martha." Lucy handed my plate back.

When we finished eating, we washed the grease off our hands and examined Claire's quilts again.

Finally Lucy stepped away from the table and looked at me. "I'm not seeing anything new."

Birdie shook her head. "Me neither."

I took several photos of each quilt with my digital camera and then folded them back up. "We need more data. I'm going back to Claire's house and search for the list of quilts Siobhan mentioned."

"We'd offer to go, but both Birdie and I need to get back home."

"Tomorrow's Quilty Tuesday anyway. Let's meet here at the usual time, if that's okay with you. I should have the list by then."

Birdie picked up the empty pink bakery box and put it in the recycle bin next to my sink. "Don't worry about getting goodies. I'll bake something tonight."

"Great. Thanks," I hoped Birdie would either make her coconut ginger cookies or my very favorite, her applesauce cake. She was very liberal with the sugar and the butter, just the way I liked it. I hugged each one before they walked out the door. "See you *mañana* at the usual time."

After they left, I put the quilts back in the pillowcases. I was afraid if the thief ever figured out the quilts were in my house, he wouldn't hesitate to come after them, so I put them at the bottom of the laundry hamper under some dirty clothes. I was pretty sure he wouldn't go through my dirty laundry. Another chess move. What I didn't realize at the time was although thieves can come when you're not at home, they can also come when you're there.

I arrived at Claire's around two and let myself in with the key. The cat ran up to greet me. "Come on, kitty. Let's check on your food." I entered Claire's sewing room five minutes later and immediately saw something was very wrong. The quilt cupboard I emptied yesterday and relocked had been jimmied open. Siobhan was right about the thief coming back for Claire's quilts. I looked inside the empty cupboard but didn't touch anything. If my plan worked, the thief's prints would be all over it.

If I got the heck out of the house and called Detective Beavers about the open cupboard, he'd make this a crime scene again, and I'd never get to finish my search. The quilts were due to go back to the Terrys in two days, but first I wanted to make sure I was alone. I picked up a pair of eight-inch sewing shears to defend myself and tiptoed through the house, my heart pounding in my throat. The cat padded right beside me. "Why couldn't you be a Rottweiler?" I whispered.

There was a broken window in the guest room, with glass all over the floor. The window faced the front of the house and was hidden behind a tall, dense hibiscus—the perfect secluded entry point. The thief broke the stationary side of the window in order to reach in and unlock it. Then he removed the screen and slid aside the moving half of the window, creating a smooth entryway. A five-minute search of the house confirmed the thief was long gone. I definitely ought to call Beavers. Just not yet.

I headed back to the sewing room to look for a quilter's diary. Many quilters kept a sort of journal with photos and histories of each of their quilts—like when it was made and who it was made for.

A journal might also contain small samples of the

fabrics used or anecdotal comments such as *This quilt took me three years to complete*, or *The floral fabrics came from my daughter's little dresses and my grandmother's feed sacks*. I kept thick loose leaf binders with separate pages of photos and text about every quilt I made. I was on my fifth binder.

I searched the wall of books first but didn't find anything. I opened the drawers and cupboards one by one. Nothing. Where could Claire's journals be?

The cat and I walked back through the bedroom to Claire's office, passing again the luxurious silks and Mary Cassatt painting. *Funny the thief didn't take the painting. Maybe he didn't know what it was worth.* A four-drawer metal file cabinet stood against the office wall.

I hesitated to touch Claire's personal files. I reminded myself I was only after the list of her quilts, so I shouldn't snoop into anything else. Right. Like I was really going to listen to myself.

The files were color coded and neatly labeled. I went to the green Income section first, thinking that since she had sold many of her quilts, she would have filed the list there. Wrong.

Well heck, since I was already there, I might as well take a teensy little peek at her financials. I knew from watching lots of crime shows that money was one of the main motives for murder. So, who might benefit from her death?

Claire kept a huge investment portfolio managed by J.P. Morgan and had a half-million-dollar annual income from something called the Terry Family Trust. I could have lived on the income from her CDs alone and still had enough left over to buy a new Corolla every year.

Claire had been very wealthy but she hadn't flaunted it. She seemed so shy at the guild meetings and liked talking to Birdie. From her modest behavior, I would never have guessed she was worth so much. If the rumors about her messy divorce were true, I could see why. A lot of money had been at stake.

In the purple tax section, there was a folder with some check registers going back a couple of years. She made out checks to a Jerry Bell on a monthly basis, ranging from one thousand dollars to ten thousand dollars, as far back as the record went. Who was Jerry Bell, anyway? Her lover? If so, did he manage to con a small income out of her? Or maybe he was a blackmailer. What could he have blackmailed her about? I made copies of the registers on Claire's copier and put the originals back in their folder.

Then I found a folder labeled Jerry Bell. Inside was his name, phone number, and address, which I copied into my notepad. Strange. Why such a dearth of information? Claire was an obsessively detailed person. Why wouldn't there also be a record in his file of the payments she made to him? This was beginning to smell more and more like blackmail.

I noticed she paid for appointments at a well-known spa located near Little Armenia in Hollywood. Los Angeles was known to have natural hot springs made possible by the unique geology of the area; something having to do with the subducting of the Pacific tectonic plate beneath the North American plate. Back in the 1920s and '30s, a number of Turkish bathhouses around the city tapped into the various hot springs and capitalized on the natural steam and mineral water.

As the city grew and developed, the pipes were eventually capped off and the bathhouses disappeared under high-rises. To my knowledge, this spa was the only one of its kind remaining in LA. A person could soak in the hot bubbling water or get a massage, body scrub, acupuncture, mud wrap, or facial. Judging from the weekly checks, Claire liked her little luxuries on a regular basis.

On spa days, Claire also wrote a check to Mai's Nail Palace. What a life. Go to the spa, get a massage and a facial, and then go get a mani-pedi. Must be nice.

There were also weekly checks in her check registers made out to a Dr. Alexander Godwin, but they stopped about eight months ago. What kind of doctor did someone see on a weekly basis? A chiropractor? Acupuncturist? Psychiatrist?

I pulled out a folder with his name. Dr. Godwin was a shrink. Why was Claire in therapy? Knowing why might lead straight to the killer. Godwin could be a gold mine of information, but I doubted he'd divulge anything to me. I wrote down his name, address, and phone number anyway. I could always give him a shot.

I looked through the folders in the yellow section marked Charitable Contributions and found one for the Blind Children's Association. There were several receipts for thousands of dollars she donated on a regular basis.

At the back of the file was a letter on the association's stationery thanking Claire for including them in her "long-term giving" plan. Claire named BCA as a beneficiary of her will. Some nonprofits were relentless in their pursuit of bequests. Looked like BCA managed to snag a big fish with Claire. Did someone in the organization get tired of waiting for her to grow old and die?

In the left-hand margin of the BCA letterhead was a list of board members. At the top of the list was the name of the chairman: Alexander Godwin, MD. Well, well . . .

I went on to search the orange section marked Miscellaneous. Bingo! A folder labeled Quilts. My heart sped up a little as I opened it.

Empty.

Darn! The thief must have taken the list of quilts. How did he know the list existed? He might have known Claire or known about the custom of keeping a quilt journal, like another quilter would. Carlotta Hudson's sour face popped into my head.

Was Lucy right? Did Carlotta Hudson kill Claire

in a fit of jealousy? Carlotta couldn't have stolen the quilts from the show, but an accomplice could have. Was she the one trying to get her hands on the rest of Claire's quilts?

I hoped Claire kept a backup copy of the missing list somewhere on her computer. I booted up the laptop on her desk. Password protected. *Darn again.*

Then I realized—whatever the thief touched in the filing cabinet I also touched. If he left any fingerprints, I just screwed them up. Detective Beavers was going to be really, really mad. The only thing I hadn't touched was the sewing room cabinet, so maybe they could still get fingerprints from that.

I looked at my watch; nearly six. I closed the file drawers and stuffed the copies of the check registers and the notepad in my purse. I took the laptop out to my car and put it in my trunk. If only I could find the password, I could look at her document files. There was sure to be a copy of the list there.

I sat on the bench outside the front door. The card Detective Beavers gave me at the quilt show was still in my purse. I called him on my cell phone.

"Arlo Beavers."

"This is Martha Rose. I'm afraid someone has broken in to Claire Terry's house."

"How do you know?"

"Because I'm here, at her house."

"Impossible. How did you manage to pop up at yet another crime scene?"

I didn't much care for his tone of voice. "I came

to get something Claire's mother wanted and discovered someone broke in. The window in the
guest room was shattered. The door to her quilt
cabinet was jimmied open. I think the thief came
looking for the four quilts I took home with me."

"Sit tight. Don't touch anything. I'll be there in
fifteen minutes."

I called Siobhan next.

"Siobhan, this is Martha Rose. I'm at Claire's
house looking for the list of quilts you mentioned."

"Did you find one?"

"No. Someone else beat me to it. The folder
where she kept the list was empty. The thief came
in through a window and broke into her quilt cabinet. You were right about his coming back for the
rest of her quilts."

"Are you all right?"

"Yes, but I'm concerned about the Mary Cassatt
painting in her bedroom. The thief apparently
didn't know enough to take it. Shouldn't you move
it to a safer place?"

"Oh, I forgot all about that painting. Thanks for
reminding me. I'll have Will take care of it."

"Another thing, Siobhan. Did Claire have a
boyfriend?"

"If she did, she didn't say. After her divorce from
James years ago, she didn't seem interested in
dating."

"Did you say James?"

"Yes. James Trueville."

"Did Claire ever call him Jamey?"

Siobhan sighed. "Yes. That was her pet name for him."

"I know this sounds weird, but was he ever unfaithful to Claire?"

"Yes. His infidelity was the primary reason for the divorce. Why do you ask?"

"It has to do with one of the quilts. I'll tell you more when I can. Meanwhile, the police are on their way so I don't have much time. Do I have your permission to take Claire's laptop home to search for the list?"

"Of course. When you find it, please fax me a copy at this same number."

"Right. Do you have any idea what her password is?"

"I'm sorry. I don't know anything about computers."

I looked up. The cat stood at the front door. "One last thing—what do you want to do about her cat? The police are probably going to seal off the house again."

"Heavens. I forgot all about Bumper. Could you take him? I'm allergic to cats."

When my daughter, Quincy, was growing up, we adopted a succession of hamsters, dogs, and cats. Quincy even kept a garden snake she named Buttons when she was twelve years old—a love offering from one of the many neighborhood boys who had a crush on her. I had to persuade her to return him to the wild where he could be reunited with his family, who worried about him. We drove up Topanga until we found a dry, grassy area and released him, chanting "Good-bye dear Buttons. You're free to be."

When Quincy went away to college, three cats and a dog stayed behind with me. One by one they aged and died. The last of them, a timid Siamese cat named Mazda, after Quincy's first car, died about a year ago. I really missed him.

I looked over at the ginger ball of fur smiling at me. "No problem. I think we've bonded."

I headed back in the house. The cat kept bumping his head against my leg and purring as I gathered up his gear from the laundry room. "Now I know how you got your name." I scratched him behind the ears and under his jaw where his scent glands were. I found his carrier and put him and his stuff in my car. Then I sat down on the bench by the front door to wait for the police.

Again.

CHAPTER 12

The familiar silver Camry pulled into the driveway behind my car. Detective Beavers got out and strode over to me with a scowl on his face.

Oh God. I dreaded the confrontation that was a nanosecond away.

"I just got off the phone with Mrs. Terry. She confirmed your story."

"My *story*?"

"Tell me what happened."

"Siobhan Terry told me there was a list of all the quilts Claire made and who owned them."

"Did you find it?"

"I was too late. The file was empty."

"Was there anything else missing?"

"How would I know? The thief was too dumb to take the Cassatt painting hanging in Claire's bedroom, but that's all I noticed. I can tell you if I hadn't taken her quilts home with me last night, they would now be long gone. The thief broke into the locked cabinet where they were stored."

"Did you take anything else out of this house, like a laptop?"

"Did the police leave a laptop behind?" I deftly skirted his question.

"A simple misunderstanding. Forensics thought Kaplan had taken care of it and Kaplan thought they had taken it. We were about to rectify the situation when I got your call. Please tell me the laptop is still here."

"It is not." Still not an outright lie.

"I did take the cat and his gear." If Beavers got hold of Claire's laptop before I had a chance to find the list, I could kiss my research good-bye. Besides, Siobhan said I could have it.

"How long were you in there?"

"A little more than three hours."

His scowl deepened and I could tell he was about to get all pissy with me again. Fortunately a patrol car pulled into the driveway behind the Camry. Beavers walked over to them. "Secure the house until CSU gets here."

Then he walked back. "I'm going inside to look around. I want you to go home and lock your doors. I'll be by your house later this evening, so stay put."

This was the second time in less than an hour he'd given me an order. I stood as tall as I could and looked at him. "You need to be specific about the time you'll be there. I have better things to do than sit around and wait for you."

His eyes darkened. He hooked his thumbs in his belt and leaned slightly forward. "My ETA is somewhere between now and midnight. Be there."

I drove down Canoga when it hit me. Statements were usually given at the police station. At least that's how it was done on television. What was he up to?

I stopped at Crazy Chicken Takeout and got some wings, thighs, and a side of coleslaw to go. When I got back in the car, Bumper was yowling. He told me in no uncertain terms he wanted out of his carrier. "I'm sorry, Bumper, but California law says cats have to stay in their cages while riding in a motor vehicle. My hands are tied."

I made three trips to carry everything into my house from the car. I put Claire's laptop in the closet in my office. Then I set up Bumper's food, water, and litter box in my laundry room. When I let him out of the carrier, he made a beeline for the litter box. Cats were smart that way.

I took a Coke Zero from the refrigerator and ate my Crazy Chicken $4.99 special while Bumper loudly crunched his star-shaped kibble. "It's been a while since I've eaten dinner alone with a man. What do you think about taking our relationship to the next level? Are you ready to commit, because I am." Bumper answered by jumping up on my lap and purring. I smiled and scratched him under the chin.

After dinner I pulled my blue and white quilt out of the tote bag and started to quilt the curving lines of the Bishop's Fan pattern. Quilting by hand always calmed me, almost to a meditative state. Soon the rhythm of the needle biting through the fabric made me forget about Claire and her quilts. My focus was on following the gently curving lines of the Bishop's Fan.

I was known in the quilting community for my tiny quilting stitches. My secret was in the needle I used—a size eleven "between," which was only one inch long because a short needle made small stitches. The higher the number the smaller the needle. The size eleven was a hybrid combining the short length of a size twelve with the bigger eye of a size ten to accommodate the thicker dimension of quilting thread.

At eight Beavers knocked on my door. I looked into his big brown eyes, noticed the way his mustache softened the line of his upper lip, caught a whiff of his Me Tarzan cologne, and remembered again why I found him attractive.

I shrugged. "Come in and let's get this over with." He followed me to the kitchen where I had already put a kettle of water on to boil.

"Exactly when did you arrive at the crime scene today?" He slid onto a stool at the island.

"Around two."

"Yet you didn't call me until after five? What were you doing?"

The kettle was boiling. I poured two mugs of steaming hot black tea and brought them over to where he sat. "Research."

"What the heck does that mean?"

"No need to get huffy, Detective. Milk and sugar?"

He took the cup. "Sugar, and please answer the question."

I brought spoons along with a jar of agave syrup and a cream pitcher and sat on the next stool over. "It means I was there at the request of Claire's mother, looking for a list of Claire's quilts. Like I told you earlier."

He picked up the bottle of sweetener. "What's this?"

"Sweet syrup from the agave plant. It's natural and much better for you than refined sugar. One teaspoon is usually enough."

"Agave, the same plant they make tequila from?"

"Exactly."

He squeezed a spoonful into his cup and stirred. "Which rooms did you go into?"

I put milk and syrup into my cup. "All of them."

He blew on his tea and took a sip. "When did you discover the quilt cabinet had been tampered with?"

"Almost as soon as I got there."

He narrowed his eyes. "Why didn't you call the police then?"

"I needed a little more time to look for the list. I looked through all the bookshelves and drawers in her sewing room, but I didn't find a journal or list of any kind."

"What did you do after you left the sewing room?"

"I went to her office where I eventually found her empty Quilt folder."

"What time was that?"

"I don't remember exactly. I spent quite a while looking through her files."

"Why didn't you call the police when you discovered the file was missing?"

"I thought maybe Claire filed a backup copy somewhere else, so I kept looking."

"Are you sure you didn't see her computer?"

"Heavens." I stared at my tea. Could I get away with answering a question with a question? "Do you think the intruder took it? I was focused on the papers in the filing cabinet."

"For more than three hours? What were you doing all that time?"

"You know, Detective, you need to be more trusting. I'm neither the thief nor the killer. I was there legitimately. Everything I did was with Mrs. Terry's approval, and when I was done, you were the first person I called."

I was on a roll. "And, by the way, locking the quilt cupboard yesterday was my idea. I thought if the thief came back to Claire's house, looking for quilts, he'd be forced to jimmy open the lock and leave his fingerprints. What do you know—I was right. So, if you lift any prints from the cabinet door, you have me to thank." I leaned back and felt as self-righteous as a politician's campaign ad.

"Did it ever occur to you the thief will eventually figure out where Claire Terry's quilts are and come after them?"

"Of course. This morning I hid them where no *man* would think of going."

"Where?"

"In the dirty laundry."

"Are they still there?"

Oh my God. I couldn't say for sure. Since arriving home, I'd been too busy to check on them. So far, the thief was one step behind me. The possibility of the quilts having been taken from my house made my face feel like it was dissolving into a gazillion swirling molecules. My lips went numb and my pulse rate shot up. I got up and walked quickly toward the laundry room. "I don't know." *Please, God, let the quilts be there.*

I exhaled. The bundles were still where I left them. Darn that Detective Beavers, scaring me to death. I took a couple of calming breaths and walked casually back into the kitchen and sat down. "They're still here." I sipped my tea noisily.

"You need to give them back."

"I will, Detective, day after tomorrow. Meanwhile, I made a promise to Siobhan that I intend to keep."

"Listen to me very carefully, Martha Rose."

The tiniest thrill of pleasure went through me in the way he used my whole name. It seemed somehow intimate, despite the sharpness in his voice.

"I don't know what you think you're doing, but I do know you better stop right now."

My bully radar started pinging and my brief sense of pleasure evaporated. This man just loved to throw orders around, but he didn't intimidate me. "Just what do you mean?"

Beavers never took his eyes off my face. "You knowingly tampered with a crime scene, a misdemeanor. By touching everything he touched, you've compromised our ability to collect his fingerprints. If you're holding anything back, that's obstruction. A felony."

"Well, how was I to know he stole the office files? If I messed up the prints, I didn't mean to. Besides, I was careful not to touch the quilt cupboard door."

"Listen carefully. This is not TV where crimes are solved in one hour minus the commercials. This is the dark side of LA. Poking around in people's lives can be dangerous. You can get killed. You can get sued. You can also get arrested for playing amateur detective."

He didn't scare me.

In the 1970s, in my antiwar protest days, I used to call the police "fuzz" and "pigs." They were much scarier back then, before sensitivity training and dash cams. "Just who the heck do you think you are, talking to me that way? I'm not afraid of you. My friends and I are going to find the messages in Claire's quilts. When we do, we'll likely find her killer."

Beavers spoke slowly, in a barely controlled voice. "There is someone out there who is after something you have. He may be the same person who killed Claire Terry. If he's killed once, he could easily kill again. Do you think you and a couple of senior ladies are any match for such a person?"

"That does it!" I jumped off the stool, shaking my finger. "The truth finally comes out. Just because we're older, you think we're stupid and incompetent. Any woman with gray hair is written off by society. We become invisible. A lifetime of achievement and wisdom is erased with a roll of the eyes and a patronizing smile."

Bumper must have sensed I was upset because he jumped up on the island, pinned his ears back, and stared at Beavers.

"I'm not a social worker or a shrink. If you feel you're invisible, call the AARP."

"Very funny."

My problem was that at one time, I had been very visible. As the only child raised in an extended family household, I was the center of everyone's world. Marriage to Aaron Rose changed all that. I felt invisible after years of his emotional abuse. Then, when the arrogant little jerk finally left me for another woman, he took what was left of my self-esteem. It took years of hard work to find myself again. I wasn't about to let another man treat me badly. Even if he was really, really hunky.

Beavers got up to leave. "Get off your high horse, Ms. Rose, and take my advice. Give the quilts back and stop playing Jessica Fletcher." He opened the front door and turned to me. "Make sure to keep your doors locked."

Bumper hissed at him from across the room.

Beavers's sarcasm raised my hackles, but at the same time my heart skipped a little at the look he gave me—almost as if he really cared.

My God, Martha, stop being so pathetic! The attraction is probably only in your mind.

TUESDAY

CHAPTER 13

The next morning was Quilty Tuesday, one week after we discovered Claire Terry's body. Bumper perched on the back of the sofa and looked out the window to survey his new home. He didn't run away when Lucy and Birdie arrived at ten. A good sign.

"Where'd you get the cat?" Lucy put her tote bag down beside her favorite easy chair. She was dressed in grass green pants, a green and yellow print silk blouse, apple jade earrings and bangle bracelet, and yellow sandals. She smelled like Jungle Gardenia and with her bright orange hair reminded me of the tropical plant section at Home Depot.

"He was Claire's. Siobhan asked me to take him, so Bumper and I are an official couple now."

Birdie handed me a plate covered in foil. The cinnamon and cardamom of the applesauce cake underneath wafted into the room. Then she stepped over to the sofa and caressed the soft ginger fur ball. Bumper burst into an ecstatic purr.

I served coffee with the cake as we all sat. Birdie made it with lots of plump, sweet raisins—just the way I liked it.

Lucy took a sip of coffee. "So, did you find the list?"

"No, unfortunately. The thief got there first." Between bites of cake I told them all about the empty folder and what Claire's other files revealed.

Birdie was an avid fan of crime dramas and spoke forensics as a second language. "Looks like you may have uncovered some possible perps, dear. Jerry Bell, who is either her lover or blackmailer, and a nonprofit organization headed by her psychiatrist, no less, which stands to gain by her death."

"It appears so."

Lucy reached for another piece of cake. "Let's not forget Carlotta Hudson. Who else but another quilter would know to look for a journal or a list?"

"Did you find out who stands to inherit Claire's money besides the Blind Children's Association?" asked Birdie.

"I didn't see a will anywhere in her files. Oh, there's one other thing." I told them about taking the computer home and fibbing to Detective Beavers.

Birdie grabbed the end of her braid. "Oh my goodness, Martha. Won't you get in big trouble?"

"Well, Siobhan said I could take the computer

and I didn't exactly lie. I just kind of asked him if he thought the intruder might have taken it."

"I don't know," said Lucy. "What you did was pretty risky. Not telling him you took home Claire's computer was an important detail. What do you think he'll do when he finds out?"

"He won't. I'll give the computer back to Siobhan as soon as we're through with it."

I retrieved the laptop from the closet. "Well, we've got to find her password in order to get into this thing."

Lucy reached out her hands. "Let me." Of the three of us, Lucy was the most computer literate, thanks to the patient tutoring of her son Richie, who'd earned a degree in computer science. We crowded around Lucy's chair and stared at the black screen while Lucy pressed the power button.

A familiar four-note melody sounded as the screen turned blue and asked for a password. Lucy typed in *Claire, Claire Terry, Claire's Laptop, Quilter, Quilts, Quilting*, but nothing worked. "This could take forever."

"Does Richie have some software that could get us in?"

"Probably. He's in San Francisco this week, though." That was Lucy's code for something she rarely talked about: her middle son was gay and regularly visited Silicon Valley to be with his boyfriend.

I'd known Richie since he was in Little League. He was like every other boy. Loved to play sports and excelled at baseball. Richie was also the brightest of Lucy's five boys, majoring in the hot new science of computers when he went to college. Lucy thought his reluctance to start dating girls was just due to shyness.

So, when Richie "came out" in college, Lucy and Ray were caught completely off guard. Ray had the hardest time accepting his son's sexual orientation, but he eventually reconciled himself to Richie. Lucy supported her son from the time she found out but still seemed to feel a little embarrassed. I once reminded her there is little stigma anymore, at least in the liberal community.

"Yeah," she'd replied, "but we're Republicans, Martha. It's still a big deal in our world."

"Well, if you're so Republican, why didn't you vote for George W. Bush?"

"There are limits to everything."

So, here we were, trying to get into Claire's computer on our own. "We'll just have to figure this thing out. Try her address, ninety-three hundred Rosario Road."

"Nothing."

"What do you normally use for a password?" asked Birdie.

Lucy paused for a moment. "Usually something that you won't forget easily. I use the names of quilt blocks for my passwords, like Monkey Wrench or Log Cabin."

"What name did Claire give to her latest quilt?" asked Birdie.

"Ascending, I think. Right, Martha?"

I nodded. "Try it."

Nothing happened.

"We'll try the names of her other quilts, just in case." Lucy typed in variations of Mother's Asleep, Midnight Garden, Secret Garden, Wandering Lover, and Jamey I Hardly Knew Ye, but the screen stayed stubbornly blue.

Birdie persisted. "Wait. What's the cat's name again?"

"Bumper. Passwords are never that obvious, Birdie. You need to make it really hard for someone to hack into your computer."

"Why not just try it anyway?"

Lucy typed in *Bumper*. Nothing happened. She looked up. "Sorry, hon'. Good guess, though."

I put my hand on Lucy's shoulder. "Wait a minute. Maybe it's case sensitive. Try all uppercase or all lowercase."

When she typed in *BUMPER* all caps, Lucy got a hit. Yes! At last we were in, and Birdie, who knew nothing about computers, beamed.

Claire kept hundreds of documents and e-mails. We carefully scrolled down until we spotted a folder titled Quilts.

We found only one document in the folder—three pages recording in chronological order the names of all her quilts and dates of completion.

When Claire sold a quilt, she listed the selling price and the buyer's name and contact information.

"Martha, what is your wireless password? I want to use your printer."

I thought I was pretty creative with my password. I used something easy to remember—my daughter's name. "Quincy."

Lucy snorted. "Talk about the obvious."

I smiled. "Not when you change the spelling to *kwinsee,* all lowercase letters."

Five minutes later we each held a hard copy in our hands. I put my copy in my fax machine, typed in Siobhan's number, and pressed the button. Then I looked over the list. "Look on page three. Claire donated her last quilt to the Blind Children's Association for a silent auction this month."

Lucy turned the pages. "Curiouser and curiouser. Which quilt?"

"Lullaby. A baby quilt."

Birdie leaned toward the computer screen. "Oh, I wish we could see what it looked like."

Lucy started typing on the keyboard. "Maybe we can. I'll look for her photo album." A minute passed. "Bingo!"

My glasses slipped farther down my nose as I also leaned in to get a closer look at the laptop screen. Each of Claire's quilts was extensively photographed both full size and up close. The baby quilt was pieced with a simple basket design in yellow and white. Claire used dark gold embroidery thread to make her French knots.

We studied the list, trying to find a pattern or clue in the quilt names, and scrutinized the photos. "Does anything jump out at you?" I asked.

Birdie sighed. "Not so far, but maybe these titles are anagrams or cryptograms. I'm pretty good with word puzzles. I'll work on them tonight." Birdie was being modest. She was an avid reader and true wordsmith, easily solving the *New York Times* Sunday crossword puzzle in ink!

Lucy sounded frustrated. "If she stitched her life's stories into these quilts, I sure don't see how. We probably should make a backup copy of everything before we have to give back the laptop. Those pictures may prove to be invaluable."

"How are you going to do that?"

"In case of a disaster, Richie told me it was important to keep backup files off-site. So I carry a ten-gig flash drive with me." Lucy dug around in her purse and pulled out her key ring. She waved her hand. "All our personal and business files."

I poured another round of coffee while she plugged the flash drive into the USB port and copied Claire's files.

"I've got an idea. I'm going to call Claire's psychiatrist. If there is a pattern or a code, she might have told him."

Lucy and Birdie exchanged a look.

I stared at them. "What?"

"Well, we just know how much you love shrinks."

Lucy was alluding to my ex-husband, Aaron Rose, the psychiatrist. We weren't exactly bitter enemies, but I didn't like the man. He was an arrogant know-it-all who could never be wrong. I helped put him through medical school and in return he transformed me into a cliché. After our daughter was born, he cheated on me and eventually dumped me for the gorgeous wife of one of his colleagues. "I've outgrown our relationship," he told me. If anyone could push my button, it was Aaron.

"I'll be fine."

Birdie didn't seem so sure. "Martha, what about confidentiality? Do you really think he'll tell you anything?"

"What've I got to lose? Time is running out. I've got to give those quilts back tomorrow." I opened my notepad and found the page with his phone number. I expected to get his answering service. He must have been between patients because he picked up the phone. I turned on the speaker so everyone could hear.

"This is Dr. Godwin." Strong voice. Authoritative but pleasant.

"Dr. Godwin, my name is Martha Rose and I'm a friend of the Terry family. We know Claire Terry was very committed to the Blind Children's Association, and that you knew her. I was hoping you might be able to shed some light on a delicate matter."

I glanced over just in time to see Lucy roll her eyes.

"Yes, I knew Claire Terry. She was a wonderful friend to BCA. So dedicated to the children. Her death is a great loss."

"Yes, we are devastated."

I let a few beats pass. "I know you must be terribly busy, Doctor, but Mrs. Terry is quite fragile and I'm running out of time. Is there any possibility I could see you today?" I knew this was a long shot because shrinks rarely made room for the walk-in trade.

"Can you tell me what the delicate matter is?"

"I'd prefer to discuss this in person." I lowered my voice to a near whisper. "I'm not alone right now and I don't want to be overheard."

Lucy smirked.

"Ah, I see." Godwin's voice was reassuring, and I hoped he'd prove to be a sympathetic ally in my search for Claire's story.

"I just so happen to have a cancellation this afternoon. I can see you at one."

Birdie gave me the thumbs-up.

"Thank you so much, Doctor. I'll be there at one."

I put down the phone and looked at my friends. "Well, today's my lucky day."

Lucy threw me an amused look. "What's this 'delicate matter' anyway?"

"Haven't a clue. I'll come up with something. Meanwhile, I'm hoping to examine the quilt to see if there is anything unusual about it." I got up to look for my digital camera, just in case.

Two hours later I parked near an upscale office building on Ventura Boulevard. Lots of windows enclosed an atrium awash in natural daylight. I walked over to a large pool in the center of the atrium to get a closer look.

A miniature waterfall splashed serenely over the lip of a stone fountain into a pool where hyacinths, ferns, and pond lilies sheltered a few golden koi swimming lazily beneath the surface. The air smelled slightly damp.

I took the elevator to the sixth floor. Godwin's office was situated in the corner of the building. The waiting room was small and beige with steel and black leather chairs. Sole practitioner psychiatrists typically didn't employ office staff, and Godwin was no exception. I looked at my watch: 12:55. I flipped through a copy of *Los Angeles* magazine I pulled from a stack on the glass coffee table.

At precisely one, the door on the far side of the reception area opened. Alexander Godwin strongly resembled that forty-something bad boy movie star who was famous for breaking his girlfriends' hearts. He looked down at me from a height of over six feet and with just the right mixture of gravitas and charm. Under the light of his smile, I felt I'd just lost about thirty pounds. "Mrs. Rose? Please come in."

"Actually, it's Ms."

I could see why Claire might have wanted to give gobs of money to BCA. Godwin's smile was *über*-charismatic. He was so charming he probably could have raised donations for the Wall Street bankers' bonus fund.

I patted my hair in place as I walked behind him, down a short hallway to his office. His stride was long and elegant. He stepped aside to allow me to enter his office first. As I passed him, the glint of his gold wedding band caught my eye.

The sunlight streamed into this equally beige room through the two walls of windows and was diffused and softened by the tinted glass.

"Please have a seat, Ms. Rose, and tell me how I can help." He gave me another reassuring smile and directed me to a soft, cream-colored sofa as he took his place in a black leather Eames chair.

I was tempted to smile back. This was the kind of man you wanted to hold your stomach in for. *Come on, focus. I'm supposed to be grieving.* I swallowed hard and visualized dead puppies. Dead kittens. Another Republican in the White House.

CHAPTER 14

A tissue box was strategically placed on the table next to the sofa. Psychiatrists bought them by the carload. I used to go to a big box store to purchase them in bulk for my ex-husband's office. Aaron possessed a true gift for making people cry.

I dared to look up at Dr. Godwin. "Claire told Mrs. Terry she sewed the story of her life into her quilts. Did she ever mention anything about them to you?"

"Well, I knew she made quilts. I gather she was quite good at it, but she never mentioned anything about stories. How would someone go about it, anyway?"

"That's exactly what Mrs. Terry wants me to find out. I was hoping maybe Claire mentioned something to you."

Godwin shook his head slowly. "I'm afraid I can't help you. Was that the 'delicate matter' you mentioned on the phone?"

I shifted uncomfortably in my seat. They say you can tell when someone is lying if they look up and to the right while speaking, so I focused on his perfect nose.

I thought about how I kept running into Arlo Beavers and convinced myself what I was about to say wasn't exactly a lie. "I've been meeting with the police every day, helping them in their investigation." I paused to see if he believed me.

"Interesting. Go on."

"We know Claire was having an affair, and we think her boyfriend may know a great deal about her quilts and her stories. Do you know who he was? Did you ever meet him? Maybe she brought him to a fund-raiser?"

Godwin leaned back in his chair and tented his long fingers, twirling his wedding ring absently with the thumb of his right hand. He closed his eyes. "I'm sorry I can't help you."

"You can't tell me because you don't know or because you were her psychiatrist?"

Godwin opened his eyes, spread his hands, and shook his head sadly. "Since you know she was my patient, you must also be familiar with doctor-patient confidentiality. Even if I knew the answers, I couldn't give them to you."

I shrugged. "Yes, I know about that rule, but I thought I'd give it a try. I was hoping the confidentiality thing wouldn't apply after someone's death."

Godwin checked his watch and moved forward

to the edge of his seat. "Is there anything else I can help you with?"

I stood. "Well, before I leave, could you tell me where to find the baby quilt Claire donated to your silent auction next week? I'd like to take a photograph before it's sold."

He looked puzzled. "Did Claire donate a quilt to the auction?"

"Her records indicate she did."

"Well, you'd have to go to the BCA office. I think all the items are being stored there. Just go down to the third floor. I'll let them know you're coming." He walked me to the door and offered his hand and a look that oozed sincerity. "Good luck, Ms. Rose."

I stepped into the hallway and his door closed softly behind me. Godwin was very skilled at avoiding my questions and slick enough to make me feel I got something when, in reality, he gave me nothing.

The elevator stopped at every floor on the way down. On the third floor a woman led a little boy by the hand into the lift. He walked jerkily, and I wondered if he suffered from cerebral palsy. Then he turned his face up toward his mother and I saw the milky film covering his eyes. My heart wrenched when I realized this little boy walked funny because he couldn't see where he was going. He was blind.

As the stainless steel doors started to close, I put my arm out to stop them. "Excuse me." I stepped around the boy and out into the hallway. Directly in front of me were the offices of the Blind Children's Association. I pulled the door open and entered.

The floor was covered with light brown speckled linoleum. Carpet samples of various textures were glued to the lower half of the walls for the sightless children to feel and explore.

"May I help you?" The young receptionist smiled with brilliant white teeth. Her straight brown hair lay in a silky sheet over her shoulders. Thirty years ago I would have been jealous. Now I was grateful for my wash and wear curls. Less to fuss over.

"Yes. My name's Martha Rose. Dr. Godwin sent me here to photograph the baby quilt Claire Terry donated to your silent auction."

"If you'll take a seat, I'll let our director, Miss Barcelona, know you're here." Another flash of white.

I sat down and looked over at a small girl with thick glasses sitting at a miniature table painted a minty green. A woman sat in an adult-sized chair and handed her a red plastic cube to put in a shape sorter box. I was fascinated when the girl felt the shape of the holes with her tiny fingers, found a square one, and pushed the cube inside the box. She smiled triumphantly. "More."

The woman handed her a triangular block. "Good job."

A minute later a large-boned, horsey woman in her forties came striding out of a doorway extending her arm like a backhoe. She pumped my hand vigorously. "Ms. Rose? My name is Dixie Barcelona. Won't you step into my office?"

We walked into a small room filled with mismatched furniture and bulging file cabinets. A Dell laptop sat open on the desk. I dodged stacks of folders to find an uncovered chair to sit on.

I immediately liked the earnest Dixie Barcelona. She squinted behind thick glasses that made her eyes appear very small. Her navy blue jacket was straight out of the L.L. Bean catalogue, conservative, somewhat shapeless, and wrinkle proof.

Dixie was clearly overworked, so I got right to the point. "I'd like to examine and photograph Claire Terry's quilt before it gets sold."

"Yes. I just got a call from Dr. Godwin. He asked me to make it available to you. All the donated items are in a room down the hall."

Dixie rummaged through the mess on top of her desk until she found a manila folder. Then she led me out of her office and down a hallway with classrooms on both sides.

"Claire's death must have come as quite a shock to you."

Dixie's words came out in a tumble as she pushed open a door at the end of the hall. "It's just awful. Claire was more than just a fund-raiser. We were personal friends. Claire was also a longtime volunteer. Worked with the children for years. She loved these kids as much as I did. She even taught some of them how to do a little sewing. Can you imagine? Teaching blind kids how to sew? She was a talented teacher with a great deal of compassion. We will really miss her."

We stepped into a small room with about fifty large gift baskets sitting on tables and the floor. Each basket was tagged with a number and filled with donated items. Dixie opened the folder and pulled out several pieces of paper with a list typed in large print. She brought the paper close to her face and ran her finger down the list. "Here. The quilt is in basket number twenty-three."

We went through the baskets one by one checking the numbered tags on each one. Basket number twenty-three was under a table in the far corner.

Dixie bent over with a grunt. "Wouldn't you know it, the one you're looking for is always the last one you find." She pulled out the basket and set it up on the table.

It was empty.

We looked at each other for a long moment. Dixie's lips were opening and closing like the koi in the pond downstairs, but no words came out. Beads of sweat began to collect on her upper lip. "There must be some mistake. Probably got into one of the other baskets."

Her arms flailed as she started randomly going through donations.

I put my hand on her shoulder. "Let's do this

methodically. Let's use the list and go through these one by one."

A half hour later, Dixie's jacket was rumpled, her hair was plastered against her forehead, and beads of sweat ran down the sides of her reddened face. We'd searched all the baskets, but the quilt was gone. "I don't know what to say, Ms. Rose."

"Call me Martha. In a way, I'm not surprised. The thief stole a list of Claire's quilts from her house, so he must have known about this one. You need to call the police."

Dixie took a tissue from her pocket and wiped her face. She looked at me with pleading eyes. "Do we have to? The publicity will be awful. If our donors think we're careless with our resources, we might lose their support. I can't help but think of the blind children who will be affected if we're forced to close our doors."

"We can ask the police to be discreet, Dixie, but this is probably connected to Claire's murder. They need to know. I have the number of the detective handling the investigation. I'll give him a call."

She slumped into a folding metal chair and put her hands on her knees. "I hope you're right, Martha. I hope to God you're right."

I took out my cell phone and dialed Beavers's number. Voice mail. "Detective Beavers, this is Martha Rose. I'm calling from the offices of the Blind Children's Association. The quilt Claire Terry donated for their silent auction next week is missing. Looks like the thief has struck again."

As we headed back to Dixie's office, she turned to me. "What should I do now?"

"Well, you'll probably be contacted by Detective Arlo Beavers as soon as he gets my message. Just tell him what you know. Of course, you'll also need to inform Dr. Godwin. Apparently he didn't know Claire donated that quilt in the first place."

"No, he wouldn't. He leaves all the details up to me." She smiled and gestured toward the rest of the offices in an attempt to lighten the mood. "I'm the brains of this outfit and he's the pretty face. His job is to get the large donors that keep us going."

I chuckled. "You're right about the pretty face. Dr. Godwin is quite a hunk. I imagine he's pretty good at pulling in the donations."

"You don't know the half of it. Still, it's bad enough Claire's quilt is missing. We could have raised a lot of money from the sale. Frankly, I'm worried we won't be able to pull this auction off without Claire's help. We count on these fund-raisers to keep us going."

I was moved by Dixie's distress, so I sat down and pulled my checkbook out of my purse. "I know what a blow this must be. I can't attend the auction, but I'd like to give you a donation in Claire's memory."

In Hebrew, the letters spelling the word *chai*, or "life," also stood for the number eighteen. Giving eighteen or multiples of eighteen to charity is considered to be a compound blessing in Jewish tradition. Thinking about the little boy with the milky eyes and the little girl feeling the shapes with her fingers, I wrote a check for ten times chai.

Dixie gushed and pumped my hand. "Oh, Martha, thank you."

Outside in the hallway again, I pushed the call button for the elevator and ran my finger over the Braille embossed beneath. Things became much easier for the visually impaired once elevators, restrooms, and other public facilities were required to post signs in Braille.

At the first floor, I stepped out of the elevator and bumped into a tall man waiting to get in. "Oops. Sorry." I glanced up.

Arlo Beavers took my elbow and steered me over to the koi pond. He strode with grim purpose, and I took two steps to his every one.

"You certainly showed up fast."

"I was on my way over here anyway when I got your message. Talk."

I told him about my visits to Godwin and Dixie Barcelona and the missing baby quilt. The more I told him, the darker his eyes became.

"It's the darnedest thing—you showing up at another crime scene."

"Well, how was I supposed to know there was going to be another crime scene? I was just following a new lead to another of Claire's quilts."

"Where did you get this lead?"

Oh no. I couldn't let him find out Claire's computer was at my house. "Birdie remembered something Claire told her from before."

"How can I convince you how dangerous your snooping is, Ms. Rose?" He pointed his finger. "You need to stay away from this investigation because if you don't, you could end up in jail or worse."

"What could be worse than jail?"

"The back of a coroner's van."

I pictured Claire's body again, and for once in my life, I kept my mouth shut. I left the building and walked toward my car, parked on the street. Parking spaces were hard to find, and I'd been lucky to get one half a block away from Godwin's office. The building was on a stretch of Ventura Boulevard where other new, tall office buildings hovered like bullies next to aging strip malls. Several Middle Eastern restaurants populated the area, sending the spicy aromas of cumin and chili into the air.

Near my car a bag lady with tangled hair sat on an overturned bucket outside a sixties era strip mall. Her shopping cart was laden with bulging black trash bags. "'Scuse me." She rattled a Styrofoam cup filled with coins. "Can you spare some change?"

I usually tried to avoid the homeless. Several shelters had sprung up in the city in the last decade, and help was available for the truly desperate. I also knew many of the homeless preferred to live on the streets or to camp out inside the bushes under freeway bridges or along the overgrown banks of the Los Angeles River.

Still, the woman clutching the white cup in her grimy fingers could have been one of those newly displaced Americans, a victim of the bad economy. I reached in my purse and pulled out a five-dollar bill. Today was turning out to me my *tzedaka* day— my day to be charitable.

She took the money from my hand. "God bless you."

She watched me curiously as I glanced at her cart. Hanging from the handle was a black Hefty bag stuffed with aluminum cans. "Takes me a whole day to fill up one of those bags." She smiled affably.

"What do you do with them?"

"I go over to the recycle in Ralph's parking lot and turn 'em in for cash money."

"Do you get much?"

She shrugged. "It's a living."

"Where do you find them?"

"Trash, Dumpsters, streets, alleys. I have my reg'lar places." She pointed to Solomon's, a deli down the street. "The owner of the deli over there, Sol, he saves 'em for me."

I was about to walk away when a piece of yellow and white cloth sticking out from a greasy looking bedroll attracted my attention. "What's that?" I pointed to the cloth.

"Oh, it's something I found in the Dumpster behind that building last week." She pointed a dirty finger toward Godwin's building.

"You'd be surprised what you can find in a Dumpster. Once I found a brand new sweater with the tags still on. See?" She smiled proudly and opened her coat to reveal a hideous purple and yellow Fair Isle sweater with snowflakes and reindeer encircling her torso in horizontal stripes. Some places were dark with old grease spots.

"Great find." I pointed to the cloth. "How about that thing?"

She eyed me warily. "It's my towel."

"Could I see it?"

She frowned. "I didn't steal it. I found it fair and square."

I smiled and took a twenty out of my purse. "Please show me the towel."

She grabbed the twenty and with her other fist pulled Claire's baby quilt out from the bedroll.

I tried to control the excitement in my voice. "What's your name? Mine's Martha."

"Hilda."

"Well, Hilda, I'd like to buy the towel from you."

She eyed me shrewdly. "It'll cost you."

I gave her another twenty. She took it and just looked at me, not moving. I reached in my wallet and took out my last twenty. "This is all I have."

She smiled and handed over the missing quilt. "God bless you."

I briefly thought about going back to the BCA office to find Detective Beavers, but I knew once Beavers got hold of this quilt, he'd seize it as evidence. As I walked toward my car, I wondered why the thief would go to the trouble of stealing the quilt only to throw it in the Dumpster.

If there was any forensic evidence on the quilt, it had long been obliterated by Hilda's rough treatment. I didn't see how the police could find any meaningful clues on it. So I decided to clean it up at home and take a closer look. Who knew what I might find?

CHAPTER 15

All the drama made my head hurt. A flare-up was coming on. On the way home I stopped at Yum Yum and got ten ounces of frozen vanilla yogurt with only eight calories per ounce. Then I loaded the top with crushed Heath bars for a dollar extra. I deserved it.

When I got home, I took a Soma and one of my migraine pills. Bumper followed me into the laundry room for a pit stop. I checked to make sure the other quilts were still in their hiding place. Then I put the foul-smelling baby quilt in the washing machine to soak and added some Orvis soap.

Washing quilts with ordinary detergent faded the colors and weakened the cotton fibers. Serious quilt owners tried to use a pH neutral soap if they had to wash their quilts. Orvis, a gentle liquid soap, was originally developed for shampooing horses. Used to be you had to go to the feed store to get Orvis soap, but now it was also available in quilt stores.

Back in the living room, I took the yogurt and a plastic spoon out of the bag and plopped on the sofa. Bumper jumped up and settled into my lap purring. I closed my eyes against the throbbing in the right side of my head and only opened them to scoop up the next sweet mouthful.

The thief had the same list we did and knew where to find this quilt. So, how did he get into the offices of BCA? Could he have come in during the daytime disguised as a workman? He could have pretended to be repairing something while he searched the rooms.

I'd seen that scenario on television hundreds of times. Nobody paid attention to a guy in overalls with a tool belt. He could have stuffed the little quilt inside his shirt and nobody would have known. So why did he go to so much trouble just to throw it in the Dumpster?

By the time the spoon scraped the bottom of the Styrofoam container, the meds were kicking in. I felt deliciously detached and floating out of my body a little, the way I always did after taking my medicine. I looked at my watch. Two-thirty.

I took out my notepad and flipped through the pages. The name Jerry Bell jumped out at me. This was the guy who received monthly checks of a thousand dollars or more from Claire for as far back as her check registers went. Why? Was he blackmailing her? Was he a lover who was being subsidized?

Claire hardly seemed the type to go for a boy toy, but you never knew.

I decided to find out, and dialed his phone number. He answered on the fourth ring, "Mr. Bell, my name is Martha Rose and I'm a friend of Claire Terry's. I hate to bother you under the circumstances, but I'd really like to talk to you about her death."

"Claire's *dead*?" The shock was unmistakable.

"Oh dear. You didn't know? Her death has been all over the news for the last week." The media loved to report on tragedies involving celebrities and the very wealthy. It was hard to imagine anyone could miss all the publicity.

His voice choked. "I've been out of touch with just about everything these last two weeks. When did she . . . What happened?"

He sounded genuinely upset. Would a blackmailer sound that way?

"She died last week. Mr. Bell, I really need to talk to you. Could you possibly meet with me this afternoon? I'll be happy to drive to where you are."

"Yeah, I guess so, although it has to be soon. I'm working the night shift, and I start at five. We can meet at Dinah's on Sepulveda near the airport. Do you know it?"

I knew the LA landmark well. Dinah's was famous for crispy fried chicken and apple pancakes the size of hubcaps. "I can't get there for another hour, so let's plan on three-thirty. How will I recognize you?"

"I'll be wearing green scrubs."

Three minutes later I was on my way to Culver City to meet either Claire's blackmailer, her lover, or both.

Traffic on the 405 south was heinous as usual. For once, traveling cautiously at fifteen miles per hour was a good thing. I was still feeling the effects of the pill. I pulled into the parking lot of Dinah's at three twenty-nine. Low-flying jets roared overhead, coming into their final approach at LAX and fouling the air with the acrid smell of jet exhaust.

Dinah's was decorated in typical 1950s coffee shop style with red vinyl booths and brown laminate tables. In the mornings the place smelled like coffee and maple syrup. In the afternoon it smelled like hamburgers and fried chicken.

I spotted a blond man in green scrubs standing near the cashier. He looked to be around thirty, the same age as my daughter. I walked up to him. "Are you Jerry Bell?"

He turned toward me. "Yeah. You're Claire's friend?"

I was stunned at how much he resembled Claire. He looked like he could be her younger, blonder brother. I didn't remember Siobhan mentioning she had any other children, though. Also, Jerry's last name was Bell, not Terry. *Who would name a baby Jerry Terry anyway?* So, if this man wasn't Claire's brother, who could he be? I began to entertain another possibility.

Jerry Bell looked sleep deprived and his eyes were puffy and red, as if he either recently had cried or smoked weed. His lips slightly trembled. It wasn't weed.

"Yes. I'm Martha Rose. Thanks for meeting me." I extended my hand.

His grip was firm but brief. "Uh, I want to find out what happened to Claire." He teared up and seemed so pitiful that my Jewish mother hormones started to surge.

I put my hand on his arm and suggested the one sure remedy for everything. "Let's get something to eat. I find it's always easier to talk over food."

We sat in a booth toward the back and Jerry ordered a coffee and hamburger. I was still full of yogurt and crushed Heath bars, so I just ordered coffee. I hoped the caffeine would help my headache.

"Ms. Rose . . ."

"Call me Martha."

"Yeah. Okay. How did Claire die? When?"

"We discovered Claire's body a week ago today. She died of an overdose."

Jerry stared at me, horrified. Just then the waitress arrived with a thermos full of coffee and two cups. He waited for her to leave.

"An overdose of what? I could swear Claire would never abuse drugs."

I poured the coffee for both of us. "The police don't think she took the drugs voluntarily."

His jaw dropped. "*Holy . . .* ! What are you saying? Are you saying someone poisoned her?"

"Would you know of anyone who might want her dead?"

All the color drained from Jerry's face. He put his elbows on the table and grasped his head. "No." Then he looked at me suspiciously. "I don't get the connection. What is your involvement in this?"

"Claire invited us to quilt with her last Tuesday morning. When my friends and I got there, we found her body and called the police. They later determined she was murdered."

With shaking fingers, Jerry added two packets of sugar and stirred his coffee slowly. "How do they know it wasn't accidental?"

"There was blood on her hands."

"Oh my God."

Jerry's obvious distress could be for a number of reasons. If he was a blackmailer or a boy toy, he would have to say good-bye to those monthly checks. However, if he was Claire's true lover, he'd understandably be upset by her death. I didn't know what to believe about him yet. Of course, there was that third possibility I was beginning to think was even more likely.

The waitress returned with Jerry's burger. He vigorously shook salt all over his French fries and then squeezed a blob of ketchup on the side of his plate. "I haven't talked to Claire in about two weeks. Normally we talk every few days, but I've been working all night and studying for the boards on my time off." He picked up a fry and stirred it absentmindedly in a slurry of ketchup.

"Boards?"

"Pediatrics. I'm a resident." He shook his head slowly. "I can't believe she's gone." He put down the fry and swiped at his tears with the palm of his hand.

"I'm so sorry, Jerry." I didn't know what else to say.

We sat in silence for a while. He worked on his burger.

I used my fingertip to push around the white salt crystals that spilled on the brown wood-grained plastic of the tabletop.

"I have to ask you one thing. Were you and Claire lovers?"

"What the . . . ? Is this some kind of sick joke?"

"I'm sorry if I upset you, but I have to ask. It seems Claire had a boyfriend, and we're trying to find out who he is."

"Who is 'we'? What are you doing, anyway?"

He started to slide out of his seat, but I put up my hand to stop him. "Wait, Jerry, just give me a minute to explain."

He settled back down while I told him about my quest to break the code in Claire's quilts. "I thought maybe her boyfriend might know, that's all."

"I'm not her boyfriend. What made you think I was?"

"Well, this is a little awkward. I saw your name in

her um, address book." I wasn't going to tell him I'd been snooping in Claire's files, let alone her panty drawer. "Since none of us knew who you were, we thought you might be the one. So I decided to call and find out."

Jerry's laugh was mirthless. "Sorry to disappoint you."

I waited a beat. "There's one more thing. Why did Claire give you so much money?"

He shook his head in disbelief. "How do you know about the money?"

I decided to take the direct approach. "Were you blackmailing her?"

He looked like he wanted to hit me. Then he closed his eyes, threw back his head, and laughed too loud. People around us stopped eating and stared.

I lowered my voice. "Well, were you?"

He stopped laughing and glared at me. "Not that it's any of your business. Claire gave me money to help me through med school. I wanted to make it on my own, but sometimes things got too hard. I promised to pay her back when I finished my residency and started to earn some real money. She always said I didn't have to, but I would have." He picked up his hamburger and took another large bite.

Although I thought I knew the real answer already, I still wanted to hear him to say it. "Well, if you're not her lover and not a blackmailer, what were you to Claire?"

Jerry swallowed. "I found her through adoption registry dot com. They help people locate their birth mother."

Bingo. "Can you tell me more?"

"I was adopted." He shoved a couple of French fries in his mouth. "My dad died when I was twelve, and my mom died while I was still an undergrad at Loyola. My girlfriend at the time urged me to look for my birth mother. That's how I found Claire."

"Siobhan Terry told me Claire never had children."

"I know. That was the official story. Claire had me when she was fourteen. Since they're Catholic, abortion was out of the question. They sent her away until I was born and made her give me up for adoption. They couldn't have me around. I was a social embarrassment."

I waited until he finished another bite. "How did Claire react to seeing you?"

"She was happy when I first contacted her, but she said her father would be furious if he knew. I think she was really intimidated by him."

I remembered my conversation with Will Terry and how pushy he was. I suspected he could be quite a formidable adversary when he wanted to be.

"I told her times have changed and people change. Maybe they were ready to accept me, but she was adamant about not telling them or anyone else. I figured she knew them better than I did, so I just went along."

"I appreciate your being so open with me."

"To be honest, I don't know why I'm telling you so much. I mean, you're a stranger and all, but this is such a shock and, well, you seem to care."

"Thank you, Jerry. I do care. I have another question. Did Claire ever say who your birth father was?"

"Well, I asked, of course, but she only said he was some boy in her class. She told me she didn't even remember his name."

"Did you believe her? Seems to me the father of your child would be someone you'd never forget."

Jerry sighed. "Claire was a very private person. I had the feeling she had many secrets. I never pressed the issue."

I concealed my hands in my lap, crossed my fingers, and leaned forward. "Did she ever mention a lover to you?"

Jerry shoved the last of the burger in his mouth. "I think there was something going on, but she never talked to me about that part of her life. Still, she did seem unusually happy lately."

"One last thing, Jerry. Did she ever tell you anything about her quilts?"

"She offered me the one hanging in her living room."

"Secret Garden?"

"Yeah, I think that's the one. I don't really have a place in my apartment to hang something so fancy. I told her I'd take the quilt when I got a real job and a real house of my own."

"Did she say why she wanted you to have that particular one?"

"Yeah. Let me think." He closed his eyes. He opened them after a minute. "Claire said Secret Garden was 'our story,' whatever that meant." He dragged some more fries through the ketchup and dropped them in his mouth.

Things were beginning to make some sense. Claire's teen pregnancy was a secret the family wanted buried. Yet the beautiful images of living things sewn into the Secret Garden wall hanging suggested a joyful and peaceful place of repose— possibly about secretly reuniting with her son after all those years.

I thought about the father I never knew, the one who died in a train wreck before I was born. What if I found out he was alive? Would I try to find him? Searching would take a lot of courage. What if he didn't want to know me?

Those same doubts must have burdened Jerry before finding Claire. Yet theirs was a happy reunion. She wanted to know him and obviously wanted him in her life. How sad for Jerry that with her death he'd lost two sets of parents.

Jerry wiped the grease off his hands and mouth with a white paper napkin. He looked at me sadly, his voice cracking. "I don't guess anyone knew to contact me since I was such a big secret. Has there already been a funeral? Do you know where she's buried?"

"There hasn't been a funeral yet. They had to wait to complete the autopsy. I think the wake is this Thursday evening and the funeral is on Friday. I can find out the specifics from Claire's mother and call you, if you'd like."

"Yeah, thanks. Only please don't tell them about me just yet. I want to meet my grandparents, but I honestly don't know if this is the right time to approach them. What do you think?"

I thought Siobhan might welcome contact with her grandson after all these years, but after what Jerry had just told me, I wasn't so sure about Mr. Terry. "It's not my place to say anything, but there will come a time when they'll want to know about you. You might turn out to be a big comfort to each other."

I didn't know for sure if Jerry Bell was telling me the truth. My friend Lucy raised five sons, and she would've been able to figure out right away if he was lying. The only thing I had to go on was my gut reaction, and I felt sorry for this kid.

I thought about Quincy. If someone were to call her out of the blue and tell her about my death, she probably would've reacted the same way Jerry Bell did. Shock, horror, and grief. I pulled a piece of blank paper from my notepad and wrote down two names and phone numbers. "Here. This is the detective handling the case. This is my number. Please call if you can think of anything else, or you just want to talk."

On the drive back to the Valley, I realized Jerry might very well benefit financially from Claire's death as next of kin. If he knew the Secret Garden hung behind Claire's sofa, he must've been familiar with her house. He'd probably been there many times and maybe even knew about the quilts in her sewing room and the files in her office. Maybe he even had a key to her house. Also, he was a doctor. Doctors had access to all kinds of drugs. Oh God. Had I just been played? Was Jerry Bell the thief and murderer?

CHAPTER 16

As bad as the drive to Dinah's was, the drive on the 405 north back to the Valley was worse at four-thirty. The half hour trip took three times longer because our elected officials would rather squander millions of dollars studying the traffic problem than actually doing something about it.

During the slow crawl toward the Sepulveda pass, I called Siobhan on my cell phone. I gave her the abbreviated version of my visit with Godwin, the Blind Children's Association, the missing baby quilt, and my encounter with the bag lady. Although I was tempted, I didn't tell her about Jerry Bell.

"Claire made a baby quilt? I've got to have that quilt, Martha. I must have that quilt." Siobhan sounded on the verge of hysteria.

"What is it?"

"I just now got a call from Detective Beavers with the autopsy results. Claire was four months pregnant." She started to cry. "I need to have the baby quilt."

I was stunned. Jerry said Claire had been unusually happy. Was her pregnancy the reason? "Of course. As soon as I finish cleaning the quilt, I'll bring it right over to you, but we have to tell Detective Beavers you have it. Right now everyone thinks it's still missing."

Could Claire's pregnancy have been the motive for her murder? Did someone want to make her child go away? Did the baby's father, her lover, get rid of them both? Did Jerry Bell want to eliminate any competition for a possible inheritance?

Siobhan's wave of grief passed. "How did you find out about the baby quilt in the first place?"

"We were able to hack into Claire's computer this morning. We found a copy of the list the thief took along with photos of all her quilts."

Siobhan sighed. "Yes, of course. I received the fax you sent of the list. That reminds me. The detective thought the thief also stole Claire's computer."

My heart raced as I realized I'd forgotten to warn her not to tell Beavers I had the computer. "What did you tell him?"

"I told him not to worry, that you'd taken it home with you."

Oh no! "What did he say?"

"Not much. He seemed a little vexed."

This was very bad news. The quilts were going

back tomorrow, and I wasn't any nearer to cracking the code. I planned to search Claire's other documents tonight for more clues, but I knew Beavers would be coming after the computer soon.

Then I broached a painful subject. "Siobhan, do you want me to notify the guild members of the wake and the funeral so they can come and pay their respects? I can e-mail a notice to the membership tonight."

Her voice cracked. "That's very thoughtful of you." She gave me the details and then dissolved into tears again.

"I'll get the message out right away."

I called Jerry Bell's number and left the information on his answering machine. My next call was to Lucy. I gave her the same info about Claire's wake and funeral. "Could you send an e-mail to the members this evening?"

"Sure thing. What happened with your visit to Godwin?"

I told her about the missing baby quilt, my meeting with Jerry Bell, and my conversation with Siobhan.

"Get out! Claire was pregnant and also had a secret son?"

Just then a geezer in a Dodgers baseball cap driving a brand new Beamer convertible roadster cut in front of me. I stepped on the brakes, leaned on the horn, and yelled, "Moron!"

"What was that?"

"Some old jerk just cut me off. He's giving me the one-finger salute. So mature."

Lucy laughed. "Tell me more about Jerry Bell."

"On one hand, he seems genuinely grief stricken. He cried in front of me, poor kid. On the other hand, he probably knew about her quilts and where to find her files. He's got easy access to drugs, which could also make him a suspect. Frankly, I don't know what to think. I wish you'd been there. You know boys much better than I do and you're so good at sussing out the truth."

"Wish I'd been there, too. Are you going to tell Mrs. Terry?"

"I think that's up to Jerry, and he's not ready. By the way, Siobhan told Detective Beavers I've got Claire's computer."

"Uh-oh. What are you going to do?"

"I suspect he'll be over soon demanding I hand over the computer. It's a good thing you thought of making a copy of the photos."

"I copied *all* of the files, Martha."

"All the files—as in all the documents on her computer?"

"Yup."

"How?"

"I have a ten-gig flash drive. Easier to just dump all the documents at once than go cherry picking. I figured we'd sort through them later. The flash drive is still in my purse."

"Lucy, you really are a genius."

"I know." She laughed. "Gotta go make dinner for Ray."

I pulled into my driveway sometime after six. I was relieved not to see a silver Camry parked nearby, but I was also sure Beavers would show up sometime soon. When I stepped inside, Bumper ran up to me and rubbed against my ankles. I scratched him behind the ears. "Hey, handsome. How's my main squeeze?"

I headed straight toward the laundry room and activated the washing machine, turning the handle to the rinse and spin cycle. I'd put the quilt in to soak about five hours ago, and in another ten minutes I'd find out if all the stains were gone.

I walked back into the kitchen. The light blinked on my phone. I checked the messages. The first one was from Quincy. "Hi, Mom. Haven't heard from you in days. Are you okay? Still bummed about your Civil War quilt? Give me a call and let me cheer you up with some interesting news. Love you." I smiled, wondering what her news was going to be this time. New boyfriend? Promotion at work?

There was a time when I seriously worried whether Quincy would ever get over my divorce from Aaron. She was furious with him for breaking up the family and causing us to give up our home in Brentwood and move to Encino—a social step down in Quincy's opinion. She resented giving up her friends in private school for the dubious advantages of our local public schools.

She also struggled to adapt to my becoming a working mother. In the past I'd always been at home to greet her at the end of her school day. After moving to Encino, Quincy fended for herself until I came home from my job at UCLA. All her familiar support systems vanished with the dissolution of our marriage. Who wouldn't be pissed?

Fortunately, Quincy made friends easily and soon she'd created a new support system with the other brainy kids in school. With each of Aaron's successive marriages (two more), Quincy grew increasingly bitter. She became a biting critic of both her father and me. In her eyes, we'd each failed her on a fundamental level.

Attending college back East gave Quincy a new perspective. After her first year, her anger cooled into a grudging acceptance. By the end of four years, she was once again my friend and admirer and staunch ally. My baby all grown up.

I played the next message. "Ms. Rose—Martha, this is Dixie Barcelona from the Blind Children's Association. I hope you don't mind, but I got your phone number off your check."

What could Dixie be calling about?

"As I was leaving this afternoon, I ran into Hilda in front of the building. Hilda is a homeless woman who regularly patrols this part of Ventura Boulevard with her shopping cart.

"Anyway, she bragged about how she sold a little yellow blanket she found in the Dumpster behind our building for sixty dollars. From her description, I was sure the blanket she found was Claire's quilt.

"At any rate, I'm beside myself with worry. I can't believe the thief just threw Claire's pretty little quilt in a Dumpster. Hilda also described the woman who bought the quilt. It sounded a lot like you, and I'm hoping against hope that it was. This is a terrible mess. Please call right away."

I dialed the number she gave.

"Oh, Martha, I'm so glad you called. Please tell me you were the one who bought the quilt from Hilda."

"Relax, Dixie. The quilt is safe with me. I'm washing it now because apparently Hilda was using Claire's quilt as a towel."

"Oh, thank goodness. Do you think you can fix it?"

I laughed. "The quilt wasn't broken, just dirty and smelly. Everything's intact—no rips or cuts. I'm sure with a little effort I can restore it."

Bumper meowed, and I put the phone on speaker so I could talk to Dixie and still have both hands free to feed the cat. I shook some kibble in a bowl.

"I can drive right over and pick up the quilt."

I filled his water bowl with fresh water. "Oh, the quilt's still in the washing machine." I picked up the slotted scooper and mined the sand in the litter box, filling one of the old plastic produce sacks I saved for just that purpose.

"Well, I could drive over tomorrow and save you the trouble of returning the quilt to the Terrys."

"Not a problem. I'll be returning all of Claire's quilts to the Terrys tomorrow."

There was a pause and then Dixie blew out her breath. "Okay then. I really owe you one."

The washing machine wound down and shuddered to a stop at the end of the spin dry cycle. I retrieved the quilt and examined it closely. The soaking had done the job; all the dirt was gone.

I didn't put the quilt in the clothes dryer because heat damages the fibers. Instead, I spread it on a towel and draped the two layers over a drying rack, a contraption made out of wooden bars that unfolded like an accordion. Then I disguised the quilt by placing a lightweight tablecloth over it, folding the rack back up, and shoving the whole thing inside the space between the wall and the clothes dryer. No one would suspect the quilt was hiding underneath.

I returned to the kitchen and called Quincy next, speaker still on so I could talk while fixing myself something to eat. "Hi, honey. What's the news?"

"Dad's getting remarried."

Now, for most women, being single while their ex remarries could be bitter news. Watching him make a new life for himself could make the ex-wife feel lonely—not to mention insanely jealous.

In a small number of cases, women are completely over their exes and such news wouldn't even raise an eyebrow. I personally hadn't met any of those more evolved women. I landed somewhere in the middle of hostility and indifference. However, I felt a perverse sense of vindication at the thought of Aaron messing up another marriage. Right now he was 0 for 3.

Was Quincy concerned about having yet another stepmother as a rival for her father's affections? I opened the peanut butter jar and spread a huge glob on a slice of challah. "How do you feel about this? Do you know her?"

Quincy surprised me when she laughed. "I met her for the first time at dinner last night. They were in Boston for some kind of conference. She's another psychiatrist. All they did was try to top each other. Each one of them jockeyed to have the last word. They've got the same disease."

"What disease is that?"

"Alpha dog syndrome, or in her case, alpha bitch."

I chuckled and dipped my knife into the jar of raspberry preserves. Maybe Aaron had finally met his match. "Are you going to be okay with it?"

Quincy laughed again. "I give them less than a year." Bless her cynical little soul.

The next call I made was to my uncle Isaac, who was the closest thing to a father I ever had. I usually checked on him twice a week. Uncle Isaac was in his eighties but still had a zest for life. "Hi, Uncle, what's up?"

"Oh, hi, *faigela*." I loved it when he used my bubbie's pet name for me—"little bird." Bubbie was more like a mother to me—cooking, cleaning, and keeping a kosher house. Uncle Isaac was more like a father. He owned a tailor shop and never came home at the end of the day without a piece of candy for me. He brought me scraps of couture material so I could sew clothes for my dolls.

On the other hand, my mother didn't come out of the bedroom until ten every morning, walking around in a daze smoking cigarettes and listening to the top ten hits on the radio. When I was little I rushed home after school and went straight to where she sat in an attempt to get her to notice me and love me.

"Mommy, mommy, look what I drew." Or, "Mommy, look. I got an A plus on my spelling test."

The most I ever got in return was a brief glance and a vacant smile. "That's nice." Then she'd turn away and go back inside a secret world that no one else could enter.

Once I asked her, "Who's my daddy? Where is he?"

"His name was Quinn. He died before you were born. You look like him."

"That's enough, faigela," my bubbie warned. "Leave your mommy alone now and come into the kitchen and help me make dinner." That was as much as I ever learned. In my house, the subject of my father was verboten.

Uncle Isaac's voice brought me back to the present. "Are you okay? How's my Quincy girl?"

"We're fine. I just talked to her. I wanted to check in and see if you needed anything."

"No. I'm fine, but I can't talk. Morty and the boys are here for poker. We're really livin' it up. Got a six-pack of Budweiser and a bowlful of popcorn."

I chuckled. "Go for it, Uncle. I love you."

As I cleaned up the kitchen, the doorbell rang. The digital clock on the microwave showed twenty minutes after eight. The doorbell rang again, and someone knocked loudly. I hurried to answer the door. "For heaven's sake, who is it?"

An unfamiliar voice barked, "Los Angeles police."

I looked through the peephole, but all I could see was a silver and brass badge. "Step back and let me see your face."

CHAPTER 17

I opened my door to two uniformed officers. "Can I help you?"

Their brass name tags identified them as Garcia and Cheng. "Are you Martha Rose?"

"I am."

"Would you step outside, please?"

"What for?"

Officer Cheng pointed to a blue Ford Mustang parked in my driveway. "Detective Kaplan would like to speak to you."

I recognized the young man getting out of the driver's seat. He came with Detective Beavers the day we discovered Claire's body. He approached with a swagger and handed me a paper. "Mrs. Rose? This is a warrant to search your house."

I wasn't sure I heard him correctly. Why in the world would anyone want to search my house? "You're kidding, right?"

"Just step aside, please."

Another little bully. This was getting beyond tiresome. "What are you looking for?"

He indicated the paper in my hand. "It's spelled out right there."

"Where's Detective Beavers? Aren't you his partner?"

"Beavers isn't here. Step aside, please." He brushed past me.

I couldn't believe he was being so rude. I was going to give Detective Beavers an earful about this.

Officer Cheng stayed beside me in the doorway while I scanned the warrant. I came to the part that read: *stolen property, one laptop computer belonging to Claire Terry.* "This is bogus! Why don't you just ask me for her computer? Why use a warrant?"

Cheng was silent.

I looked up to see a group of neighbors clustered under the streetlight, seeming to strain to hear what I was saying. Sonia Spiegelman, the neighborhood yenta, was already whispering behind her hand to several of the curious. Sonia lived across the street from me and patrolled our neighborhood at least twice a day looking for morsels of juicy gossip like a cockroach crawling through garbage. In her gauzy blouses and dangly earrings, she reminded me of some of my fellow travelers in the antiwar movement in the 1970s. She didn't seem to realize the world had moved on and I always felt vaguely embarrassed for her.

She broke away from the group and started

walking toward me with a smile designed to make me believe she was only there to help. She craned her neck to look into my house. "Martha dear, is everything all right?" Like I was going to confide in her, of all people.

"No, Sonia. They found out about the terrorist cell I've been harboring in my basement." All our houses were built on raised foundations. With the frequent ground shifting from earthquakes and the mild year-round weather, basements were uncommon in California and totally nonexistent in our midcentury homes. I still couldn't resist. "I hope to heck they don't find the arsenal I've hidden down there, too."

Her eyes shone. "I didn't know you have a basement."

I blinked at her, gave my head a little shake, and walked back inside my house.

Kaplan didn't take long to find Claire's laptop since it was sitting in plain sight on my coffee table. He also found my computer and handed them both to Officer Garcia to put in large plastic evidence bags.

"Hey." I pointed to my laptop. "That's mine. You can't take that."

Kaplan ignored me. "Until I can determine which is which, I'm taking them both."

"Well, I'll tell you which is which. Anyway, why did you have to create such an embarrassing spectacle? All you needed to do was simply ask me for the computer."

"You don't fool me with your sweet little old lady act, Mrs. Rose. I received information you were in possession of a laptop that might turn out to contain important evidence in the murder of Claire Terry. When I realized this was the stolen laptop, I put two and two together."

I wanted to slap the smug smile right off his face. "First of all, I resent your calling me a 'little old lady.' Second, your report was wrong. I didn't steal her computer. Siobhan Terry, her mother, gave me permission to take it."

"Tell it to the judge, Mrs. Rose." Detective Kaplan grabbed my wrist, spun me around, and handcuffed me. "You're under arrest for theft, tampering with evidence, and interfering with a police investigation."

A fuzzy black circle started closing in on my vision and my ears started to ring.

". . . the right to remain silent. Anything you say . . ."

"Wait. There's been a huge misunderstanding. Call Siobhan Terry. She'll tell you."

"You have a right to an attorney . . ."

My voice rose a few notches. "Call Detective Beavers. He knows I'm innocent."

Cocky little Detective Kaplan was the conductor

of an express train heading straight to jail, and I was his only passenger.

I'd been briefly incarcerated once before. Back in the early seventies I was arrested at an anti-Vietnam War protest in front of the Federal Building on Wilshire Boulevard. That's where I met Aaron, another protestor. They put thirty of us in a holding cell and Aaron and I talked all night. When dawn broke the next morning, I was in love. Now, however, I was no longer a college student and certainly didn't relish a night in the slammer.

Garcia and Cheng marched me toward the back of their patrol car. One of them put his hand on my head, maneuvered me into the backseat, and fastened the seat belt.

I looked over in time to see Detective Kaplan closing and locking my front door. Sonia walked up to him. She announced, loud enough for the neighbors to hear, "Officer, you'd better check her basement. I happen to know she's hiding guns and bombs down there."

Kaplan looked surprised. "She has a basement?"

For the next ten minutes I rode in a fog, too dazed to speak. Officer Cheng took my upper arm and guided me into the brand new state-of-the-art police station on Vanowen and Wilbur.

The walls of the detention area were painted a cool blue gray, and the lights were dimmed. I stumbled in disbelief toward a row of individual holding cells, all of them empty.

Officer Cheng opened the door to an eight-foot-square cell. "This will be your temporary home for the next hour or two." He unlocked the handcuffs.

With a surprising detachment, I took inventory of the room. I was amazed there were no bars. Instead, the cell was enclosed in Plexiglas, frosted partway up to give prisoners some privacy when using the one-piece stainless steel toilet. The only other place to sit was a concrete ledge built into the far wall.

The fog began lifting from my mind, and I started to panic. Could this really be happening? "What's going to happen to me now?" I massaged my wrists.

"Detective Kaplan will fill out the paperwork in a room next door. When he's done, you'll be transported to the Van Nuys station where you'll be booked and detained overnight. In the morning you'll be arraigned."

Arraigned? My heart was trying to bang right through my chest wall. I struggled not to let him hear the fear in my voice. "This is totally unjust. There's been a huge misunderstanding here."

Officer Cheng must have heard those words a thousand times before. He just shrugged and turned to go.

I glanced at the hard bench and felt anger

pushing at my craw. "I know my rights. I'm entitled to a phone call. I want to post bail."

"You can invoke your right to a phone call only after you've been booked and processed. That won't be for a few hours yet, so enjoy these accommodations while you can. Compared to Van Nuys, this is a five-star hotel." He locked the cell door.

"Come on! Call Detective Beavers. He can vouch for me."

Cheng just walked away.

In the solitude of my cell, I started to cry. How did I end up here, anyway? I didn't deserve to be here. All I was trying to do was help an old lady through the death of her daughter. What did I get in return? Humiliation and imprisonment. So I fudged a little with the truth about taking the computer. Was that such a terrible thing? It wasn't like I stole it.

Beavers thought the thief took the computer. Then Siobhan told him it was with me. Could he really have told Detective Kaplan I was a thief?

My body began to ache, and my stress headache returned with a vengeance. I attempted to lie down on the narrow bench but my size-sixteen hips were too wide and the bench was too hard to be comfortable. There was nothing I could do but sit up and wait until I could make my phone call. Right then I would have given anything for a diversion, even an out of date issue of *Sailing Life* from the table in my doctor's office.

I could only think of the injustice of all of this

and how surprised I was Beavers resorted to having me arrested. How could I be so wrong about sensing his interest in me? Granted, I wasn't the best judge of men, but I genuinely thought there was a little chemistry between us.

Technically, I supposed you could say I lied when I pretended not to know where Claire's computer was. Would that be enough to charge me with a crime? Would I have to go to trial? What if they found me guilty? Would I have to spend time in actual prison? This would kill Uncle Isaac for sure. If only my quilting were here with me. Nothing could calm me down like the rhythm of my needle as it glided through the fabric.

I thought about who I should call when the time came. I wouldn't call Quincy because she was too far away to help, and I didn't want to alarm her. Uncle Isaac wouldn't know what do and besides, the shock might give him a heart attack. My lawyer did mostly estates and contracts. He wasn't a criminal lawyer. Siobhan had the necessary clout to send a lawyer to get me released, but she might not answer her phone so late at night.

I'd call Lucy. She was likely to answer her phone no matter what time of night, and she'd do whatever was needed. I could trust Lucy with my life.

My throat closed up as I thought about how strong our friendship had grown over the years. I first met Lucy at a PTA meeting. Quincy and I had just moved to Encino and neither one of us knew anyone in her new school. Lucy noticed I was fresh meat and strode up to me with a big smile and an assignment to make one hundred cupcakes for the bake sale.

I thought about how many boxes of cake mix I had to use to make that many. "Seriously? One hundred?"

"Might as well jump in with both feet. I could've asked for two hundred, but I didn't want to scare you off, you being new and all."

"I can do two hundred."

Lucy stared at me for a moment and then gave me a warm hug. "We're going to be great friends. I just know it."

When I finally found a job at UCLA, it was Lucy who insisted on watching Quincy after school until I came home. Quincy loved playing with Lucy's boys, especially Richie. He called her Buddy and taught her how to shoot hoops.

When I took a disability retirement because of my fibromyalgia, Lucy reintroduced me to quilting to help distract me from the unremitting pain. It was through quilting that I met her neighbor Birdie and we started our weekly sewing circle. You couldn't meet weekly with someone and not learn about their struggles and triumphs. Ours became a mutual support society.

When Lucy was diagnosed with breast cancer, I took care of her every day during her chemo and recuperation so Ray could go back to work. Quincy was away at college by then, and only Lucy's youngest son, Joey, still lived at home. Birdie did all the cooking. I helped Lucy pee and eat and shower and throw up. Medical marijuana, a powerful anti-nausea drug, would have saved her from the puke bucket, but weed was still illegal back then.

Yes, Lucy would rescue me from jail. I could count on her.

Around ten, a different patrolman opened the door to my cell. I glanced at his name tag. Officer Yoder looked to be in his early twenties and spoke almost deferentially. "Okay, Mrs. Rose. We're going over to Van Nuys now. Please turn around."

"What for?"

"Handcuffs, ma'am."

"Don't make them too tight." I used as much maternal authority as I could muster.

"Yes, ma'am."

We took Vanowen Street east to Van Nuys. This patrol car smelled strongly of urine and body odor. A spit screen made of stainless steel mesh and crusted with dried phlegm separated the front and back seats and obscured my view out the front window. This was definitely not Lucy's Caddy.

My skin crawled at the thought of the bugs and lice that might be burrowing into my hair and clothes as I sat there. I thought about my fastidious grandmother, who scrubbed and cleaned until you could eat off the floor. Bubbie would die all over again if she saw me now. I leaned forward in the seat, trying to minimize contact with the interior surfaces of the squad car.

I was glad for the darkness of night. With the exception of the earlier scene in front of my house, few people would be able to witness my disgrace. How many times had I passed a police car with a prisoner in the backseat and tried to get a glimpse of who he/she was?

We parked behind the Van Nuys precinct and my heart began to pound again. I saw what Officer Cheng meant. The building was at least fifty years old, and the windows were still barred. We took the elevator to booking, on the second floor. The walls were painted an industrial tan and the fluorescent light was relentless. Unlike the new station in West Valley, this place smelled. Bad.

"I don't belong here. Release me at once!"

Officer Yoder walked me over to a wooden bench and unlocked the handcuffs. "Please sit down, ma'am."

I looked him straight in the eye. "I demand to speak to your supervisor."

"Yes, ma'am." He pressed down on my shoulder, forcing me to sit. Then he cuffed my right hand to a steel ring in the bench. He took a sheaf of papers to the desk, handed them over, and pointed in my direction. "Rose, Martha. She's the older lady sitting there."

Older lady my foot! Just because I didn't dye my hair or work out. Everyone in LA had an opinion.

Something cylindrical rolled under my right foot. I looked down. A small disposable syringe with an orange plastic plunger—probably a piece of evidence someone managed to get rid of.

Oh God, I'm in hell.

In front of me was a row of clerical stations, almost like the teller windows in an old-fashioned bank. Railings separated each station, and the detainees walking to the windows to get booked reminded me of cattle walking down chutes to the slaughter.

I stared straight ahead, trying not to make eye contact with the other people sitting on the bench. There didn't appear to be any white collar criminals in Van Nuys that night. Most of the men wore tattoos and one of them spat at another one, causing an outbreak of swearing and threats. What was it with men and their mucous?

The women looked no more wholesome than the men. I assumed most of them were hookers, by the way they were dressed. Why else did women get arrested? Oh, that's right. For stealing laptop computers.

"What're you in for, bitch?"

I looked into the watery bloodshot eyes of a woman high on something. She sat to my right and could have been fifty, could have been twenty. It was hard to tell. The skin on her face was an unhealthy color of gray and covered with sores. She grinned, and there were gaps where her teeth should have been.

I was fed up with people being rude to me. I didn't like being called bad names. I looked her in the eye. "You should consider seeing a dentist."

"Forget you," the woman said with her one front tooth.

Around midnight a voice called out, "Rose, Martha?"

I looked at an officer coming toward the bench. "Here."

He released me from the bench, and I got up stiffly. I limped unsteadily for a couple of steps. The officer took my elbow and walked me down one of the cattle chutes. I couldn't stop the tears from rolling down my cheeks. Did cows feel this way? I made a mental note to stop eating meat. Except maybe for the brisket on Rosh Hashanah.

I was fingerprinted, photographed, and sent to women's detention where I was greeted by a female sheriff's deputy who looked fresh out of the academy. Her long brown hair was pulled back into a French braid.

She took me into a small room. "Take off your clothes."

I almost fainted when she put on a pair of latex gloves. In another couple of minutes, after the body cavity search, my humiliation would be complete.

Afterward, I demanded to know, "When do I get my phone call?"

"Right now if you want." The guard peeled off the latex gloves and dropped them in a red plastic biohazard container. She took me to a phone bolted to the wall.

My hands shook as I frantically punched in Lucy's

number. The phone rang six times and switched to an answering machine.

"Lucy, it's Martha. I'm sorry for calling you so late, but I've been arrested for taking Claire's laptop. I'm in the Van Nuys jail. Please, can you get me out of here? Lucy? Ray? Please, someone pick up the phone." I waited a little longer, but nothing happened. My stomach slowly turned over as I realized I was actually going to have to spend the night here. I hung up the phone and slumped against the wall.

The guard asked, "Done?"

I nodded. She led me to the woman's dormitory, a cell with a row of double decker steel-framed military bunks. A webbing of springs supported soiled mattresses no thicker than two inches. The jailer reached into a cardboard box and handed me an old gray wool blanket that smelled like vomit.

I looked at her. "This place could definitely use a few quilts."

The other women were already sleeping on cots. Most of them took the top bunks. I leaned toward the guard and asked in a low voice, "Do you have private accommodations?"

She just put her hand on my shoulder, shoved me inside, and closed the steel door.

I slept fitfully that night. Two of the women snored, and one had a hacking cough. The toothless drug addict talked earnestly with God, who apparently sat at the foot of her bed. I wondered how many more hours would pass before Lucy could get me out of here.

WEDNESDAY

CHAPTER 18

About six the next morning, a guard distributed a paper bag of food to each of us. I threw off the scratchy blanket and sat up. My eyes stung from lack of sleep. Inside the bag was an eight-ounce serving of two percent milk. A sandwich was entombed in plastic wrap. When I pulled apart the slices of white bread, I saw there were a couple of pieces of mystery meat. No lettuce, no tomato, no mayo. Not even a soupçon of mustard. I drank the milk straight out of the carton and put the sandwich back inside the bag.

A voice next to me asked, "Aren't you going to eat that?"

I looked over. God's handmaiden pointed to my bag.

"You'd actually eat this?"

"Heck yeah." She reached over and grabbed the repulsive package. "You never know where you're going to be at lunchtime. Sometimes this crap takes all day."

"You've been through this before then?"

She threw back her head and laughed. I could see what was left of her rotten brown teeth. "What are you, some kind of diva? What'd you do, anyway?"

The hair bristled on the back of my neck as I realized I was now the center of attention. One of the other inmates, a tough-looking blonde with a tattoo of barbed wire around her neck watched me with a predatory interest. I looked around but couldn't see the guard. I frantically tried to think what I could use to defend myself. I only had the clothes on my back and an empty paper bag. Now I understood why they didn't include any plastic cutlery with our meal.

I took a deep breath for courage. "They claim I stole a laptop computer and interfered with a police investigation, but this is all a misunderstanding. I had permission to take the computer."

Someone mused, "A computer can score enough crank for a couple of days."

I shrugged. "I don't do drugs."

The blonde walked over, shoved me on my collarbone, and sneered. "You too good for jail? You think you're better 'n us?"

I looked around but the guard was still nowhere in sight. I looked the blonde straight in the eyes, hoping my mouth wouldn't start quivering. "No way. This is my second arrest."

Blondie looked unconvinced. "Yeah? What was the first one for?"

"Antiwar protest. Back in the seventies."

"Well, la dee dah." She flapped her hand. "What did they give you? Community service?" She looked at the other women, who now stood in a circle around us, probably waiting for a fight to start.

"Worse. I took home the booby prize." I paused for effect until I had their full attention. "My ex. Jail is where I met my ex-husband."

After a beat, they all exploded into laughter.

Blondie slapped me on the back. "You got that right." She smiled.

Ten minutes later everyone was handcuffed and moved from the jail to the courthouse. We were put in a holding cell, a cage made out of steel mesh— like the spit screen in the patrol car. There were no windows, just white fluorescent lights sucking the color out of everything.

I started to sweat at the thought of having to sit there for hours. Male inmates in a neighboring cell shouted profanities and threats at each other. Guards barked at them to be quiet but were largely ignored. The air was stale and the stench of un-washed bodies was overpowering. I surreptitiously sniffed my armpits. It was official: I was a bona fide member of the "great unwashed."

What if Lucy didn't get my message? Nobody

knew I was here. I might lose it if I were forced to stay another night. Already my clothes smelled sour from the blanket, and my body smelled worse. I looked at the blonde. "What happens now?"

"They call us one by one into court, and we have to plead. Then they set a court date. We post bail and we're outta here."

I needed someone to arrange for the bail. I prayed Lucy would be in the courtroom when my turn came. Just then a guard called, "Martha Rose?"

I jumped at the mention of my name. "That's me." I turned around and looked into the face of a young body builder dressed in a crisp brown sheriff's uniform with a neck that looked like a size thirty and shirt sleeves that strained over bulging biceps.

"Come with me."

The blonde looked him up and down. "You must be a rookie. I've never seen you before."

"Ooo, *papi*! I'd party with you for free," someone else piped up.

The women hooted and made kissing sounds. The young deputy's ears turned crimson as he led me down the hall. I looked back over my shoulder at my cell mates, smiled, winked, and wiggled my hips. They started to clap and Blondie gave me a thumbs-up.

The guard led me to an empty interview room with a small metal table and four metal chairs. He took off my cuffs and left. I collapsed into one of the chairs, feeling sticky and oily. I closed my eyes and imagined standing in a hot shower with a bar of lilac-scented soap in my hands.

A minute later the door opened. Arlo Beavers wore blue jeans, a blue and white striped cowboy shirt with pearl snaps, and boots. His thick gray hair was neatly combed, his moustache freshly trimmed, and he smelled fresh and clean like I wish I did.

As soon as I saw him I jumped up and yelled, "You bully! How dare you have me arrested. I'm going to sue you for kidnapping and false imprisonment. Just wait until I see the judge. Someone is going to pay. I want my computer back!"

Beavers held a paper cup of hot water with the tag end of a Lipton teabag dangling over the side. He put the cup on the table. "It's the best I could come up with on short notice. I remembered you take both of these." He placed two packets of sugar and a thumb-sized plastic container of fake cream next to the cup.

Tears of anger blurred my vision as I sat down. I tore open the packets and doctored the bitter tea, trying not to cry as I sipped the comforting hot liquid. Beavers took a seat across from me.

When I could speak again, I looked at him. "Why'd you do this?"

He held up his hands, palms forward. "I had no idea Kaplan was coming after you."

"You must have told him the computer was at my house. How else would he have known?"

"That's true. I left a message on his cell phone."

I wiped the tears from my eyes. "Didn't Siobhan tell you she gave me permission to take Claire's computer?"

"Yeah, but Kaplan's cell phone must've cut off in the middle of my message. He says he never got to hear that part."

I glared at Beavers. "I was humiliated in front of my neighbors and thrown in a filthy dungeon." With each word, my voice rose another notch. "And for what? Because Detective Kaplan didn't get his facts straight?"

Beavers spoke calmly. "If you remember, Ms. Rose, I cautioned you several times to leave the investigation to the police. I also warned you could be arrested if you went too far. Kaplan was only doing his job."

"Baloney!" I jumped up again and waved my arms. "As soon as I get out of here, I'm getting a lawyer."

"That's your prerogative, but a good attorney will probably advise you, given the facts as he knew them, that Kaplan had probable cause to arrest you. False arrest cases are hard to prove because there's a lot of room for reasonable doubt." He paused. "Especially with someone who has priors, like yourself."

"Priors? What are you talking about?"

"I know about the Federal Building." There was a twitch at the corner of his mouth. "Seems you've been a menace to society more than once in your life."

"Very funny. Besides, that was ages ago."

"If it makes you feel any better, as soon as I found out Kaplan arrested you, I went straight to the DA's office to get the charges dropped. Then I hurried over to get you released."

"How did you find out?"

"At about oh six hundred hours, Mrs. Mondello picked up your message and then called me. I told her I'd fix this, even though today's my day off."

"So I'm free to go? Is Lucy here to drive me home?"

"I promised Mrs. Mondello I'd see you safely back to your house." Beavers stood. "Are you ready?"

"You can't get me home fast enough. I need to take a shower and wash off all these cooties. Oh, by the way? The breakfast here sucks!"

On the way back to Encino, he interrogated me about finding the baby quilt and about my meeting with Jerry Bell. Fifteen minutes later we pulled into my driveway.

"Oh my God." I suddenly realized that last night I was forced to leave without my purse. "How am I going to get inside my house?"

Beavers reached into his pocket and pulled out

my keys. "Detective Kaplan took this from your hall table yesterday to make sure your house was secured. They were logged into the property room last night. I retrieved them right before I came to get you. Your laptop computer has been logged in as evidence. Getting your computer back to you will take a while longer, but I'm working on it."

I grabbed the keys from his hands and got out of the car. Beavers followed me up onto the porch. I turned to him and growled, "Now what?" I just wanted him to go away.

"I made a promise to deliver you safely."

I turned my back to him and opened the front door. The moment I walked into the living room, I stopped. The sofa and chair cushions were on the floor. As my eyes traveled farther back to the kitchen, I saw that every cupboard and drawer hung open. I knew Kaplan had quickly found the laptop computers last night and left the house as neat as he found it. I remembered seeing him leave at the same time I did.

Every opening scene I ever watched on *Law and Order* came flooding into my head. I turned toward Beavers. "Kaplan didn't do this. Someone else has trashed my place."

Beavers stepped in front of me and pulled a small handgun out of the top of his boot. He put one finger to his lips and then gestured for me to go back out the front door. He watched me until I was safely outside and then disappeared farther into the house, holding the gun with two hands.

Five minutes later he came to the door. "You're lucky you weren't here last night."

"What do you mean?" I pushed past him into the living room. "Where's Bumper? Where's my cat?"

"Didn't see him. Listen, someone really doesn't want you to be messing around in the Claire Terry case."

At the mention of Claire's name, I remembered the quilts. I hurried past him and ran to the laundry room. The drying rack was still shoved against the wall, concealing the baby quilt underneath the tablecloth. The clothes hamper was knocked over and some of the dirty laundry was on the floor, but the other quilts were undisturbed in their pillowcases, safely at the bottom.

I heaved a sigh of relief as Beavers walked up behind me. "They're still here."

"That's not what I mean," he said. "In your bedroom. Come with me but don't touch anything."

I thought that under other circumstances, an invitation to accompany Detective Arlo Beavers to the bedroom might not be such a terrible thing.

Looking down the hall, my stomach flipped over at the thought of what could be waiting for me in there. A bloody horse's head on the sheets? Oh, please don't let it be Bumper . . .

I walked in front of Beavers down my hall, barely

able to process the mess. I stopped to pick up some of the towels and bedding that the intruder threw out of the linen closet. Someone had violated my home, taking away my sense of security and leaving me exposed and vulnerable. I stood in the middle of the hall, folding towels in a trance. "I'm going to have one heck of a time cleaning all this up."

Beavers gently took the towels out of my hands and urged me toward the bedroom. "You can do this later."

I stopped at my bedroom door, scarcely able to take in the mountain of clothes that had been ripped from my drawers and closet and thrown into piles around the room. Then I saw a huge butcher knife sticking straight up out of my pillow, pinning some kind of note there. My knees felt like rubber and I sagged backward into Beavers's chest. He stood solidly behind me and grabbed my shoulders.

"Oh my God." I turned slightly and looked at him. "Who did this? What does the note say?"

"It says 'Back off or die.'"

I shook. The killer had finally caught up with me just like Beavers predicted. I was in over my head, just like he said I would be. He'd been right all along. God, I hated when that happened.

"How'd he get in?"

"Bathroom window. Broken." Beavers took out his cell phone and called in the CSU.

"Darned if you haven't done it again," he said,

turning me around and gently guiding me by the shoulders back into the kitchen.

At this point I was grateful he'd insisted on seeing me safely home. I was even glad to have him take charge, but I barely heard him through the pounding in my ears.

"What's the story with you and crime scenes?"

I just stared at him. Then I remembered Bumper again. "My cat! Did you see him? If Kaplan let him run out of the house last night, I'll kill him!"

"I'll pretend I didn't hear you say that."

My whole body trembled and I couldn't sit still. I started pacing and shaking my wrists. "What do I do now?"

"Why don't you call Mrs. Mondello and go stay with her?"

"I need to find Bumper. Take a shower. Get some clothes. My medications."

"You can get a few things to tide you over, but you can take only a minute or two. Forensics won't want you to disturb anything."

"Like nothing has been disturbed already? Like my whole house isn't upside down? What about Claire's quilts? I promised the Terrys I'd give them back today."

"Giving them back is the first good idea you've had in over a week. And, Martha?"

Whoa. Did he just use my first name? An arc of

electricity sizzled somewhere in the region of my shoulder blades.

He stood in front of me, put his hands on my shoulders, and looked at me intently. "The fact you spent last night in jail? Detective Kaplan probably saved your life."

CHAPTER 19

I stood in Lucy's shower for twenty minutes, exhausted and achy, shampooing the filth from my hair and scrubbing until my skin turned pink. Lucy had provided a silky bar of triple-milled French soap smelling like a field of lavender in Provence.

After I dried myself off, I swallowed a Soma. The strong muscle relaxer eases some of my muscle pain and stiffness and makes life bearable. It also gives me a brief, fuzzy high and a feeling of well-being.

The worst time of year for fibromyalgia was winter when the barometer dropped before every rainstorm and cold front. During approximately six months out of the year I relied heavily on all my medications for relief. However, stress could also cause a flare-up of fibro. So even though it was now springtime, a relatively pain free time of year for me, the stress of going to jail drove me straight to my bottle of medicine.

I put on some clean clothes from my hastily packed overnight bag and followed my nose into the kitchen. I'd already decided not to call Quincy and tell her about my ordeal because I didn't want any of this to get back to my ex. I also decided not to tell Uncle Isaac as he would certainly become upset and worry.

When I was first arrested in an anti-Vietnam War demonstration, Uncle Isaac told me, "We're not a family of Cossacks and thieves. We're not a family that gets arrested."

"But, Uncle Isaac, this war is all wrong. We're sending our young men to die for Southeast Asian oil, pure and simple. Nobody's fooled. We need to get out of Vietnam and stop this unrighteous war."

"You're a good girl, faigela, but a young lady doesn't get herself arrested. This is going to be on your record for the rest of your life. How will you get a decent job or find a decent husband if you're a felony?"

"It's *felon*, Uncle. Felony is the crime, felon is the criminal."

He threw up both his hands. *"Vey iz mir!"*

Lucy and Birdie sat waiting for me at the table. They'd fixed me a breakfast of waffles, fried eggs, turkey sausage, sliced cantaloupe, and coffee.

As soon as she saw me, Birdie jumped up and gave me a long hug. She spoke into my ear while she patted my back. "I'm so sorry, Martha dear. You're safe now, here with Lucy and Ray."

Tears stung my eyes. Dear, sweet Birdie.

I sat down and Lucy put a heaping plate in front of me. Just an hour earlier she drove to my place, helped me pack a bag, and drove me back to her house. "Feeling better?"

I gratefully thought about my twenty-minute shower. "I'll never take hot water for granted again." I shoveled a hunk of waffle into my mouth. The crispy edges of the little squares dripped with melted butter and sweet maple syrup. I closed my eyes and the food and I became one.

Birdie poured the coffee. "I tried for hours last night, but I just couldn't come up with a pattern in those quilt names. I'm sorry, Martha."

"Thanks for trying. Actually, what you did isn't a complete loss. At least we can now rule out cryptograms and anagrams as part of a hidden message."

Birdie nodded. "I can't believe that young detective actually arrested you. What was it like? In jail, I mean."

I moved on to a bite of juicy sausage. "Pretty awful. Dirty. Vulgar. Disgusting. Smelly and scary." I stopped for a sip of coffee.

Birdie was a huge fan of crime dramas and mystery novels. She leaned toward me and lowered her voice. "You didn't have to be somebody's girlfriend, did you, dear?"

Lucy rolled her eyes.

I thought about my confrontation with Blondie.

"Well, I did have a near miss with a big, blond biker chick, but everything turned out okay."

As I devoured my breakfast, I filled them in on everything, beginning with Godwin, Dixie Barcelona, and the baby quilt; meeting Jerry Bell; getting arrested; and ending with Bumper's disappearance and the knife in my pillow.

Lucy threw her hands in the air. "Why can't you just make quilts like a normal person?"

"Don't worry. When I return Claire's quilts, that's just what I intend to do. Quilt like a virgin."

"When the time comes, we'll help you put your house back together again, won't we, Birdie?"

"Absolutely!"

I shifted uncomfortably in my seat, fighting the urge to cry. "I don't know if I'll ever feel safe enough to go back, especially with Claire's murderer coming after me." I looked at Lucy and my voice quivered. "I just don't want to jeopardize you and Ray by staying here."

"Oh, please." She waved her hand. "Ray and I are from Wyoming, remember? We own guns and we know how to use them."

"Wasn't Dick Cheney from Wyoming?" asked Birdie.

"Right!" I nodded. "And he practically shot a man to death while hunting. Guns can be dangerous."

Lucy started gathering the dirty dishes. "I rest my case."

A moment later Lucy answered her telephone. "Just a minute." She handed the phone to me.

"This is Arlo Beavers." When did he become "Arlo" and not "Detective"? I could almost smell his cologne through the phone.

"I'm wrapping up here and will be at Mrs. Mondello's house in about fifteen minutes. Don't go anywhere."

I stood up and handed the phone back to Lucy. "Detective Beavers is on his way over."

"Oh, this should be interesting." Birdie smiled. She exchanged a knowing glance with Lucy.

"What?" I suspected they talked about me while I was in the shower.

Lucy stopped loading the dishwasher and examined me for a full ten seconds. "Your hair is still wet."

"So?"

Lucy put her hands on her hips. "So, you should dry it."

"I'm not stupid. I know what you two are doing, and you can stop right now. I'm not interested in him, and he's not interested in me."

Lucy put her arm around my shoulders and propelled me down the hallway. "You should still dry your hair, girlfriend. Let me show you where the blower is."

She shoved me into the guest bathroom and pulled a hair dryer out of one of the vanity drawers. "You'll feel better if you do this." She was right, of course; I was just vain enough to want to redeem myself from the sorry sight I was after spending a night in the Van Nuys jail.

For the next five minutes I scrunched my curls with one hand while aiming the dryer with the other. At some point Lucy came back armed with a bottle of perfume, which she sprayed all over me, despite my protests. "Don't forget lipstick."

I smoothed my pink T-shirt, adjusted my glasses, and took one last inventory in the mirror. So what if I was a little on the zaftig side. I still had a recognizable waist, curvy hips, and a generous bosom that was 100 percent natural. Some men would find me irresistible. Maybe not in LA, but somewhere on this planet.

When I walked back into the kitchen, Lucy looked me up and down. "Better." Birdie just smiled.

My face heated when the doorbell rang.

Detective Beavers walked in holding a cat carrier with Bumper inside, and a bulging plastic trash bag.

"Oh, Bumper!" I took the carrier from him.

Lucy raised an eyebrow. "I hope you brought his litter box."

Beavers smiled at her and pointed to the trash bag. "Also a sack of litter and a bag of kibble I found in the kitchen."

Lucy took the bundle to her laundry room and came back with a cup of coffee for Beavers, who accepted it gladly.

Bumper purred in my arms, clearly happy to be reunited. "Where was he?"

"I sent a patrolman door to door. Turns out one of your neighbors took him home last night."

"Who?"

"Spiegelman. Sonia. She insisted she saved him from being blown up by the bombs you kept in your basement." He looked at me over the rim of his coffee mug. "Would you happen to know what she was talking about?"

I opened my eyes wide and shrugged. "Not a clue. I don't even have a basement."

The hot shower, the Soma, and a stomach full of comfort food were working together to finally relax me. My eyelids felt too heavy.

Beavers must have noticed. He stood up and handed his cup to Lucy. "Thanks for the coffee, Mrs. Mondello."

He turned to me. "CSU will be finished in a few hours. You'll want to get the bathroom window fixed as soon as they're done. I also strongly advise you to get a security system. Or a big dog."

"And a gun." Lucy pointed her finger at me.

"Only if you know how to use one," he warned.

Birdie cleared her throat. "Detective, do you have any leads on our missing quilts?"

"I'm sorry, Mrs. Watson. Not yet."

My body felt leaden as I walked with him to Lucy's front door. "Thank you for making the effort to find Bumper. I haven't forgotten this was supposed to be your day off."

"Get some sleep." He opened the door. "You've been through a lot."

I vaguely remembered walking to Lucy's guest room and putting on my pajamas. I crawled under a lovely Dresden Plate quilt Lucy's grandmother made using feed sacks she saved during the Depression. Lucy told me her grandmother raised chickens and sold the eggs to help support the family. The chicken feed came in cotton sacks printed with colorful patterns. In those days, nothing was wasted, and the feed sacks were repurposed to make clothing and quilts.

I pulled the quilt up to my chin and turned on my side. Bumper jumped up on the bed and curled into the crook behind my knees. Feeling cozy and safe, I snuggled deeper into the bed and closed my eyes.

The next thing I knew, it was dark outside and the little hand on the bedside clock was pointing to seven. I debated whether to get up and be sociable or just roll over and go back to sleep. Snippets of something I dreamed came floating through my brain behind wisps of gray fog: I stood near a bank of elevators in a crowd of people; Claire was standing in the midst of the crowd holding a needle and thread; the little girl with the thick glasses and the shape sorter box fingered the elevator call button. She turned toward her mother and smiled excitedly. "It's a rectangle."

My eyes flew open and I sat straight up in bed.

That was it! Oh my God! No longer sleepy, I jumped up and threw on some clothes. I wanted to consult an expert for confirmation, but I was dead certain I was right.

Then it dawned on me. This was Wednesday night and I'd promised Will Terry he'd have the quilts by now. *Darn!* I needed to keep them a little bit longer. Just until I knew for sure. Then I'd give them back.

I turned on my cell phone and discovered several messages from Siobhan Terry. *They probably think I'm a flake.* I called her number.

"Siobhan, this is Martha Rose. Please forgive me for not getting back to you earlier today. I was kind of incapacitated."

"Thank goodness you called. Are you all right? Will sent a driver to your house earlier to pick up the quilts. The driver reported when he got there he saw crime scene tape and police cars. No one would tell him where you were. I've been calling your cell phone for the last several hours. What happened?"

I told her about my arrest, the break-in at my house, and the threatening note. "Detective Beavers says if I'd been home last night, I might have been killed."

"Mother of God! Where are you now?"

"For the moment I'm staying with my friend Lucy Mondello and her husband, Ray. I was so exhausted from everything that's happened, I slept the entire day. I just woke up, in fact."

"I'm so sorry I ever got you into this, and I'm really sorry you were arrested. I was stupid to tell the detective about the computer. If you give me your friend's address, I'll have someone come right over and pick up the quilts. You do have them, don't you?"

"They're here. Whoever broke in to my house didn't find them." By now I was pacing the bedroom. "I'd like to keep them just a little longer—say until noon tomorrow? I need to test a hunch."

Siobhan's voice dropped to a whisper and I had to strain to hear her. "Have you found something?"

"Yes, Siobhan, I have. I think I know exactly how Claire sewed her story into her quilts!"

CHAPTER 20

The pillowcases containing Claire's quilts sat next to my overnight bag on the floor in the corner of the bedroom. I pulled out one of them at random: Midnight Garden, the one with the navy blue background. No good. The background was too dark to see what I was looking for.

I pulled out another one: Mother's Asleep, the one with the white cloud background. This one was much easier to examine. I needed an expert to decode what I was looking at, but I was confident I was right.

I took the quilt out of the guest room and went looking for Lucy. Bumper jumped off the bed, followed me out of the bedroom, and made a beeline for the litter box. Lucy sat in the kitchen with a glass of wine reading the newest issue of *Pieces* magazine. She wore a white blouse with a sailor collar, blue capri pants, and red and white striped espadrilles (which kind of matched her hair). Little gold anchors hung from her ears. For a minute I wondered if this was Memorial Day.

When Lucy saw me, she got up, still holding her wineglass, and gave me a one-arm hug. "Hi, hon'. Did you get a good sleep?"

"Not only did I sleep like a log, I had an incredible dream."

Lucy pointed to an empty chair. "Sit. Ray and I have already eaten, but I saved some dinner for you."

"Okay, but first I have to . . ."

She took the quilt out of my hand and put it on a chair. "Sit. Before you do anything, you're going to eat."

I sat obediently. "Are you sure you're not Jewish?"

"Italian by marriage. Same thing. If you're thinking about calling someone to fix your bathroom window, forget about it. Ray is over there now with Joey doing the repairs."

She poured me a glass of red wine and prepared a steaming plate of meat loaf and gravy, mashed potatoes, and spinach sautéed in garlic and olive oil while she talked.

Suddenly I was famished. "I can't thank you and Ray enough," I mumbled through a mouthful of spicy meat loaf, "but I have to go back to my house tonight."

"Are you kidding?"

"No. I have to get a phone number. I think I've

figured out how Claire sewed her stories into her quilts."

"Get out! How? When?"

"Well, it actually came to me in a dream. Right now I need to talk to an expert who can read the code."

"Code?"

"Yes, Lucy. I need to talk to Dixie Barcelona. She's a Braille expert."

Lucy looked puzzled for a moment and then her eyes lit up. "I get it! You're brilliant." She stood and went for the quilt on the chair. "The code is in the French knots, isn't it? You think the French knots are Braille."

I smiled and nodded as Lucy spread out the quilt and fingered the bumps in the background.

Lucy looked closely. "I see what you mean. These knots appear to be clustered in tiny groups and are oriented in even rows. To the casual observer, they'd just look like random embellishment."

Then Lucy got a funny look on her face. "Do you think the killer is blind?"

"No, of course not. Claire may have confided to the killer what she was doing. The killer wouldn't have to actually read Braille in order to want to destroy the quilts and the stories they tell."

"So you think anyone could be the killer?"

"At this point, yes. That's why I have to find someone who can actually read this stuff. I got voice mail from Dixie Barcelona on my landline last night.

I need to play back the message to get her telephone number."

"Can't you access your phone remotely?"

"I never learned how."

"Well, you can't go home by yourself. I'll call Ray and make sure he waits for us. I don't like the idea of our being in your house alone at night."

"Okay, but let's hide the quilts before we leave. We can't be too careful."

"I've got the perfect hiding place." She picked up some plastic trash bags from under the kitchen sink. "Follow me."

We gathered the quilts and walked down the hall to Ray's office. A six-foot-tall cast iron cabinet stood against one wall, painted with shiny black enamel embellished with gold curlicues and a big golden eagle.

It reminded me of an old-fashioned bank vault. "What is this? This thing must weigh a ton."

"Half a ton, actually. Took six men to install. It's a gun safe, among other things." Lucy punched in a digital code and the small red light on the keypad turned green. She rotated a steel handle that looked like the spokes of a wheel and the heavy door swung open. Inside were several rifles neatly lined up, standing vertically on their stocks. Handguns rested on the shelves.

I stared at Lucy. This was a side of the Mondellos I'd never seen. "What is all of this for?"

"You're looking at Ray's collection. Kind of an

investment. Some of these are antique, some rare, and some for personal use."

"When would you ever use these guns?"

"Hopefully never, but where we come from, guns are a part of everyday life. Living in Wyoming meant you owned guns for hunting and for protection against predators."

"Even the two-legged kind?"

"Especially them."

I peered inside. Several other shelves and drawers were filled with boxes. "What are these for?"

"Some are for ammunition, some for cash and documents, and some for my jewelry. It'll be a tight squeeze, but I think we can stuff these pillowcases between the rifles. First let's put them in the plastic bags. We don't want any gun oil to get on the fabric."

Once the quilts were safely stowed, Lucy closed the heavy door and turned the wheel, locking them safely inside.

I breathed a sigh of relief. "Okay. Let's get over to my house."

Lucy called Ray and told him we were coming. Just as she hung up, her phone rang. "Hi, Birdie. Yes, she's up. I'm taking her back to her house to get something. Listen. Martha discovered the secret of Claire's quilts!"

Lucy put her hand over the phone. "Birdie's coming with us. She wants to hear what you found."

From the backseat of Lucy's Caddie, I explained everything to Birdie.

"And the answer came to you in a dream?"

"Yes."

"Ah . . ." She tapped her head. "The little gray cells. They never rest, *n'est-ce pas?*"

We laughed.

When I opened my front door, Ray Mondello was waiting for us in his flannel shirt with the sleeves rolled up. Ray was a few inches shorter than Lucy. At sixty-six years old, he still had a full head of dark, straight hair. He smiled at me and winked, as if to say, "I've got your back."

I looked around and, even though I'd already seen the destruction, I was still shocked by the mess the killer made of my house. I walked over to Ray and he wrapped me in a big hug.

"How's my girl?" He patted my back. Good old Ray. Heart of gold and utterly dependable. "I hope you don't plan to stay here tonight."

"No. I just came to listen to my messages, then I'm going to drive myself back to your house."

"That's my girl."

I carefully picked my way through the debris in the kitchen. The floor was filled with breakable items that had shattered when they hit the hard brown ceramic tiles. Ray located my broom and began to sweep up the mess. I found my phone upside down on a pile of what used to be my white coffee and tea canisters. I picked up the handset lying nearby and miraculously heard a dial tone.

I pulled my notepad and a pen from my purse and replayed Dixie's message, writing down her number.

While Ray swept, Lucy and Birdie drifted into the living room. They replaced the cushions on the sofa and picked up the books that the killer pushed out of the bookcases.

Then Joey walked into the living room. He was the only one of Lucy's five boys with light hair and blue eyes. The others all got Ray's dark hair and eyes. "Hi, everyone." Joey turned to his father. "I finished the window, Pops."

"Okay. We're outta here."

They waited for me while I picked up some clothes for the wake and funeral. As we walked to the front door, I hugged Joey. "Thank you so much for your help."

Joey was the only one of Lucy's boys who didn't finish college. Like his father, Joey was most comfortable working with his hands. By the time he was twenty, he was a licensed carpenter, and by twenty-five he owned his own contracting business.

"A piece of cake, Aunt Martha, but it sucks this happened to you. Dad and I agreed I'm gonna install an alarm system so you'll be safer. I'll have you hooked up by Friday."

Joey brushed off my offer to pay. "You're family."

I drove my car back to Lucy's. On the way, I

punched in Dixie's number on my cell phone. I got her voice mail. "Dixie, this is Martha Rose. I really need to talk to you right away. I think I've figured out something about Claire's quilts, but I need an expert's help. This is urgent because I have to give the quilts back to the Terrys by noon tomorrow. I'm staying with friends at the moment, so please call me on my cell."

I gave her the number and then hung up. Now I just hoped she'd get the message before I returned the quilts tomorrow. While there was still a chance, I wanted to find out what secrets were hidden in the Braille—secrets terrible enough to kill for.

CHAPTER 21

Back at the Mondello house, I installed myself in front of Lucy's computer and downloaded Claire's files from the flash drive. Little pieces of paper flew from one folder to the next on the screen when Lucy came into the room. She handed me a steaming mug of French roast with milk. "There's a fresh pot of this in the kitchen, and the quilts are back in your room."

"Thanks, Luce. I'm going to be up for a while."

"So, what are you looking for?"

"While I'm waiting for Dixie's call, I'm going to dive into Claire's files and see what I can dig up."

Lucy yawned. "Well, unlike some people we know, I didn't sleep all day. Ray and I are going to turn in now. Feel free." She gave a generous wave toward the house. I knew this was Lucy's shorthand for *Take what you need. Mi casa es su casa.*

A melodic prompt from the computer told me

the files were downloaded. Scrolling down the list I stopped at the James Trueville folder. Would Claire's ex-husband have a reason to want her dead? I double clicked on the folder and read the most recent document first.

> *March 13*
> *James:*
>   *I trust the enclosed documents will finally put*
> *an end to all the wrangling of the past. I'm glad*
> *you've found happiness. I, too, have finally found*
> *a measure of my own.*
>
>   *Claire*
>
> *Cc: John Doud, Will Terry*

The happiness she was talking about must have been her pregnancy and her love affair. According to the gossip at the board meetings, the wrangling of the past was over her divorce settlement.

I took a sip of caffeine and looked at an earlier message.

> *February 2*
> *James:*
>   *I'm glad you've reconsidered your demand for*
> *Palm Beach. I've already signed over Aspen and*
> *I'm prepared to sign over your choice of either the*
> *villa in Hanalei or St. Feliu—if that means we're*
> *finally done.*

*Just call John Doud and let him know your
decision. He's prepared to execute the documents.*
                                              Claire

Cc: John Doud, Will Terry

Holy crap. Claire owned places in Aspen, Palm
Beach, Hawaii, and somewhere called St. Feliu?
Where the heck was St. Feliu?

Three clicks into Google and I stared at a me-
dieval town with sunny beaches on the Costa Brava,
the Mediterranean side of Spain. Must be nice.

Their earlier correspondence was full of postur-
ing and demands. Eventually they'd settled the last
of their financial differences. Jamey boy walked
away with at least two luxury houses, a wad of cash
in the eight figures, and a smile on his face. Somehow I couldn't see this guy needing Claire dead.

Since I was logged into Google, I typed in *Braille
alphabet* and got tens of thousands of hits, all revealing the same thing. A Braille cell was the basic unit,
oriented like a tall rectangle made up of two
columns. The first column had spaces numbered
from one to three top to bottom. The second
column had spaces four to six numbered top to
bottom. Each letter of the alphabet occupied one
cell and had a unique pattern of one to five dots
arranged within the six spaces.

Could I decipher the quilt on my own? I'd have
to choose a quilt with dots that were easy to see, like
the one with the white cloud background. I printed

out a copy of the alphabet and took it along with a ruler from Lucy's desk and the Mother's Asleep quilt to Lucy's kitchen.

I spread out the quilt on the table and peered closely. Where was the beginning? I used the ruler to help me find the line of text and started in the upper left-hand corner with the printout right alongside for easy reference.

The first dot was in the number six position, which meant, according to the printout, the next letter should be a capital letter. After painstakingly searching the printout, I discovered the first letter was an *m*, so I wrote a capital *M* in my notepad. The second letter was a *y*. It took five minutes to read the first word, *My.*

Oh my God. I did it. I cracked the code! I leapt up and dislodged a ginger-colored fuzz ball sleeping in my lap. Bumper looked at me scornfully while I did a little victory dance with a lot of hip action.

At this rate, it would take three weeks to read the quilt, but I was almost out of time. I needed Dixie. I looked at my watch. Midnight. *Darn!* Why hadn't she called?

I sat back down and Bumper jumped up in my lap again. With the help of a ruler to keep track of the lines of text, I got better at reading. Thirty minutes later I'd written on my notepad:

My mother alcoholic.

Whoa. This wasn't what I expected. What kind of

story was Claire telling here, and did I really want
to know more? The elegant Siobhan didn't strike
me as a drinker. She looked pretty well put together
for a woman in her seventies. There was no sign of
booze when she served tea on Sunday. She must be
sober now.

I pressed on. In another thirty minutes I came
up with:

M never there 4 me when I child.

This was beginning to sound like a typical adoles-
cent's diary—lots of complaints about Mom. I
glanced at my watch. One-thirty in the morning.
I was hyped up on caffeine and not at all sleepy,
so I continued to read.

M pass out every night 9 pm.

I looked up from the quilt and rubbed my eyes.
What was it like for Claire to have a mother who
wasn't there for her? Must have been pretty lonely.
My mother had been so traumatized by my father's
death, she was incapable of taking care of herself,
let alone a daughter. I'd had my bubbie and Uncle
Isaac. Who'd been there for Claire?

I stepped back and looked at the quilt again. A
nude woman slept on clouds with teardrop-shaped
beads dripping down. Of course. This quilt wasn't
about rainmaking, as I'd first thought, but absent
mothers and sadness, lots of sadness.

After two in the morning, I freshened the coffee
in my cup and started again to slowly read the en-
crypted words.

Daddy's night visits

The hair on the back of my neck bristled. Uh-oh. What was I reading here? What did she mean, *night* visits? I hoped this wasn't leading anywhere bad.

began when I 10yo.

Okay, okay. So maybe he came in to read her a story or tuck her in, things her mother would have done if she hadn't been passed out.

He say I love of his life.

Okay. Love is a good thing, right? Wasn't he just making up for the love and attention she didn't get from her alcoholic mother?

I was hooked. The time was now after three, but I couldn't stop reading.

He only wore bathro . . .

Oh my God. I stopped reading. Something acid crept up from my stomach, and I felt as if I'd just taken a dirt bath. Was this real? If so, Will Terry was a child molester! I fingered the teardrop-shaped beads Claire had sewn so extensively on this quilt.

These messages must be why Terry tried to talk me out of examining the quilts and gave me so little time with them. He said if I came up with nothing, he was afraid of what the disappointment might do to Siobhan, but he didn't give a crap about Siobhan. He just wanted to keep the truth hidden—a terrible, damning truth.

If Claire was a victim of incest, that would be a huge motive for Will Terry not wanting the information in the quilts to get out. He could have been behind the theft of the quilts, the attempted theft at Claire's house, and the break-in at my house. Still, was he capable of murdering his daughter, the "love of his life"?

What about Siobhan? If she knew about the incest, would she really have wanted me to discover the secrets in Claire's quilts? Most families wanted to keep such awful secrets hidden from the outside world.

I looked back down at Mother's Asleep. There was much more to decode, but I was so done. I'd become an unwitting voyeur to an appalling tragedy and wished I'd never agreed to help.

I looked at my watch. Four. A wave of revulsion and emotional exhaustion washed over me. I folded the quilt and put it back in the pillowcase. There was still enough time to grab a couple hours of sleep.

I walked back to Lucy's office, but before I turned off the computer, I opened Claire's digital photo album and briefly examined the pictures of her quilts. Fortunately, she'd taken extensive close-ups clearly showing the knots on all the quilts, except those with a dark background. Good. Even though I had to give the quilts back tomorrow, I might still be able to study the Braille from the photos if I needed to.

Claire's secrets were compelling. She was robbed of her innocence and endured the unspeakable, and now she was dead. Her molester walked around a free man. I vowed to find some justice for Claire if it was the last thing I did.

THURSDAY

CHAPTER 22

At six that morning, I heard Lucy and Ray starting their day, so I got dressed in my uniform of blue jeans and a white V-neck T-shirt, ruffled my curls with wet hands to get rid of the bed hair, and joined them in the kitchen. I poured myself a steaming mug of dark French roast while Lucy set the table for three. She still wore a baby blue chenille bathrobe, but her short orange hair was brushed, her eyebrows were freshly drawn, and her mascara was expertly applied. Dame Judi Dench never looked so good.

"How'd you do last night?"

I told her about the divorce settlement, but I was reluctant to talk about the incest with Ray in the room. "I went on Google and downloaded a copy of the Braille alphabet. I've been studying it."

She put plates of scrambled eggs, hash browns, and toasted English muffins on the table. "Did Dixie Barcelona ever call you back?"

I sat down and opened a jar of raspberry jam. "No, but I don't think I'll be asking her to help after all. I really think I'm getting a handle on this Braille thing."

After breakfast I gathered the dirty dishes from the table as Ray kissed Lucy good-bye. With the difference in their heights, Lucy bent her head a little. This was an endearing and graceful gesture she'd perfected over the years. Ray popped her affectionately on the behind. "See ya later, babe."

"Love you." She kissed him.

I smiled at their tender daily ritual of nearly fifty years. How was it some women were lucky enough to find the perfect mate, while the rest of us either ended up alone, like me, or in a loveless arrangement like Birdie?

Whenever we were around Ray, he always gave Lucy a touch, a hug, a kiss.

Then he smiled. "You babes stay out of trouble today." We liked being Ray's *babes*.

I'd never seen Russell touch Birdie, let alone kiss her. Whenever we were at Birdie's house, he nodded his head. "You girls carry on." Girls. The way he said it I always felt dismissed—the same way Birdie must have felt every day of her married life.

Birdie once confided they hadn't been intimate in years. "Do you think he has another woman?" She'd had tears in her eyes.

Lucy reached out and touched her arm. "Did

you ever consider that he might be gay?" Because of Richie, Lucy was developing quite a gaydar.

Birdie's mouth dropped open. "Frankly, I don't know what is worse, the idea of Russell having an affair with a man or a woman."

"Why do you stay with him?" I asked.

"I'm too old to change now. I resigned myself a long time ago where my marriage is concerned. I try to fill my life with other things, like my gardening, my friends, and my quilting. I don't know what I'd do without the two of you." Then she cried.

Lucy and Ray smiled at each other in the secret way lovers did. Their marriage was an unlikely success. They'd been sweethearts in high school and, despite the fact they married in their teens, neither Ray nor Lucy seemed to think they'd ever missed out on anything—college, parties, dating, travel. Their life together was exactly what each of them wanted and they were happier than anyone else I knew.

Fingers of envy and self-pity squeezed my heart, and I turned toward the sink to hide my teary eyes. If I could go back and make my life's choices all over again, I'd do it their way.

Lucy's voice jolted me out of my reverie. "I can finish those, hon'."

I scraped off the last of the plates. "I'm almost done. Anyway, now that Ray's gone, I need to show you what I found." I dried my hands and handed my notepad to Lucy. "I started decoding Mother's Asleep. Here's what I've discovered so far."

Lucy clamped a shocked hand over her wide open mouth as she read. She looked at me with eyes the size of baseballs. "Martha! Are you sure? You really read this?"

Just then her phone rang and she looked at the caller ID. "You answer it, Martha. I don't think I can talk right now."

"Hi, Birdie. What? Are you all right? Did you call the police? We'll be right over."

Lucy looked at me. "Now what?"

"Russell walked out the front door and stepped on a note for Birdie taped to a small paper bag full of dog crap."

Lucy whooped out an incredulous "No! Dog poop? What did the note say?"

"Just two words: *You're next.*"

Neither one of us said another word as we rushed to get to Birdie's. Lucy opened the front door, and I yelled, "Stop! Don't move."

Lying there on the porch, just outside the threshold where her foot would have landed, was a note taped to a small paper bag.

"Dang!" Lucy never swore.

I bent down to examine the angry letters scratched in black marking pen on plain white paper. *Lucy Mondello is a dead woman!*

I stood up. "When Ray left this morning, I wasn't

really paying attention. Did he leave by the front door? Because if he did, someone just put this here."

"No, he left through the kitchen door straight into the garage like he always does."

"Then this could have been placed here any time during the night. Oh, Lucy, I told you I didn't want to bring you trouble by staying here."

Lucy narrowed her eyes, pulled herself up to her full height, and put her hands on her hips. "This guy picked the wrong woman to mess with. I'm going to call Ray and wait for the police."

"Right. I'll go see if Birdie's okay."

As I walked across the street, my stomach clenched with a sick realization. By seeking refuge at Lucy's house, I'd put both my friends in jeopardy.

CHAPTER 23

Birdie must have seen me walking across the street as she opened the door and pointed to the porch. "Be careful, Martha dear. Don't step in the mess."

"Looks like someone beat me to it." I took a large step over the smelly brown smear.

Birdie twisted her braid furiously. "Russell, and he's madder'n a wet hen."

"Don't you mean rooster?"

"I said what I meant, Martha. Come on in. I just got off the phone with Detective Beavers. He's on his way."

Russell walked into the living room, his white hair perfectly groomed. I never could get over the contrast between earth mother Birdie and this fussy little man dressed in a blue business suit and silk tie. He smiled tightly at me and nodded once, slightly disturbing a strand of hair on his forehead. "Hello, Martha."

"Hi, Russell. You okay?"

"Just fine. Just fine." He took Birdie's hands in his, looked at her over the top rim of his gold wire-rimmed glasses, and spoke to her, slowly enunciating every word as if he were addressing a child. "I wish I could stick around, but I've got an early meeting at the bank with the federal regulators. You know how critical this is." Russell looked at me with desperate appeal in his eyes. "I'm hoping Martha can stay with you until I get back." I nodded, and he turned his attention back to Birdie.

"I'll make an effort to get away the moment the auditors leave. Meanwhile, try to be brave. I'm sure the police are on their way."

Russell gave her a rare, perfunctory kiss on the cheek. "By the way, my shoes are on the back porch."

Birdie looked like a thundercloud, clenched her teeth, and lowered her voice into an uncharacteristic snarl. "I'm not touching those shoes, Russell."

He glanced nervously at me and I looked away, pretending to find some important lint that needed removing from the front of my shirt.

Without another word, Russell Watson walked out the front door for the second time that morning, this time stepping over the mess on the porch and leaving his wife to clean it up.

At eight a silver Camry pulled up in front of Birdie's house, followed by a squad car. Detective Beavers barked some orders to the two uniforms, who fanned out toward the neighbors' houses. Then he knocked on Birdie's door. When Beavers saw me sitting on her sofa, he shook his head a couple of times. "Where were you last night at eleven?"

"Across the street at Lucy's. Why?"

"There was a robbery in Pacoima, but when I got to the crime scene, you weren't there."

"Very funny. Listen, Birdie's not the only one who got hit. Lucy also got a threatening note taped to a bagful of dog crap on her porch. She's waiting for you across the street at her house."

Birdie gasped. "Why didn't you tell me? What did *her* note say?"

"That she was a dead woman."

Birdie started to rub the middle of her chest.

Beavers's frown deepened. He dug his cell phone out of his pocket, punched some buttons, and turned away as he spoke. "I need you to go over to Martha Rose's house and see if there's a bag of dog crap on her porch with a note taped on it. If there is, bag it and bring it in. No, just the note. No, I'm not kidding, Kaplan. Just do it."

I sat next to Birdie and held her hand while she told Detective Beavers everything she could remember about the morning. At one point she got up and produced a plastic baggie with the note inside. The white paper was smeared brown and ripped from when Russell made contact with his shoe, but the menacing words printed with a black marker were clearly readable.

At about eight forty-five Beavers received a call. "Yeah, Kaplan. Thanks." He put his phone back in his pocket and looked at me. It wasn't good.

"What?"

"Three for three."

"You mean I got one, too?"

Beavers nodded.

"What did it say?"

He glanced at Birdie and then cleared his throat. "Uh, he called you a know-it-all in not such nice words."

Then he stood. "I'm sorry about this, Mrs. Watson, but my gut tells me this is probably an unrelated prank. Dog excrement isn't usually a killer's weapon of choice, but I'll order a patrol to swing by here for the next few days." Then he looked at me. "Ms. Rose, can I speak to you for a minute?"

We stepped outside, avoiding the brown mess, and when I glanced across the street, Ray's car was there. Then Joey drove up in his truck. He jumped out and hurried inside his mother's house. In a short time, Richie and the other boys would arrive to complete the circle of protection. If anyone wanted to harm Lucy, they were going to have to get past six Mondello men.

"Where exactly are you staying?" He looked at the activity across the street.

"I'm still at Lucy's."

"Good. That's the best place for you right now." He looked back at Birdie's house. "I don't think Mrs. Watson should be left alone to wait for her husband to come back from wherever he went."

"Yeah. I'll stay with her."

Beavers nodded and turned to go across the street.

"What about my laptop?"

"In the works."

Should I tell him about reading the quilts? I'd wait until after the funeral, for Siobhan's sake. I wanted to spare her this new grief for as long as possible, and I needed to plan the best way to break the awful news. I went back inside with Birdie. "I'll stay here with you until Russell gets home."

"You might be waiting here for hours."

I looked at my watch. Nearly nine and I knew Birdie wasn't exaggerating. No matter what Birdie might need, Russell wouldn't come home until Russell was ready. This meant, of course, I'd just lost my last chance to examine the other quilts. Thank goodness for the photographs. An incomplete record was better than none at all.

I looked at my friend still nervously twisting her

braid and forced a smile. "That's okay, Birdie. There's no other place I'd rather be right now. Maybe I could help you cut pieces for your Grandmother's Fan blocks."

As we worked in her sewing room, I told Birdie the story I deciphered in Claire's quilt the night before.

"Oh, Martha, how awful! Poor, poor Claire. Do you think her father is behind her death and the disappearance of her quilt?"

"While he has a strong motive for stealing and destroying the incriminating evidence in those quilts, I find it hard to believe he'd kill her. Why would he steal our quilts from the quilt show, too? That piece doesn't seem to fit anywhere in this puzzle."

At 11:45, Russell Watson returned home with a pint of Birdie's favorite Chocolate Cherry Cordial ice cream. I suspected this was as close as he ever got to an apology.

I left Russell and Birdie, but before I walked back to Lucy's house, I turned on the Watsons' garden hose and washed off their front porch. The crime scene people didn't need the dog crap anymore.

Back at Lucy's I was greeted warmly by all the boys. I turned to Lucy. "Are the quilts ready to go?" She pointed to the pillowcases stacked neatly near the door.

Just then the doorbell rang. As Joey walked to the front door, Ray warned, "Be careful, Joe." A driver in gray livery stood on the porch with a white Bentley parked at the curb. Two minutes later he drove away.

I sighed and hooked my arm into Lucy's. "Well, they're gone," I whispered so nobody else could hear me. "But after all this trouble, I'd sure like to know what other stories those quilts have to tell."

"You and me both," she whispered back.

In the afternoon the Mondello men worked out a schedule for one of them to be with Lucy at all times. They each chose a gun from the safe.

Ray put his arm around my shoulder. "Your house is fixed now, Martha, but for the time being, I think you should stick with us rather than take your chances on your own."

"Thanks, Ray, but I can't stay here forever. I plan to go back home after the funeral tomorrow. I won't be terrorized into staying away from my house."

Richie turned to Joey and muttered, "No wonder she and Mom are such good friends."

Ray handed me a pistol. "Then I insist you take a handgun to protect yourself."

"I don't even know how to work one of these things." I turned the weapon over in my hands. "I'm a Democrat."

"Joey is going to take you to the shooting range

this afternoon and make sure you know how to use the gun."

"But . . ."

"No arguments, please. We'd all feel better if you had some self-protection. Right, Lulu?"

Lucy nodded. "This was my idea, really."

I started to protest, but Joey grabbed the gun and led me by my hand to his pickup like a parent leading a child who doesn't know how she feels about the first day of school.

"Come on, Aunt Martha. I'm taking you to an indoor shooting range. In an hour or two you're going to know all about gun safety and, more important, you're going to know how to use this little baby."

Joey sheepishly grabbed all the empty fast-food bags off the passenger side and stuffed them behind the seat.

I hoisted myself into the elevated cab of the white pickup by holding on to the door with one hand and the grab bar with the other.

The inside smelled like onions and motor oil.

The shooting range was in the foothills of the San Gabriel Mountains to the east of the Valley. Straw bales with paper targets were set up outside for people with rifles. Inside a building with extra thick concrete walls, the range was shorter and looked like all the shooting ranges I'd seen on the cop shows on TV. It smelled like gun oil and sulfur. The gray room was divided into lanes with zip lines to move paper targets toward the back wall. Thousands of spent bullets with shiny copper and steel jackets littered the concrete floor.

Joey pinned up a paper target with a body silhouette on it and sent it down the line about twenty feet. He picked up the gun. "This is a Browning semiautomatic twenty-two caliber pistol." He showed me how to release the safety, chamber a round by sliding back the top, and sight down the barrel. The gun was heavier than I expected and I had a hard time holding it—even using both hands.

Joey put a headset on me to protect my ears. Then I heard a voice say, "Commence fire."

I'd never shot a gun before, but I was pretty sure I could hit the target. After all, it was only twenty feet away. Guns exploded in the lanes all around me. I aimed, sighted, and pulled the trigger. The kickback sent my arms down and back.

I looked at Joey. "Whoa."

"You're doing fine, Aunt Martha. Just try to keep your arms and wrists straight."

When the voice commanded, "Hold your fire," I put the empty gun down on the shelf in front of me.

Joey pressed a button and the paper target came back. I'd shot fifteen bullets and there were seven holes in the paper. Four of those didn't even hit the silhouette, but the other three hit pay dirt. Two in the torso and one in the crotch.

"Awesome, Aunt Martha. We'll make a sharp-shooter out of you yet."

"Do I have to change political parties?"

Joey, like the rest of his family, was a Republican. He looked at me and grinned wickedly. "You should do that anyway."

CHAPTER 24

In the evening, Ray drove Lucy, Birdie, and me to Clancy Brothers Mortuary on Olympic Boulevard in West LA. for Claire's wake. Lucy looked like a Mexican mourner in her black linen dress, long string of black beads, and a black lace mantilla over her flaming hair. Ray wore a dark suit jacket concealing a handgun he'd tucked into his waistband. Before we left, we agreed to not tell Birdie about the gun for fear of alarming her.

This was one of those rare times when we got to see Birdie out of her overalls and Birkenstocks. She wore a plum-colored polyester dress and jacket and limped a little in her black leather walking shoes. Russell declined to join us, claiming fatigue. That man was about as supportive as a flat tire. He probably thought the Chocolate Cherry Cordial ice cream bought him a long-term pass.

At 6:45 we pulled into the driveway of a two-story red brick colonial with white columns in front. The valet opened the door and I stepped out of the car, smoothing the wrinkles on my black Anne Klein skirt and readjusting the collar of my silk blouse where the seat belt twisted it.

Ray insisted on parking his vintage Mercedes himself. One of his passions was restoring old cars, and he wasn't about to trust his baby to a twenty-year-old valet. So we waited for him on the sidewalk.

All around the building, decorative shutters flanked tinted windows you couldn't see into from the outside. The small strip of front lawn was trimmed to the last blade of grass, and pink and white petunias bordered the short brick walkway from the sidewalk to the broad front steps.

A few minutes later Ray joined us. As we approached the double doors, white-gloved ushers in black suits opened them for us, and we stepped into a lobby with hallways leading in several directions. A sign on a stand in the shape of an arrow read MILLER and pointed down the hall to the left. Another sign pointing to the right read TERRY.

We followed the wood-paneled hallway until we came to a large room. At the far end was a bier draped in dark blue velvet. Lying on top was a polished mahogany casket with oiled bronze handles. It was open at one end and covered at the other end with a spray of white calla lilies and roses. Dozens of other bouquets filled the air with the sweet and spicy fragrances of tuberose and carnations. A string trio plus flute and harp sat off to the side playing Bach's "Sheep May Safely Graze."

I wasn't used to open caskets. In the Jewish tradition, the casket is always closed. I wondered if at some point tonight I'd be required to file past and look at Claire's dead body. I'd already seen it the day we discovered her. I really didn't want to see her again, but I also didn't want to offend her mother. Hopefully Lucy could guide me through the unknown waters of Catholic wake etiquette.

I scanned the room. Two walls were lined with Claire's quilts: those that I'd saved and others I recognized from her files as having been purchased by private collectors.

"Where did all these quilts come from?" asked Birdie. "I don't recognize some of them."

"Some of these are privately owned. Somehow the Terrys must have been able to borrow them for the evening."

"They certainly are displayed professionally. Look at the care with which they've been hung. All the clips along the tops are precisely the same distance apart." I counted three security men on each side of the room. Then I spotted Siobhan in the front row of seats. She seemed diminished, a fragile starling in an elegant black faille suit. "There's Claire's mother. Let's go and pay our respects."

As soon as Siobhan saw me, she reached up and pulled me down to her for an embrace. "Oh, Martha, thank you for coming." The musicians switched to Albinoni's "Adagio in G Minor," a piece poignant enough to make even Cruella De Vil cry. Siobhan glanced at Claire's casket a few feet away with an expression of grief so profound it sliced into my heart. Even if she'd been a negligent parent during Claire's childhood, she was a devastated mother now.

She turned in her seat toward a dapper older man sitting at her right. The fine wool of his black bespoke suit fit him perfectly. Hand stitching around the edges of his lapels screamed money as well as the initials embroidered in tiny blue letters on the cuffs of his crisp white shirt. "This is my husband, Will."

Will Terry was a prisoner of his Irish genes and reminded me faintly of a leprechaun with his small stature, long upper lip, and ruddy complexion. And like a leprechaun, this impeccably dressed little man was sitting on top of a huge pot of gold— not to mention a sewer full of shameful secrets.

I could barely bring myself to look at him as he stood up to greet me. Before I knew what was happening, he grasped my hand in both of his. Eww. Just his touch made me feel dirty all over.

Terry's grip remained firm and strong while he searched my face. The muscles in his square jaw bulged as he clenched his molars and sized me up. Was he trying to guess whether I knew? Well, I was sizing him up, too, wondering if he could've murdered his only child.

He thrust his jaw forward. "Miss Rose, let me say how grateful we are. My wife told me about the unpleasantness with the police."

Yeah. I was in the place you ought to be. Jail. However, all I could bring myself to say was, "I'm sorry for your loss."

He nodded gravely, let go of my hand, and sat. Lucy cleared her throat.

I reached behind me and waved them over. "I'd like you to meet my friends. This is Birdie Watson, Lucy Mondello, and her husband, Ray."

"You must be the other ladies who discovered . . ." Siobhan stopped and cried softly.

Birdie, her long white hair neatly wrapped in a conservative bun, leaned forward and touched Siobhan's arm. "I really admired your daughter. I was looking forward to getting to know her better. I'm so sorry for your terrible loss."

Siobhan nodded graciously. "Thank you."

The musicians stopped playing and we looked up. The priest stood nearby apparently waiting to speak to the Terrys.

Siobhan turned to me and pulled me down again so she could whisper, "Martha, before we leave tonight, you must tell me what you know about the messages Claire sewed into her quilts."

"Absolutely." Would I really be able to? We walked away and I turned to my friends. "Does anyone have a hand wipe?"

Ray looked at Lucy with a big question mark on

his face as she dug a small bottle of Purell out of her purse and handed it to me. She gave him a look that clearly warned, *Don't ask.*

I squeezed a blob into my palm and scrubbed until my skin was dry again. "Let's sit in the back of the room. I want to see who shows up."

From our seats we counted twenty guild members, including Carlotta Hudson, who wore a homemade number looking like something straight out of the 1940s with little puff sleeves, shoulder pads, and a sweetheart neckline. The bandage I saw on her forearm several days ago was still there, but smaller. When she saw us looking at her, Carlotta's mouth twisted into an unattractive smirk.

Birdie looked hurt. "What's with her?"

"Probably came to gloat. You know, *one down and one to go.*" Lucy was referring to her theory that Carlotta was knocking off the competition so she could finally win first place in the appliqué category at the quilt show.

Birdie had a horrified look.

"Oh, hon', I'm just kidding."

I pointed out Alexander Godwin, who came in with a beautiful brunette. She looked about six months pregnant. Godwin held her elbow and gently guided her to a row in the middle of the room. He briefly smiled at her when they sat down. Then he took her hand and kissed it.

Everyone seemed captivated by this glamorous couple so obviously in love.

"That's Claire's shrink and, I assume, his wife."

Lucy raised her eyebrows. "They make a perfect-looking couple—she looks like a model and he looks like the actor, whatsisname."

Ray, who'd remained silent up to now, nudged Lucy and gestured toward the front.

The priest had taken his place and was about to start the rosary.

I watched fascinated as Ray's large hands, slightly stained with engine grease and oil, gently fingered the black beads of his rosary.

My heart gave another powerful squeeze.

Lucy was so lucky to have a man who had a spiritual side. Ray was a rock with a humble soul.

Aaron was a Sunday-morning-at-the-deli-lox-and-bagels kind of Jew. He attended services only on the high holidays at the most assimilated congregation in the city. The man didn't know the Shema from the Kol Nidre. What would it be like to be married to a man of real faith like Ray?

I closed my eyes and listened to the Hail Mary being recited over and over by a hundred voices. The chanting was calming and reassuring. The closest thing I could compare it to in Judaism was the Mourner's Kaddish. The Kaddish prayer wasn't repeated over and over like the rosary but was recited once at a funeral, three times a day during the period of mourning, at every anniversary of the death, and on solemn holy days thereafter. Reciting the Kaddish gave me great comfort after the death of my bubbie.

During the service, Dixie Barcelona slipped quietly into the room. She walked over to the yellow baby quilt I'd rescued and reached out her hand to touch it. A security man quickly intercepted her with a smile but a firm shake of the head. Nobody was going to get near those quilts. I tried to get her attention as she looked for a seat, but she seemed oblivious.

How close had Dixie and Claire been? Dixie had given me the impression they were close friends and she'd relied on Claire for years, not only to raise funds but to help teach the children. With her death, Dixie had not only lost a personal friend but an important supporter and advocate for the Blind Children's Association. I'd just have to wait until after the service to find out why she never returned my call, although now I was glad she hadn't. The fewer people who knew what Claire wrote in those quilts, the better.

After the service we joined a line of people walking toward Claire's casket. There was a tap on my arm. I turned around. Ingrid, Claire's next-door neighbor, smiled. With her blond hair falling softly on her dark green dress, she was a knockout. Ingrid gave me a weak smile. Was it just my imagination or were her lips a tad plumper than the last time I saw her?

"Hello, Martha. This is really sad, isn't it?"

"Unspeakably sad."

Ingrid leaned close and growled in a low, angry voice, "I see Claire's boyfriend is here."

What did she just say? I looked wildly around to see who she was talking about.

"Over there." She scowled and pointed a brightly painted acrylic fingernail. "Can you believe it?"

My mouth fell open in shock. "How do you know?"

"I saw him come to her house once. I was on my knees weeding in my yard, so they didn't see me. The way she greeted him at the door . . . well, it was obvious."

"How?"

Ingrid whispered, "They, um, you know, kissed and sort of fondled each other as they went inside the house."

"Have you told this to anyone else?"

"Nobody has asked, and anyway, I don't know his name."

I looked at Claire's boyfriend and putative father of her unborn child. "It's Godwin. Doctor Alexander Godwin."

CHAPTER 25

As we moved forward toward Claire's casket, I slipped out of line and hurried for the door. I couldn't face looking at Claire's body. I also wasn't ready to tell Siobhan what I knew about the quilts. I needed time to figure out what to do about Ingrid's shocking disclosure. Doctor Alexander Godwin had now soared to the top of my suspect list.

I walked briskly down the hallway, my mind racing. Godwin's wife was pregnant. Did he know that his lover, Claire, was also pregnant? Had Claire wanted to keep the baby? Had she expected him to leave his wife? Had she threatened to go public with their affair? What if she threatened to withdraw her bequest to BCA? Godwin might stand to lose everything. With Claire dead, his problems would be solved and his secrets would be safe. Maybe.

I started pacing in the lobby. If Claire had told him she sewed her stories into her quilts, Godwin would have good reason to want them to disappear. He didn't match the physical description of the quilt show thief but, like Will Terry, he could have hired someone else to steal them. Godwin could also have easily gone to the BCA office when nobody was there, taken the quilt and thrown it in the Dumpster, never dreaming it would be rescued by a homeless woman.

There was something else: Alexander Godwin was a doctor with access to drugs. He had both the motive and the means to kill Claire.

I waited in the lobby for my friends as departing mourners streamed past me and out the front doors. I caught a glimpse of Godwin and his wife. That phony. That lying psychopath. There was his wife, tenderly shielding her belly with her hand as they made their way through the crowd. Smiling. Hanging on his arm. Trusting him. What would the awful truth do to her?

Exposing Godwin was going to devastate his poor young wife, and exposing Will Terry was going to devastate Siobhan. Each man wouldn't have wanted the information in those quilts to become public, and either one could be Claire's killer. The time had come to call Detective Beavers and tell him what I knew.

How had I gotten myself into this position? Lucy was right. Why couldn't I just make quilts like a normal person? Right now I would have given anything to be sitting quietly at home running my size-eleven needle through the layers of my blue and white quilt while listening to a good audio book.

I pulled my cell phone out of my purse and looked for Beavers's business card when Lucy walked up.

"There you are. Where did you go? One minute you were standing in line and the next you disappeared." She studied my face for a moment. "You look awful. What happened?"

"I'll tell you everything once we're out of here."

As we waited outside for Ray to bring the car, I quickly told them about Ingrid recognizing Godwin as Claire's lover.

Birdie gasped. "But his wife is pregnant."

Lucy made a disgusted noise. "What a sleaze."

"Yeah." I punched in Detective Beavers's number. "He has plenty of motive to silence Claire." After the fourth ring, I got voice mail. "This is Martha Rose. You need to call me back right away. I think Dr. Alexander Godwin could have killed Claire. I just found out they were lovers, and there's more. Claire's father also had a good reason to silence her. The information is all in the quilts. Call me back and I'll explain everything." I left my number and then disconnected.

Lucy bent her head and whispered, "Don't look now, but a foul wind is blowing."

Carlotta Hudson breezed up to us with her usual sour expression. She examined her fingernails, then focused on Birdie. "This is a real shame, isn't it? The death of someone so talented. Let's hope this isn't some kind of trend."

Birdie looked puzzled.

Carlotta leaned closer, her crow's beak just inches from Birdie's face, her eyes glittering behind her lavender glasses. "I mean, someone is killing quilters and stealing their prize-winning quilts. Did you ever wonder if you might be next?" Then Carlotta looked at Lucy and smiled. "Of course, you won't have any reason to worry, Lucy. Only the good quilters seem to be in danger."

"Well, you must also be greatly relieved. Didn't the thief leave your quilt behind?"

"Witch!" Carlotta murmured as she turned and walked away. She headed for another group of quilters and as she got closer, she pulled a tissue out of her pocket and dabbed at her dry eyes.

Birdie put her hand on Lucy's arm. "You know what? I do believe you might be right about Carlotta killing the competition."

Lucy squeezed Birdie's shoulder. "Hon', Carlotta Hudson would have to kill off half the guild to be the best quilter around. She's not that crazy. She's just an out and out poor loser. Don't you worry about her."

I looked around. "I wonder what's keeping Ray."

Dixie Barcelona strode toward me with the same energy I remembered from before. Her short, frizzy hair looked slightly deranged and the dark circles under her eyes suggested she wasn't getting much sleep.

Dixie thrust her arm forward, pumping my hand in a hard grip. "I'm so glad I found you, Martha."

After a round of introductions she peered at me through the thick lenses of her glasses. "I'm sorry I didn't get back to you before. My cell phone was out of juice, and I didn't realize it until this evening. You said you needed help, something about Claire's quilts?"

"Oh, false alarm. I figured out what I needed to know and, as you can see, the baby quilt made it safely back to the Terrys. How's the silent auction going?"

"Lots of work, especially now Claire's gone." She looked at us eagerly. "You know, I'm still looking for donations to the auction. This is one of our major fund-raisers, and the people who attend are looking for unique and beautiful items to buy. All proceeds go to programs teaching Braille to children. I wonder if any of you ladies have a quilt you'd like to donate?"

Birdie shook her head.

Lucy shrugged sympathetically. "Not right now, but if you let me know with enough time before your next event, I could probably whip up a baby quilt."

A picture of the little blind boy walking awkwardly into the elevator flashed through my mind. He clung to his mother's hand, trying to navigate through unseen territory. "I actually have a small quilt I can donate. You should be able to get a few hundred dollars for it." The quilt was a wall hanging I'd entered in last year's show, featuring a center medallion with appliquéd fruit in a basket and borders pieced with one-inch patches. The thing was only about thirty inches square but represented dozens of hours of stitching.

Dixie gushed. "You ladies are unbelievably generous. Martha, when can I come over to pick up your quilt?" We settled on Sunday evening.

Back at Lucy's house, I stood at the refrigerator giving Bumper a late night snack of cheese when my cell phone rang.

"You're still playing amateur detective?" asked Beavers.

"Nice to talk to you, too." I tore open a small package of M&Ms and spread the contents on the kitchen table.

"So . . ." The tinge of amusement in his voice really annoyed me. "What evidence did you uncover implicating Dr. Godwin and Will Terry? The entire homicide division of the LAPD would be grateful to know."

I refused to rise to the bait. He'd be singing a different tune soon enough. "It's complicated." I crunched a red M&M and lined up another. I preferred to finish one color at a time.

"Well, let's start with Godwin. How did you find out he and Claire were lovers?"

I told him what Ingrid saw as I separated out all the green ones. "Godwin was Claire's lover and is presumably the father of her unborn child, but he already has a pregnant wife."

By the silence on the other end, I was pretty sure Beavers was considering the implications much the same way I did.

"Of course," I continued, "her father also had a strong motive to get rid of her quilts. He could have killed Claire out of desperation to protect the secrets hidden in them."

"Her father? What possible evidence . . ."

I told him about deciphering Claire's quilts and what was hidden in the Braille of the French knots. By the time I'd finished talking, all that were left were the yellow and brown M&Ms.

Silence again. "First of all, I gotta admit I'm really impressed with how you figured that whole message thing out, Martha. You really do know quilts. But you aren't an expert in Braille. Are you absolutely certain that is what you read?"

"Disgustingly certain."

"Have you told anyone else about this?"

"Just Lucy and Birdie."

"What about Mrs. Terry? Have you told her?"

"She knows I've cracked the code, but she doesn't know the code is Braille or what the messages are.

Frankly, I don't want to be the one to tell her, so I've been avoiding her."

"Good. I don't want the three of you talking to anyone about this. I need some time to check this out. If you're right about Godwin, he's murdered once and would probably murder again."

"What about Will Terry?"

"You don't want Will to suspect you know about him and Claire. He's a very powerful man. If he could kill his daughter, he wouldn't think twice about having you killed. You'd be wise to stay at the Mondellos for now."

I put the last brown M&M into my mouth. "I admit I was terrified at the thought of someone breaking in to my house and stabbing me. Now I'm just mad! My new alarm system will be hooked up tomorrow, so after Claire's funeral, I'm going back to my house. I need to start cleaning, and I want to sleep in my bed again."

Beavers sighed. "I didn't think I could talk you out of going back home, so I've arranged for some extra protection."

"Extra protection? I won't need protection since I'm going to take one of Ray's guns home with me."

"Not! You need a permit to have a gun, and that process takes time you don't have."

Oh crap. I shouldn't have mentioned the gun. "Did I say I had a gun already? I only meant I could get one if I need it."

Beavers wasn't about to be brushed off so easily.

"Suppose you did have a gun. Are you prepared to shoot to kill? Because if you hesitate at all, the killer will disarm you and kill you instead. Trust me. Statistics show you'd be the one most likely to be hurt. What I'm proposing is better than a gun, and a lot safer."

"What is it?"

"Arthur."

"Who?"

FRIDAY

CHAPTER 26

I woke up Friday morning at eight-thirty and looked out the window to see what kind of day it would be for Claire's funeral. The weather was typical for late April in Los Angeles: the slightest breeze, aqua skies, plenty of sunshine, and dappled shade from the new green leaves of the liquidambars lining the streets. LA contained the largest urban forest in the nation, and every single tree was teeming with songbirds.

I'd attended many funerals over the years, beginning with my grandmother's when I was nine. Bubbie's casket was closed, according to Jewish law. During the service, the cantor sang El Maleh Rahamim, God Full of Compassion, and the mourners recited the Kaddish. While Uncle Isaac talked about how sweet and generous Bubbie had been, I sobbed into my mother's lap.

I couldn't imagine my life without Bubbie's soft hands coaxing my unruly curls into braids, "just like challah," or her Friday night dinners beginning with chicken soup, ending with apple crisp, and served on the lace tablecloth she crocheted as a young bride. The ache in my heart would take years to subside.

Yet that was the right order of things, the young burying the old. How much more excruciating for Siobhan to bury her daughter today? Did a parent ever recover?

After Bubbie's graveside service, we returned to the house we'd all shared: Bubbie, Uncle Isaac, Mother, and me. A pitcher of water and a towel waited for us on the front porch so, according to tradition, we could wash death and the cemetery off our hands before entering our house of mourning. All the relatives, neighbors, and friends were there eating and talking softly.

The first thing I noticed was that all the mirrors in our house had been covered with cloth according to Jewish tradition. During the time of mourning, we were supposed to focus on prayer, grief, and communion with God. To help in that pursuit, we would not be allowed to look at ourselves for an entire seven days.

I went to the table to get some deviled eggs before they were all gone. My ugly aunt Esther intercepted me and whispered, "Poor little *mamser*, no Bubbie to wipe your tushie anymore." Aunt Esther and I had been secret enemies ever since I was three. I was terrified of the large brown mole that disfigured her right cheek and once when she insisted on holding me, I screamed and peed on her lap. From then on she called me a bastard whenever nobody else was around. At such a young age I was confused about what the word meant. I knew it had something to do with my never knowing my father, but my family told me he died before I was born. Could I help it if I was a half orphan?

I put two eggs on my plate and looked up at her. Three black hairs grew out of her mole and her eyes gleamed, but not from tears. "You're the only one who hasn't cried yet," I observed.

"Feh," she spat, and walked away.

I shrugged away the memory and wondered who wouldn't be crying at Claire's funeral today.

It had felt good sleeping in, but I knew I needed to hustle to get dressed in the outfit I'd brought from home—a chocolate-colored linen dress and my good strand of Mikimoto pearls. As I put on my shoes, Lucy knocked on the bedroom door. "You up yet?"

I opened the door and smiled as Lucy, wearing all black again, thrust a cup of coffee into my hands. "Glad to see you're dressed. We're leaving in about an hour, and you haven't eaten breakfast yet. You'll need something that sticks to your ribs."

I walked to the stove and helped myself to some steaming oatmeal with raisins, sprinkling on a heaping spoonful of brown sugar and topping it off with milk. As I ate, I told Lucy about my conversation with Beavers last night. "He warned me not to take Ray's gun. Said I need a permit. Then he told me he was getting me a bodyguard named Arthur. Don't you think that's—excuse the pun—overkill?"

Lucy smiled. "Until the murderer is caught, it might not be such a bad idea. Wasn't that sweet of the detective to arrange a bodyguard? I think he likes you, Martha."

Oh God. Lucy was worse than a mother. I rolled my eyes and finished my cereal, secretly wondering if she were right about the him liking me thing.

Ray, still in protective mode, insisted on driving us. Before Birdie arrived, he tucked a handgun into his waistband, concealed under his jacket like he had the night before. "Where to?" He started the engine.

Lucy checked the paper in her hand. "St. Genesius Catholic Church on Maple and Santa Monica in Beverly Hills."

"St. Genesius?" asked Birdie. "That's not a name I've heard before. Who was he?"

Ray looked at her in the rearview mirror. "Beats me."

"I Googled him. The church was built in the nineteen thirties by the movie people. St. Genesius was the patron saint of actors, theatrical performers, clowns, and lawyers."

Ray snickered. "Like there's a difference?"

We drove over Coldwater Canyon in silence, arriving at the church with about twenty minutes to spare. St. Genesius was easy to spot—a neogothic stone building with pointed windows and slender twin towers on either side of the arched entryway.

We cruised the surrounding streets until we found a parking spot suitably safe for Ray's car. Ray offered Birdie his arm as we walked slowly up the broad front steps, blending with the crowd streaming in to the church. When we reached the bottleneck at the door, Ray positioned himself in front of us, unbuttoned his jacket and, with his head slowly moving from side to side, constantly scanned the crowd.

When Detective Beavers walked toward us, Ray's shoulders seemed to relax a little.

Beavers shook Ray's hand. "You remind me of a cop, Mr. Mondello."

"Nam. Military police."

"Right." Beavers never took his eyes off Ray. "You got a permit to carry a weapon?"

Ray returned the look, his hand moving slightly to button his jacket. "What weapon?"

"I'm not in the mood to confiscate concealed weapons today. Especially if the weapon stays concealed."

Ray nodded once.

Beavers turned to go. "Best to leave the policing to the ones who get paid for it."

Lucy covered her head with her black lace mantilla as we entered the sanctuary and filed into a pew at the back, the better to observe the mourners. Ray took the aisle seat and unbuttoned his jacket again.

The congregation rose when three boys in white robes, one holding a cross, walked in as eight pall-bearers in white gloves carried the mahogany casket into the church. Two priests dressed in white vest-ments met the coffin at the doorway and escorted it down the aisle.

Next came the Terrys, escorted by another priest. Will Terry stared straight ahead, clenching and unclenching his teeth so the muscles rippled in his square jaw. Siobhan's head was bowed in grief. I couldn't be sure because it happened so quickly, but I thought I saw Siobhan stumble slightly. Will reached out to steady her, but she quickly drew away from him, leaning instead on the arm of the priest. Then they sat down in the front row and I thought I recognized several dignitaries, including one United States senator. The Terrys were no lightweights, that was for certain.

We sat and my mouth fell open as I took in the sheer scale of the interior. Stained glass windows lined both sides of the sanctuary, depicting the stations of the cross. In the nearest window Jesus carried a cross while a crown of thorns sent blood drops cascading down his face. A woman on the side of the road held out a piece of cloth, but a Roman soldier barricaded her way with an out-stretched spear. I had learned something about the cross Claire bore in her lifetime and, in wanting to help find justice for her, I felt just like the woman on the side of the road.

I looked farther up. A graceful network of tall buttresses crisscrossed to form points high up in the vaulted ceiling. On the front wall hung a huge gold-leafed crucifix with a compassionate Jesus looking down on Claire's casket, feet facing the altar.

I was impressed to see the resident cardinal in attendance, standing near the altar with his distinctive red biretta and cape. The press often suggested he was an influential part of the Catholic hierarchy and had the ear of the pope. His presence today only underscored how well placed the Terry family was.

Off to one side of the podium was a lectern raised up higher so the priest would have to ascend a few stairs to give his homily. The whole purpose of the soaring interior space and the priest's aerie was to draw the eye upward toward heaven, the source of all hope. All very inspirational and theatrical.

I turned around. Detective Beavers stood in the back, eyes scanning the crowd the same way Ray had done outside. A few stragglers were trying to find seats. One of them was Jerry Bell, Claire's son. Beavers looked at him with keen interest as he walked to a seat two rows in front of us, genuflected, and sat far enough to the side that I could just make out his profile.

Birdie sat on the other side of me, sniffing and dabbing her eyes throughout the service. Beyond her, Lucy sat with Ray's comforting arm around her shoulders. She wore the pink and diamond bracelet he'd given her after we discovered Claire's body.

When a vocalist sang "Ave Maria," I reached into my purse for a tissue. Mothers losing children. It was too much to bear.

Remembering the way he teared up the day I told him of his mother's death, I was curious to see Jerry Bell sitting stony-faced throughout the service. I didn't know Claire very well, and yet here I was dabbing my eyes and blowing my nose. Where were his tears?

Maybe my suspicions on the day we met were true. Maybe Jerry Bell was the real killer. After all, he had a motive. As her son, he could file a claim to Claire's sizable estate. All that talk about reconciliation might have been a smoke screen to cover up anger at having been given up for adoption.

Could he be the one who broke into my house three nights ago and stuck a knife in my pillow? I turned around and looked for Beavers, but he was gone.

At the end of the service, we all stood as Claire's coffin was carried back out of the sanctuary to the hearse waiting outside. Siobhan and Will Terry walked slowly behind, Will working his jaw.

I glanced again at Jerry, who watched the Terrys with sharp interest. The muscles in his square jaw bulged as he clenched his teeth. Just like Will Terry. The family resemblance was unmistakable.

Jerry was taller than Will, but both of them shared the same military posture, square jaw, long upper lip, and blue eyes.

Wait a minute. How old was Jerry? Around thirty? Claire was fourteen when he was born. Was her father still molesting her at the time? Oh my God! My stomach did a nasty leap. I'd just stumbled onto another of Claire's horrible secrets. What if she didn't get pregnant by a boy in school whose name she conveniently forgot? What if that part of the story was to hide the fact Will Terry was Jerry's real father?

CHAPTER 27

Jerry met up with us at the cemetery, and I introduced him to my friends as we gathered around Claire's grave. At one point Siobhan looked at me and nodded a slight greeting. She stopped when she saw Jerry and stared. Then she looked back at me as if to ask, *Who is this man?* I was sure she was figuring it out.

Several times during the brief graveside service, Siobhan glanced at Jerry, but her husband didn't seem to notice him at all. Jerry seemed too lost in thought to be aware of the scrutiny, gazing the whole time at Claire's casket. At one point tears stole down his stoic face. There was no mistake he was grieving, and once again I just couldn't imagine him to be a killer.

Immediately after the service, the Terrys and their stellar entourage left in long black limousines. I turned to Jerry. "Siobhan kept looking your way. I think she may have recognized you."

He wiped his cheeks with the back of his hand, smoothed back his blond hair, and briefly worked his jaw. "Do you think my grandfather recognized me, too?"

"I don't know."

He looked at me earnestly. "Are you going to the reception? I could use a friend." Jerry looked like a sad, scared little boy.

"We'll be there, dear." Birdie was earth mother to all living things. "You will sit with us, of course."

A dozen young men in red jackets trotted up and down the street providing valet parking for the mourners at the Terrys' Benedict Canyon estate. In the backyard, tents with open sides dotted the lawn and shaded dozens of tables covered with white linen cloths. A huge buffet and bar were set up under a large tent on the tennis court, and waiters in black suits carried trays of white wine and Perrier through the growing crowd. Other servers carried hors d'oeuvres on silver trays with paper cocktail napkins.

Jerry sat with us at a table near a large fountain featuring lion heads gently spouting water from their mouths. The soothing sound of water splashing over carved stone attracted little brown towhees with tinges of orange and dun-colored sparrows.

Carlotta Hudson approached a group of quilters sitting at a nearby table. She threw a derisive look at us and then turned away. Just then, several crows cawed hoarsely and flew over her head, landing in the branches of the many eucalyptus trees surrounding the estate.

Lucy pointed to the trees. "I see Carlotta brought her posse."

A voice in back of me asked, "May I sit with you?"

I turned around.

Ingrid was dressed in a tight-fitting black jersey sheath with a torsade of pearls and jet beads around her neck.

"Of course! Please join us."

Ray and Jerry stood up while Ingrid took a seat next to me. She smiled at Jerry. "I think I've seen you several times at Claire's. I'm Ingrid, Claire's neighbor."

"Jerry." He shook her proffered hand and smiled briefly.

"I really didn't spy on Claire. I work in my garden a lot and see the comings and goings of the street. Claire and I were on very friendly terms. We drank the occasional morning coffee together. You're the doctor, right? She mentioned your name a couple of times. Weren't you related?"

"Still am."

All during lunch the Terrys were sequestered inside with their high-profile friends. They finally emerged at about two and a crowd of us normal humans swirled around them as Will shook hands and Siobhan accepted an occasional hug. When she spotted us standing on the edge of the pack,

Siobhan waved at me in a gesture more of a command than a greeting.

"Wait for me here." I set out over the lawn toward Claire's puffy-eyed mother.

Siobhan stood stiffly, clasping her elbows, the wrinkles around her mouth accentuated by the black dress she wore. A slight breeze lifted the feathers of white hair floating around her face and the diamond and sapphire earrings tugged a little at the holes in her earlobes.

Siobhan reached for both of my hands. "Martha, how nice of you to come." The next thing I knew we were walking through a set of French doors into a sunroom at the back of the house.

As soon as we were alone, she looked at me with fierce, glittering eyes. "Who is he?" A frightened look shone in her eyes.

I led her over to an overstuffed rattan sofa and sat next to her. She'd sneaked looks at Jerry all during the funeral and, from the expression on her face, I was sure she'd figured it out. "Who do you think he is, Siobhan?"

"He's Claire's boy, isn't he?"

"His name is Jerry Bell. He found Claire a few years ago after his adoptive mother died. According to Jerry, they saw each other frequently and she helped him through medical school."

"He's a doctor? Why didn't she tell us about him?"

I could think of a hundred reasons Claire wouldn't want to confide in her mother, beginning with

Siobhan's failure to protect Claire from incest. "You can probably answer that better than I, Siobhan. Jerry's resemblance to your family is unmistakable. If you doubt him, I'm sure a simple DNA test will confirm he's Claire's son."

I put my hands on her shoulders and turned her toward me so she'd have to look in my eyes. "Claire never told him who his father is. I think I've finally figured it out. However, I don't want to be the one to break the ugly news to Jerry. I'll leave that up to you, if you ever decide to talk to him."

Siobhan buried her face in her hands and started to weep. "How do you know all this? What can you possibly think of me now?"

Good question. I took a deep breath. "You know all those French knots Claire sewed on her quilts?"

Siobhan nodded.

"Well, Claire was brilliant, really. Those knots are Braille. I think each quilt represents a chapter of her life's story. I found a Braille alphabet to test my theory and started to decipher one of the quilts. I didn't get very far, but I got far enough to learn about the incest."

Siobhan moaned.

"How could you let that happen?"

She was still weeping. "I swear I didn't know about them until it was too late, until Claire was already pregnant. I drank a lot in those days and I slept a lot. I found out later he . . . they . . . it didn't happen until he was certain I was out for the night."

"What about after you found out? Why didn't you turn him in?"

"He swore to me he'd never hurt her again, and I wanted to believe him. I wasn't strong. I couldn't have made it on my own."

What about Claire? What about protecting her? Poor Claire didn't have a chance with a predator for a father and a drunk for a mother.

Siobhan dried her eyes with a tissue. "We sent Claire away to a convent to have the baby. During the time she was away, I went into rehab and stopped drinking. I don't think she ever even saw her son. His adoptive parents took him home practically from the delivery room. Will said it was best that way."

Best for whom? "What are you going to do about Jerry Bell now that he's here?"

"If he really is Claire's son, I want to meet him. I don't know how Will is going to take the news. He won't like this one bit."

"Forget Will! He doesn't deserve any consideration in this matter. You don't need his permission for anything. You can do this on your own."

Siobhan stared at me and then burst out laughing. "Don't think I haven't thought about that for the last forty-five years."

Just then the door flew open and Will Terry stormed inside. "Just what do you mean leaving me alone out there? We have guests—" He stopped when he saw me.

"If you don't mind, Miss Rose, this isn't a good time to visit with my wife. You'll have to go back outside with the rest of the people."

What an imperious little jerk. Did he think he could just order me around like he did everyone else? I sat up straighter. "I'll leave when Siobhan asks me to leave."

Will Terry pulled down the corners of his mouth and spoke through clenched teeth. "I don't think you realize who you're talking to."

I stood and looked at the reprehensible little pedophile. I'm only five feet two and we stood exactly eye to eye. "This is a free country, *Mister* Terry. Your wife can speak to whomever she pleases." I thought about this man committing the unspeakable to his daughter and getting away with it, and I couldn't hold back any longer. "You may be able to push your wife around and rape your daughter, but you don't intimidate me one bit!"

My words hung in the air like the particles of a bomb after an explosion. I'd spoken out loud the terrible truth this family worked so hard to keep hidden for three decades. Will Terry's mouth fell open and he staggered backward for a moment, too stunned to speak. Then he turned to Siobhan. "What have you been telling her?"

"Your wife told me nothing. Claire told me through her quilts. She sewed everything in her quilts using Braille. I imagine she wanted to make sure that somewhere there would be a record of what happened to her. Of how she was repeatedly raped by you when she was just a child. Of how you got her pregnant and then forced her to give up her child."

Will's face turned frigid. "Get out of my house, you fat kike, or I'll have you thrown out."

Kike. The anti-Semitic slur sent icy shards into my heart. This man was a typical narcissist with no regard for other human beings whatsoever. He was cruel and arrogant and probably not used to people standing up to him. I'd managed to push his ugly buttons.

But calling me *fat*? That was war. I leaned forward, hands on my hips. "Listen, you pathetic little pile of monkey puke. I wouldn't be surprised if you were behind your daughter's death and the theft of her quilts. Who had a better reason to want to keep the world from knowing the truth about the incest and pregnancy?"

He glanced at Siobhan, who was still crying. "I'd never kill my daughter."

"Oh no? Claire wrote all about the incest in her quilts. In details I imagine you'd do anything to keep secret."

Will waved his hand dismissively. "Until Siobhan engaged your so-called services, I had no idea Claire might have used her quilts in that way. My wife never told me about Claire's messages." He paused and said in a slightly softer voice, "The love of my life was gone."

My skin crawled as I remember what Claire wrote

in her quilt: *He told me I was the love of his life.* If he was still calling her that, had he still been sleeping with her? "This new baby she carried—was this one yours as well?"

Will remained silent, and Siobhan stopped crying and looked up sharply.

"I'm sure you didn't want to make the same mistake twice. Claire was four months along, which tells me she intended to keep this baby. So killing her would solve the problem."

"It wasn't my baby! Claire cut me off over a year ago after she went into therapy with that quack Godwin."

Siobhan was an armed missile as she jumped up and ran at her husband. She clawed at his face with her carefully manicured red fingernails, forty-five years of fury blazing in her eyes. "Bastard! You bastard! You swore to me you ended it after the boy was born. I should have known!"

Will grabbed her wrists and threw her down on the sofa. Then he stepped toward me, with blood trickling down his cheeks. "You will regret this."

I hoped he couldn't see my heart pounding in my throat. "I doubt it. The police know all about you. I made sure they did. You touch me now and they'll be crawling all over your scrawny pedophile neck."

Someone coughed in the open doorway. We looked over. Jerry Bell stood there. I could tell Will didn't recognize him. He snarled, "What do you want? This is a private conversation."

Jerry looked at me and my heart sank. "Jerry, honey, how much of this did you hear?"

"Enough." His eyes were swimming as he glared at his grandparents.

Will glared back. "Who are you?"

Jerry walked into the room and over to Will Terry. "Your son."

CHAPTER 28

Will Terry fell into the nearest chair, Siobhan started to wail again, and Jerry just stood looking at both of them. What would they say to each other? I decided I didn't want to know. Enough was enough. I left quickly, closing the door behind me.

On my way to rejoin my friends, I pulled out my cell phone and left a message for Detective Beavers. "I know you told me not to tell anyone, but I couldn't help myself. The cat is out of the bag. I told the Terrys about the secrets I read in Claire's quilts, and Jerry Bell overheard everything. So now he knows, too. You have to get those quilts away from Will Terry before he destroys them."

By the time we got back to Lucy's house, my head was throbbing and every muscle in my body ached. The confrontation with the Terry family caused my fibro to flare up. I dug a Soma and a migraine tablet out of the small cloisonné pillbox I carried in my purse.

The antique box came from imperial China and featured a small peach-colored lantern surrounded by tiny pink peonies on a turquoise background. My grandfather found it in an antique store and gave it to my bubbie on her birthday, and she used it for many years. I caressed the design gently with my finger before putting this precious keepsake back in my purse. Then I took a gulp of water and threw my head back to swallow. Bumper purred and rubbed against my ankle.

Joey walked into the kitchen. "Your alarm system is in, Aunt Martha. Me and Richie straightened the mess up a little, so you might find things in the wrong place, but at least they're off the floor."

I hugged him. "Joey, you didn't have to do that." But I was secretly relieved I wouldn't have to clean my ransacked house while suffering such pain. Whatever mistakes the boys made, I could put right tomorrow. I smiled. "All I want to do now is go home and fall into bed."

"I'll follow you home then and show you how to work your new alarm system. You're being moni-tored by All City Alarm Company." Joey grinned. "I know a guy. He gave me a really good deal."

I picked Bumper up. "Great. I've already said good-bye to your parents. Just let me put this guy in his crate and gather our things and I'm good to go."

"Don't forget the gun."

"In my suitcase."

On the way home, Bumper started yowling again.

"Poor little guy. First your mommy gets killed, then you get adopted by me, then you get kidnapped overnight, then you go to live at Lucy's house, and now you're coming back home with me again. Poor kitty. I promise you this will be the last disruption in your life. From now on, it'll be just you and me."

I pulled into my driveway a few minutes later and as soon as I turned off the motor, someone tapped on my car window. Sonia Spiegelman. How did she manage to appear so fast? She couldn't even wait until I was out of the car? I opened the door and got out, still angry she took Bumper home with her the night I was arrested. I could barely remain civil.

"Hello, Sonia." I refused to look at her. I turned my back and yanked out my suitcase and Bumper's crate a little too hard, hoping she'd take the hint and leave. She didn't. When I turned around, she blocked my way.

"Hello, Martha." She put a worried look on her face as transparent as a politician's promise. "Have you been in jail all this time?"

What an idiot. Like I'd tell her anything? The entire Northern Hemisphere would know in about ten seconds.

I looked over her shoulder and pretended she wasn't there as I tried to walk forward, but she stayed put.

"I haven't seen you around for a few days, but

we noticed a lot of activity at your house. We called an emergency meeting and activated the patrol."

Sonia had organized a harmless but zealous neighborhood watch group that sometimes patrolled the streets at night. They even used walkie-talkies and wore matching T-shirts proclaiming they were the "Eyes of Encino."

I took a step forward, but she persisted. "The police came back here the day after you were arrested, but none of us could get them to say what was going on. Just what happened here? We'd all like to know."

I sighed. Conversation with Sonia was unavoidable. "Yes, Sonia. The bomb squad has been working like crazy to remove all the ordnance I have hidden in my basement. They're having particular difficulty disarming the ground-to-air missiles, but I think they've got them all."

While I talked to Sonia, Joey picked up my overnight bag and Bumper's crate and carried them up the walkway to the front door. I followed him with Sonia still chattering to my back. "I'm glad to see you know this young man. I saw him earlier at your house and didn't know whether or not he was the one who broke in. I was waiting to see if I should call the police."

I caught up to Joey.

He shook his head and grinned. "Ground-to-air missiles? Dude!"

I looked back. Sonia was already talking on her

cell phone. "The nosy neighbor who stole my cat right after I was arrested."

Joey unlocked my front door and turned to a new white keypad on the wall, beeping urgently. "I gave you a temporary code, Aunt Martha. I chose the number of guys on a pro football team, fifty-three, and entered the number twice. So you just press five three five three and then press 'Enter.' You can easily change the code. Just read the manual I left on the coffee table."

"Thanks, Joey." I couldn't care less about sports. I'd have to think of something easier to remember. I briefly wondered why they settled on exactly fifty-three players. Why not fifty-one or forty-eight?

I looked around at a fairly cleaned-up house. "Looks normal in here again. You boys did a really nice job."

He just grinned. "Come on. I'll show you how to set the alarm after I leave. Then you can 'fall into bed.'"

A half hour later, Bumper was curled up next to me on top of the antique blue and yellow Ohio Star quilt my grandmother sewed before I was born. As I snuggled between clean sheets, I didn't want to think about the knife stuck in my other pillow a few nights ago. I was home at last, and between the alarm and the gun sitting in the drawer beside my bed, I felt safe.

I looked at the clock before I closed my eyes. It was four in the afternoon and there was something

I ought to do tonight, but my brain was foggy with fatigue and I couldn't remember. *Never mind. Everything will just have to wait.*

Was someone hammering nails? No, they were slapping boards together. No, they were beating a drum. Why didn't they stop? I slowly swam up from my dream and realized someone was pounding on my front door. The clock read past seven.

I stumbled out of bed, put on a robe, and shuffled through the living room, eyes half closed. "Hold on!" The pounding stopped.

"Who's there?" I pulled my robe closer around me and strained to look through the peephole.

"Arlo Beavers."

I opened the door and a howl immediately pierced the air inside the house and out. My eyes snapped open and I jumped. The abort code—what was it again?

I looked at Beavers. "Quick, how many guys on a pro football team?"

"Eleven."

"No, I mean all of them."

"Uh, fifty something."

Oh yeah. I pushed five three five three Enter, and the howling stopped.

"Sorry." My ears were still ringing. "I forgot about this thing. Not used to it yet. Are they all this loud?"

"The louder the better."

We still stood at the door. "I just woke up. Was something supposed to happen tonight?"

"Yeah. May I come in?"

"Oh." I hopped backward. "Sorry."

It wasn't until he walked inside I saw he wasn't alone.

I pointed. "Who's *that*?"

"Arthur."

Then I remembered Beavers said he was going to bring over someone named Arthur for protection. "This is my bodyguard?" I was expecting someone beefy, tall, and wearing sunglasses. What I got instead was a German shepherd. Arthur cocked his head at me as if he could read my mind.

"No offense, Arthur, but I don't think this arrangement will work. I've got a new cat who's still getting used to this place."

Just then Bumper walked into the room. He took one look at Arthur and hissed. Arthur got down on his belly and put his head on his paws and whined.

I looked at Beavers and rolled my eyes. "Great! How can this dog protect me if he can't even stand up to my cat?"

"Arthur is a retired police dog with dozens of take-downs to his credit. He'll turn into a fierce fighting machine if he senses danger. Obviously, your cat doesn't scare him."

We both watched as Bumper walked over to Arthur and delicately sniffed the dog's nose in the universal cat greeting. Arthur thumped his tail loudly on the floor while Bumper executed an imperious turn and sauntered away.

Arthur thrust his head forward, and in the universal dog greeting stuck his nose in Bumper's butt. The cat jumped three feet in the air, yowling and clawing.

"See?" Beavers chuckled. "Another take-down."

I wasn't amused. Didn't I just promise Bumper our domestic bliss was only going to be about the two of us? "This definitely won't work."

Beavers shifted his feet. "Arthur's like me. He'll grow on you."

Whoa. Was he flirting with me? Hummingbirds started beating their wings inside my chest again.

"I don't know . . ." I dared not look at him. I stuck out my hand for Arthur to sniff. He sat up and started licking my fingers. "Well, maybe he is kind of nice." I scratched Arthur behind the ears and he closed his eyes. "Where'd you get him?"

"I adopted him two years ago. He's a bit gray in the muzzle, but he's still got a lot of life left in him."

I looked sideways at Beavers's white mustache. I pushed away thoughts of how much life he might have left. "This is your personal dog, then?"

"Yes, but he was trained at the taxpayers' expense. Shame to have all his training go to waste." He smiled and raised his eyebrows. "Shall I bring Arthur's food and gear in from the car?"

"Well, as long as he leaves Bumper alone, I guess

we could try this out for a while." Arthur was now on his back begging for a tummy scratch. "He really doesn't seem like much of a bodyguard to me."

Two minutes later Beavers carried in a thirty-pound bag of kibble, two giant stainless steel dog bowls, a slightly hairy dog bed, and a pooper scooper. "For the backyard. You'll want to put his bed next to yours. That way he'll be right there if you need him."

"He better not snore."

After some searching, I finally located where Lucy's boys had put things, and I was able to make some tea. We sat at the table and Beavers clinked his spoon against the blue mug as he stirred in some sugar. "I got your message. Talk to me."

I told him about the sordid events earlier in the day with the Terrys, including Will's admission he slept with Claire up to a year ago. "I was totally grossed out, and I felt so sorry for Jerry."

"Do you still think Jerry's a suspect?"

"Well, even though he's got motive, means, and opportunity, I don't think he's involved with Claire's death or the theft of the quilts. He seems to be genuinely grieving over losing her."

Beavers gulped the last of his tea. "Once we pick up Claire's quilts, we might find some more answers."

I scooted forward on the edge of my chair and put my hands flat on the table. Was I hearing him right? "Oh my God! Haven't you collected them yet? Don't you realize Will Terry has every reason to destroy those quilts to keep from being exposed as a pedophile?"

"I sent Kaplan out there this evening to pick them up, but Will Terry wouldn't cooperate. We have to get a court order tomorrow from a sympathetic judge. The Terrys have friends in high places and the DA has to be very careful about this. Meanwhile, I want you to promise you'll quit poking around and leave the rest of this investigation to the police."

I wasn't going to let him brush me off so easily. "Well, what about our stolen quilts? Are you doing anything about them?"

Beavers stood, preparing to leave. "In the grand scheme of things, Ms. Rose, a murder investigation trumps everything else. We can always hope that in the course of solving this murder we'll also find your missing quilts."

I didn't like his officious tone. I also stood and put my hands on my hips. "You wouldn't have gotten this far without my help and expertise. Surely I deserve to know what else you discover in those quilts."

"Possibly in the end the whole world will know."

I screwed up my face. "Please. Spare me the vague platitudes. And by the way, why haven't I gotten my computer back?"

"I'll bring it back to you tomorrow." Beavers reached in his pocket and handed me a piece of paper. "Here's the instruction manual for Arthur. Feeding times and all that."

I sighed and took the paper.

Then he knelt down and ruffled Arthur's head. "You be a good boy, Artie. Take care of this lady here. She's very important and we don't want anything bad to happen to her. Please go easy on the cat." The dog wagged his tail and licked Beavers's face.

"We'll take care of each other." I scratched Arthur's ears.

As I closed the door behind Detective Beavers and set the alarm, I smiled because, although he didn't know it, the photos of Claire's quilts were still in Lucy's computer. If Claire's baby wasn't Will's, then it must be Godwin's. I needed to decipher the story in the baby quilt to see if I was right.

There's more than one way to get at the truth, Detective.

SATURDAY

CHAPTER 29

I spent a restless first night at home waking up several times to Arthur's toenails clicking on the hardwood floor as he made occasional rounds through the dark house. At six in the morning, he jumped on my bed and began licking my face. I sighed, stumbled through the kitchen, punched in the alarm code on the keypad next to the back door, and let a desperate dog outside.

Then I filled up food bowls for both animals, put on a pot of coffee, and went back to my bedroom to get dressed. Rising so early wasn't on my agenda, but I was facing a long day of organizing my house. Having to get out of bed to let the dog out gave me the push I needed.

After breakfast I went into the yard with the pooper scooper and almost immediately found what I was after. Arthur was a big dog. It seemed I was becoming an expert in cleaning up dog crap. Only a couple of days ago I hosed a messy pile off

Birdie's porch. Apparently the police were unable to find anyone on her street who witnessed anything. Birdie and Lucy didn't have an active neighborhood watch like I did.

Wait a minute. Didn't Sonia say the Eyes of Encino patrolled the streets after I was arrested? Maybe one of the Eyes saw the killer leave the package of dog doo on my front porch. Or maybe they saw the killer around my house the night I was in jail, the night of the break-in. Maybe one of the Eyes had information that could lead us to the killer and blow the case wide open. Much as I hated to, I needed to ask Sonia about the patrol.

I walked across the street to her house and up the cracked cement walkway, which was planted on both sides with pansies and marigolds in a hideous mix of dark purple and bright orange. Flakes of turquoise paint peeled off her front door like bad skin. I knocked.

Sonia wore a red silk bathrobe with twin gold dragons embroidered on the front. The robe, like Sonia, had seen better days. She usually wore her long hair pulled back at the nape of her neck, but now it draped over her shoulders and down her back in a thin brown curtain. I'd always pegged her as younger than me, but seeing up close the gray roots of her hair and the bags under her eyes, I realized she was well into her fifties.

She narrowed her eyes. "What a surprise, Martha. You're not someone I ever expected to see."

She was so right. Nevertheless, I put on a smile and took a deep breath. "Hi, Sonia. I'm here because I'm hoping you can help my investigation."

"Investigation? What investigation?"

I lowered my voice to a conspiratorial whisper and looked over my shoulder. "I can't talk outside because I don't want anyone else to hear. Can I come in?"

She took a cautious step aside, and when I walked into her living room, I smelled a pungent herbal tang in the air, something vaguely familiar, mixed with the fragrance of sandalwood incense in a smoky layer of air. Sonia directed me to a worn sofa and chairs draped with printed cotton cloth from India, which had also seen better days. A framed photo of people I thought I recognized hung prominently on one wall.

"Would you like some tea? I've just brewed a pot."

"Sure. Thanks."

Sonia walked through a rattling curtain of purple beads as she entered her kitchen. I jumped up quickly and examined the photo on the wall. There was a very young Sonia snuggling up to— no way! He signed the picture *To my groovy little chick, Sonia. Luv forever, Mick.* That must have been a very long time ago because Sonia was no longer "groovy" and these days Mick looked positively wasted. Had Sonia really been one of Jagger's girl-friends? Sonia's brush with greatness, her proximity to fame—was that why she lived in a time warp, this shrine to the seventies?

Sonia walked back into the living room with two steaming mugs. "So, tell me why you're here."

I sat and took a sip. Mint and chamomile. Yuck. What I wouldn't give for a strong cup of dark French roast with cream. I took another sip. "Delicious. Thanks." Then I put the cup down and leaned forward. "I've been secretly working with the police." Not exactly a lie—the secret part was real. Beavers didn't know I was doing this.

Not convinced, she waved her hand. "The cops just busted you four nights ago. The whole neighborhood knows that."

I thought fast. "The arrest was just for show. I actually spent the night in a nice hotel, not in jail. We wanted the secret operation to look like the police were after me so I could gain the confidence of the bad guys." I could hardly believe how easily I could lie to this woman.

Sonia put her cup down, her eyes wide open. "Really?"

She was hooked. Now to reel her in carefully. "Can I count on your keeping a secret? I mean, you absolutely cannot tell *anybody*."

"I'm good. I know how to keep my mouth shut."

Yeah, like that could ever happen. Yentas are like

Google and Wikipedia in human form. Just give them a click and they'll tell you much more than you ever wanted to know.

"I knew I could count on you. You're the guiding force behind our little community. You know everything that goes on, and now I need your expertise."

She looked at me for a few seconds. "I gotta say, Martha, I always thought you didn't like me. Even when I rescued your cat, you never thanked me."

Sonia's private world seemed to be all about the past. I'd never seen a man at her house, nor much of anyone else, come to think of it. I supposed Sonia was lonely. Maybe that was why she was such a gossip, inserting herself into other people's lives as a way of getting attention and feeling important. I was ashamed of the contempt I'd shown her. She probably rescued Bumper with good intentions. Who knows what would've happened to him if the killer found him in the house. "You're right, Sonia. I never thanked you, and I'm sorry. You did Bumper and me a huge favor. It was really very kind of you."

Sonia's face softened, and she smiled. "Well, apology accepted."

I smiled back. "Sonia, I need to focus on one thing in particular. Did you see anyone or anything unusual at my house Tuesday or Wednesday night?"

"The cops came by and asked everyone on the

street the same question. I told them I hadn't seen anything. Neither did anyone else, so far as I know."

"You told me yesterday the Eyes have been patrolling the streets ever since my fake arrest."

"Right. Ron Wilson arranged shifts for all the guys."

I only knew Ron vaguely. He lived on the next street and hung out with a bunch of other geezers, some of them original owners of the midcentury homes in our tract. Those old vets loved reliving their glory days and playing soldier on our quiet suburban streets at night.

"Were they out Tuesday and Wednesday nights?"

"They were."

Yes! "I'm wondering if any of them saw any unusual activity around my house. Someone at the door? A strange car parked outside?"

"We can check with Ron. He keeps a log."

"Really? He keeps records?" My voice was two notes short of a squeal. This could be the break I'd hoped for. "Can you give me his phone number?"

"I'll do better than that." She picked up the phone. "Hi, Ron. This is Sonia. I'm bringing my neighbor Martha Rose by to talk about all the stuff from last week. No, she's been out of jail for a few days. Anyways, that was all just a big show to throw off the real bad guys. She's working with the cops right now in some secret investigation, and I'm helping her."

See what I mean? Wikipedia.

She ended her call. "Just give me a minute to get dressed."

While Sonia was in her bedroom, I wandered around looking at her dusty knickknacks. Rainbow-colored dream catchers, really old copies of *Mother Jones*, new copies of *People* magazine, and a purple yoga mat rolled up in the corner. Hello! What was this? A bong? I sniffed the mouthpiece. Yup. Exactly what I thought I smelled.

Just then Sonia walked back into the living room wearing black flowing pants, a white peasant shirt, and sandals. She pulled her long hair into a clip at the back of her neck, revealing turquoise studs in her ears. This neighborhood yenta living right across the street from me was at one time the loose-haired girlfriend of Mick Jagger. Who knew?

She looked at the bong in my hands. "It's not what you think." She gave a wry smile. "I'm legal. I use weed for medicinal purposes." Made sense. Medical marijuana dispensaries were now legal in California. I had considered using weed for my fibromyalgia pain, but so far I hadn't worked up the courage to ask my doctor to write a prescription.

Of course, marijuana dispensary staff physicians wrote hundreds of prescriptions a day. Anyone could walk in the front door without a scheduled appointment and get a prescription for about a hundred bucks. Ten minutes for the script, another few minutes to buy the weed and a bong.

Fifteen minutes later Sonia and I sat in the Wilsons'

living room looking at a hefty old guy with white hair cut military style. The floor plan of Ron's house was the same as mine. The built-in bookcases and slightly crooked finish molding around the windows and doors told me Ron was a do-it-yourselfer.

A wizened little Asian woman came into the living room and greeted us with a slight accent. Then she turned to Ron. "I go to the store now. Be back soon."

"Don't spend all my money." He smiled.

She looked at us, rolled her eyes, and went out the door.

"Been married over fifty years. Best little woman in the world. What can I do you for?"

I jumped right in. "Did the police ever come by your house to ask about Tuesday or Wednesday night of this last week?"

"No, nobody came by our street."

"I understand you arranged for patrols, though, and you keep a log. Do you know if anyone saw anything unusual around my house those two nights?"

"What's your address again?"

I gave him my address. Ron frowned and closed his eyes. "I think I remember something."

My heart started pounding as he reached over to a small table next to his chair and pulled out a spiral notebook with a worn blue cover. He moved his rather large girth in his black leather recliner and handed me the book . "Me and the boys sign in each shift and write down everything that looks out of the ordinary. Nobody's ever asked to see the log before. What's this about, anyway?"

"I'm in the middle of an investigation. I can't talk about it. It's strictly a need-to-know kind of deal."

Ron nodded and winked. "I was in the army. Korea and Nam. I know what you're sayin'."

I smiled. "I'm glad I can count on you."

I turned the pages until I found Tuesday night. Ron signed in at nine.

Neighbor Martha Rose arrested. Confessed to harboring a terrorist cell in her basement.

Eyes of Encino patrol activated.

Objective: hunt down terrorists.

Result: none found.

Oh brother. They believed the basement thing? According to the log, each man was relieved after two hours and a new man signed on, but apparently nobody saw anything useful. Just a possum crossing the street and crawling under someone's house at two in the morning.

Darn. The killer was able to break in to my house and trash it without being detected. Some patrol. I turned to the entries for Wednesday night hoping for better luck and very nearly jumped out of my skin when I read:

Zero thirty hours: Tall, slender woman leaving
    front porch of Rose house. Obviously not
    the homeowner.

Wait just a minute. What was obvious? Because
she was tall or because she was slender?

No lights on inside. Glasses. Fifty something.
    Subaru sedan. Plate # 3ARB997.

I wrote down the information. "This is exactly
what I was hoping to find. Great work, Ron. Thanks
so much."

Ron winked and gave me a thumbs-up.

As we walked back to our street, Sonia smiled
hopefully. "We could go back to my house and have
more tea, or maybe go to your house. Do you realize I've never been inside your place?"

Poor Sonia. I was as gentle as I could be. "I'm
sorry, but I've got to develop this very important
lead you've just given me. I'm afraid I don't have
time. You've been a tremendous help and I'm
going to make sure the police know about you." I
made a mental note to send her some flowers.
Purple and red ones.

Back home I closed the door behind me and
called the florist. Then I called Detective Beavers.
I explained about the Eyes of Encino. "You wouldn't
have known about them because the guy who runs
it lives on another street. They didn't see anything

on Tuesday night, the night of the break-in, but one of the guys actually saw someone at my house Wednesday night. He said she was a tall woman, which doesn't make sense. The description doesn't match the composite drawing of the quilt thief, and besides, all of the suspects are men."

"I'll have to talk to the guy who saw her. He might have been mistaken about the gender. In the dark, a tall slender man might be mistaken for a woman."

I immediately thought of Alexander Godwin. Would the elegant Doctor Godwin lower himself to place dog crap on people's porches? Hard to believe.

"This isn't much to go on. Did the guy notice anything else?"

"I've saved the best for last. He actually got a license number." I gave him the license number and make of the car.

"Great. Hold on a minute. Didn't you promise to stop poking around just twelve hours ago?"

"It's Arthur's fault."

"Huh?"

"While I was cleaning up after him, I remembered about our neighborhood patrol and wondered if they could have seen who put the dog poop on my porch on Wednesday night or who broke in the night before. Anyway, aren't you supposed to bring me my computer today?"

"I'll try. Depends on where these plates lead me."

"Well, I'll be home all day long getting my house back in order."

"How's Arthur doing?"

"He's made himself right at home."

"That would be an easy thing to do with you."

I stared at the phone for a while, trying to decide if I heard him correctly. "My goodness, Detective, are you flirting with me?"

He chuckled. "What do you think?"

What did I think? I thought I should run right down to Weight Watchers and sign up.

CHAPTER 30

I spent the rest of the morning straightening up the mess the killer made of my bedroom four nights before. After the break-in, Joey and Richie picked up my clothes the best they could, but I needed to finish the job.

I was surprised to discover I owned thirty-two short-sleeved T-shirts. Some I hadn't worn for ages because stubborn food stains sat on the front where the girls formed a shelf big enough to catch a man falling from a three-story building.

As a quilter, I knew something about stains. For instance, soaking cotton fabric in black tea would permanently give it a darker hue. Many quilters used tea dying to soften the colors of a fabric. Also some unscrupulous antique dealers had been known to take a modern quilt made with re-production fabrics and soak it in hot tea to make it look old, because antique quilts sold for a lot more money.

Another quilter's trick was to soak indigo-dyed cotton with pure Ivory Soap in very hot water to set the dye and stop it from bleeding color. Also, most quilters knew if you pricked your finger with a needle and bled on your quilt, spitting on the fabric would take out the stain because your saliva dissolves your blood.

Food stains, however, if not treated immediately, were often impossible to remove from colored cotton. So I threw twenty-one T-shirts in the rag bag.

When I finished sorting my clothes at one in the afternoon, my stomach was growling. I'd managed to edit my entire wardrobe and was bagging all the old clothes destined for Goodwill. I was wondering whether to replace them now or wait until I lost some weight when the phone rang.

"Have you eaten yet?" Beavers had an annoying habit of not identifying himself when he called.

"No, Detective, and I'm starving. What about the license plate? Did you find out who it belongs to?"

"Yes. I'll be there in twenty minutes with your laptop and the best barbeque you'll ever eat." He hung up.

I took one look at my sweaty self, tore off my dusty clothes, and jumped in the shower. Five minutes later I towel dried my curls and put on a pair of gray linen trousers and a peach-colored blouse with pin tucks on the front and little pearl buttons. I reached for the spray bottle of Marc Jacobs and this time I used it. Before I slipped into my sandals,

I put a tiny gold ring I hadn't worn since the 1980s on the middle toe of my right foot.

Arthur started barking and wiggling his body in ecstasy as soon as Beavers pulled up in front of the house. When I opened the door, Beavers grinned and handed me a large paper bag smelling of garlic and hickory smoke.

"I'll need you to sign for your laptop." He put it on the coffee table along with some kind of official-looking papers.

As I unpacked the food on the dining room table, Beavers bent down and ruffled the dog's fur. "Hey, Artie, you been taking good care of this lady?" The dog licked his face in adoration. Bumper watched without blinking from a safe distance away.

I realized when he stood from petting the dog that Beavers wore his off-duty clothes again—cowboy boots, a crisp western shirt, and jeans that hugged his body perfectly. I blinked my eyes rapidly and felt warmth creeping up the sides of my face. "I forgot this was Saturday. I've disturbed you on your day off again."

"I'm not complaining." He rolled up his sleeves and walked toward the sink to wash his hands. I caught a whiff of his woodsy cologne as he passed, and I couldn't help admiring this view of his hard bottom. Nor could I overlook his muscular fore-arms as he helped me open the food containers.

A mountain of food sat in front of us, enough for several people. "What, no dessert?"

Beavers smiled slowly and looked at me, letting his eyes roll down the front of my blouse and come to rest at my feet. I quickly turned around to get plates and forks and set the table with shaking hands. He must have been looking at my toes. Maybe I should have waited to put on the toe ring.

I put two slices of tri tip with crispy edges on my plate and then covered them with barbeque sauce, wondering how many Weight Watcher points I was going to have to pretend I didn't eat. I added crunchy coleslaw, beans, mashed sweet potatoes, and corn on the cob. I passed on the fresh baguettes—too many carbs.

"So what about the license plate? Who owns the car?"

He split open a baguette and forked on slices of tri tip. "The car belongs to a Carlotta Hudson."

Carlotta from the quilt guild! Somehow I always knew she was a little crackers. I could just see her skulking through the dark to booby-trap our front porches with dog crap and nasty notes, but I couldn't picture her actually killing someone. "Carlotta is the killer?"

"No, she was attending some kind of quilting conference in San Jose the night of the killing. She also alibied out for almost every night after. We checked them out. When we pressed her, however, she did confess to putting those packages on the porches." He smoothed a layer of coleslaw on top of everything, closed the sandwich, and before he took a bite he asked, "Do you know why she would be driven to such a juvenile act?"

"Pure jealousy and spite. She's the kind of quilter who enters a quilt in half a dozen shows in the hopes of earning a prize. The best she's ever been able to pull off is third place because she's just not that good."

I noticed a bit of sauce clinging to his mustache and stopped myself just in time from reaching over and wiping his mouth. "So did you throw her in jail?"

Beavers shook his head. "At worst it was malicious mischief. That doesn't earn you jail time."

"Well, what about trespassing?"

"She could only be trespassing if she went through a barrier onto fenced-off property. All of your houses are open to the streets."

My voice rose with indignation. "Well, what if we insist on pressing charges?"

"The DA doesn't prosecute 'mal mish' cases. At the most you'd get a referral to a dispute resolution counselor."

I put down my fork and jabbed at my chest with my thumb. "You mean I was forced to stay in that putrid jail overnight for nothing while this crazy woman gets a free pass?" I slapped the table with the palm of my hand. "How fair is that?"

He raised a bottle of Heineken to his lips. "I'm sorry, Martha. Your arrest was a mistake, but Carlotta Hudson gets to walk this time."

"When were you planning to break the news about Carlotta to Lucy and Birdie?"

"This afternoon."

I vigorously cut my meat into small pieces. "Maybe I should pay Carlotta's front porch a visit some night."

"I didn't hear that. To change the subject, how's the food?"

"Tastes really great." I wasn't ready yet to forget about Carlotta, and certainly not ready to forgive. "Are you a barbeque expert?" Judging from his western attire, I guessed Beavers probably came from some state where they ate barbeque all the time; like Texas or Kansas. Almost everyone in California came from somewhere else.

"Well, I've developed a taste for it. Where I grew up, we ate a lot of fish."

"Where was that?" I was now thinking Louisiana or the gulf coast of Alabama.

"Oregon. Siletz Reservation on the north coast."

"You're Native American?" Nothing could have surprised me more, and yet the more I looked at him, the more I saw it in his dark eyes.

"Half. My mother. Never knew my father. He was some white dude she picked up in a bar. I grew up with my grandparents on the rez near Lincoln City. They were good people." He looked at me and grinned. "I'm a good guy, too. They raised me right."

"What happened to your mother?"

"Died of an overdose in the sixties."

I don't know why I decided to tell him about myself, but hearing about his childhood made me go all soft inside. "I never knew my father either. His name was Quinn. My family always maintained he died in a train wreck before I was born, but mean Aunt Esther always called me a mamser."

"What's that?"

"Illegitimate. So I've always had my doubts. When I met Jerry Bell and heard how he located his birth mother, it started me thinking. I've never actually seen my mother's marriage certificate, so the only thing I know about my father is his first name, Quinn. I once asked my mother why my last name was the same as hers and Bubbie's and Uncle Isaac's. She just told me, 'It was easier that way.'

"Anyway, my mother never seemed to recover completely. She wasn't very functional and needed to be taken care of. We lived with my grandmother and my uncle Isaac. Bubbie died when I was nine, so my uncle Isaac just sort of took over. He even put me through college."

"Sounds like he was just as good as a father."

"Yeah. He warned me against marrying my ex. He said, 'He's not for you, faigela.'"

"What does that mean?"

"Little bird."

Beavers smiled. "That sounds Indian."

I smiled back. "My uncle is a wise man. He warned me Aaron would break my heart, but I was too young and infatuated to listen to him. I stubbornly defended Aaron because he was going to be a doctor and help sick people. My uncle said, 'Doctor, schmokter. He's a schmuck.'"

Beavers chuckled. "Maybe you should have listened to him."

"Ya think? But much to Uncle Isaac's credit, when my heart did get broken, he never said a word. He just loved me as usual and helped me and my daughter, Quincy, to get through it. He's still alive and well, and I adore him."

"I can see why. What about your mother?"

"She continued to live in her own world. She died of cancer about ten years ago. Her last words to me weren't 'I love you,' but 'Where's Quinn?'"

Beavers listened intently. "Are you interested in finding out more about your father? You're obviously good at research. Not that I approve, but look at the way you uncovered so much information about Claire Terry."

"I'm still thinking about it. I'm fifty-five years old. If there's a chance he didn't really die in a train wreck, he might still be alive. He could even still be in his seventies. But I'm not sure I'm brave enough to go there."

"I think you're brave. Reckless, but brave. But it's time for you to back off this case, Martha. I'd much rather see you researching your father's identity than digging into this dangerous murder."

I waved my hand dismissively. I wasn't going to

stop until Claire's murderer was found, and deep down I'm sure he knew it. "What about you? What was it like growing up on the reservation?"

"Well, I guess I have a similar story. My grandparents did for me what your grandmother and uncle did for you. We didn't have much, but I was lucky. My grandfather worked me so hard I didn't have time to get in trouble, and my grandmother insisted I get an education. I wouldn't be here today if it weren't for them."

"They must be very proud of you, being an LAPD detective and all."

Beavers smiled. "They wanted me to become a lawyer. Fight for Indian rights, but I decided to pursue the law in a different way."

"Are they still alive?"

"No. If they were, they'd be over a hundred."

"You were lucky to have such loving grandparents. Think of Jerry Bell and the awful situation he's facing."

Beavers nodded. "Claire Terry lived a tangled-up life."

"So you're no closer to finding the killer? What about Claire's quilts? Have you translated them? What do they say?"

"The Terrys have powerful friends. There's been a lot of pressure on my captain and on the DA to back off and leave the grieving family alone. Consequently, the DA has been reluctant to move on getting a warrant. Bottom line, the quilts are still with the Terrys."

"I don't believe it! The rich and powerful always seem to escape the rules the rest of us have to live by."

"Don't worry. We, *and I don't mean you,* aren't through with our investigation. We, *the police,* will get the guy who did this."

He cleared off the table while I rinsed the dishes. Working together seemed as natural as if we'd been doing this for years. I was pissed about Carlotta and even more pissed about the quilts. I still kept a little something up my sleeve I didn't want Beavers to know about. I wanted him to leave so I could get to it. I thrust the last dish in the dishwasher, wiped my hands on a dish towel, and looked pointedly at the clock. "Thanks for the lunch break; the food was delicious."

Beavers glanced at my foot and started to say something but must have thought better of it. "I'll get going as soon as you sign for your laptop."

I completed the release form, and he handed me a copy as I walked him to the front door.

"I'm beginning to figure you out, Martha. You've got that look that tells me you're up to something. Even though we know who is responsible for the dog poop, we still have a killer on the loose, a killer who put a knife in your pillow."

He folded up his copy of the release and put it in his breast pocket. Then he put his hands on my shoulders and looked at me so keenly I couldn't concentrate. "If you know something else, now's the time to tell me. Don't do anything stupid."

He really looked worried. Impulsively, I stood on my tiptoes to give his cheek a reassuring peck. The next thing I knew, he was kissing me. Deeply and thoroughly. I closed my eyes and lost all sense of space. East, west, north, south, up, down, all swirled around me. I could drown in this man. Finally I pulled away and we stared at each other, shocked by the electrical storm that just sizzled through us.

"Sorry." He grinned and pointed down. "That little gold thing . . ."

Hallelujah. I was happy to know that after all these years my lucky toe ring still worked.

CHAPTER 31

As soon as Beavers left, I ran to the phone and called Lucy. Three o'clock. She'd be home from her grandson's soccer game.

"Lucy, guess what?"

"Hi, hon'. How was your first night at home?"

Just then Arthur nudged me with a desperate look. As I told Lucy about the Eyes of Encino leading the police to Carlotta Hudson, I opened the back door for the dog, who immediately ran out and anointed the trunk of the peach tree. Then the cat scooted past me for a friendly game of catch the cat. Arthur and Bumper hardly knew each other, yet they were fast friends.

Why not? Arlo Beavers and I met less than two weeks ago and yet we had already kissed for the first time. I had to admit I hoped it wouldn't be our last.

"You mean Carlotta Hudson admitted pulling a dirty trick on us and they won't throw her sorry self in jail?"

"I know. When Barbara North gets back from her vacation, I'm going to petition the board to ask Carlotta to leave the guild. That'll be a worse punishment for her than jail."

"You're right. I'll tell Ray he can dismiss the boys from guard duty. By the way, did the bodyguard Detective Beavers talked about ever come to your house?"

"Yes. He's retired from the police force and he's outside right now peeing in my yard."

"You should call nine-one-one right now, Martha!"

"Relax, Luce. Arthur's a German shepherd."

Fifteen minutes later I was in Lucy's living room downloading Claire's files from her flash drive onto my laptop. "It's more important than ever we have these files. The Terrys aren't about to hand over the actual quilts, and who knows, maybe they'll even destroy them. So, whatever I can read from the file photos may be all we ever get to know."

Birdie came over with a freshly baked loaf of pumpkin-walnut bread, and Lucy made a pot of strong Yorkshire tea served with milk and sweet agave syrup. "Much healthier than sugar." Then she helped herself to a large slice of cake.

Birdie sipped her tea. "So I no longer have to worry about the threat on my life? Those nasty notes and the dog doody were just Carlotta's way of getting even for only getting a third-place ribbon at the quilt show?"

I nodded.

"Well, the fact I'm not going to be killed after all will be small consolation to Russell. He bought a new pair of shoes because I refused to clean the ones he wore when he stepped on the bag, and you know Russell. He gagged just carrying them to the trash."

We laughed hard enough to wipe away tears.

When we were quiet again, I looked at them. "He kissed me."

Both their heads snapped in my direction.

"What?"

"When?"

"Today, after lunch." I looked at my teacup. "I kissed him back."

Lucy slapped her knee. "I knew it! I just knew it. I could feel the chemistry between you two almost from the beginning."

Birdie smiled. "He seems like such a nice man, Martha. I hope everything works out for you, dear."

"It's way too soon to tell. I hardly know him." I told them what little he'd revealed about himself. "I know nothing about his history as a grown man—marriage, kids, divorce, girlfriends. . . ."

"Well, you should have fun finding out." Lucy winked.

She and Birdie were always pushing me to get out there and date. They even tried fixing me up a couple of times.

"I don't know, Lucy. Remember the car salesman you and Ray fixed me up with two years ago?"

Lucy waved her hand. "How were we supposed to know he liked to dress up in women's clothes?"

I turned to Birdie. "Or the schizophrenic podiatrist in your garden club you insisted I meet?"

"I admit he turned out to be a little peculiar, but he did have splendid azaleas, poor man."

Around five I declined Lucy's dinner invitation because I was anxious to go home and examine Claire's files. As we said good-bye, Lucy and Birdie offered to come over in the morning and help me put my sewing room back together.

As I pulled into my driveway Sonia peeked out her window at me. She waved and mouthed "Thank you." She must have received the flowers.

I smiled and waved back, then hurried inside in an effort to avoid conversation. I fed the animals and nuked a container of leftover mashed sweet potatoes for myself. Between bites of steaming comfort food, I printed a copy of the Braille alphabet from the Internet and pictures of all of Claire's quilts from her files. I wasn't sure what Beavers would do if he knew the photos of Claire's quilts were in my laptop. No one actually gave us permission to copy those files. Still, we weren't withholding any evidence since Claire's computer was at the police station with all the same evidence on it. Was it my fault I was the one who figured everything out?

I started searching for Claire's last quilt, the one that was stolen. What was the name again? Ascending?

There was nothing in her computer. No photos. Darn. Without clear photos to read, how would we ever know why it was stolen?

I thought back to the day of the quilt show and tried to picture the quilt in my mind—pink, red, and purple roses on a gray background covered with hundreds of red French knots. I remember thinking the hearts and flowers reminded me of Valentine's Day. Maybe the quilt was all about the romance between Claire and Godwin, a romance that made her heart soar, or ascend. Jerry told me she'd been noticeably happier lately. Maybe Godwin stole it to destroy any evidence of their relationship.

So why would he steal mine and Birdie's quilts, too? With a sinking feeling, I became almost certain we'd never see our quilts again. I was glad I'd taken so many pictures of them right before they were stolen. I hoped the red knots on the gray background of Claire's quilt would show up clearly in those photos. With any luck I'd find the evidence I was looking for right in my digital camera.

I wasn't sure where to start searching for my camera. I remembered putting my fanny pack in my sewing room after the quilt show, but the killer made an awful mess in there. The night of the break-in he raked through my fabric and tossed it all over the room in a futile search for Claire's quilts. Richie and Joey put everything in cardboard boxes for me to sort through when I was ready.

I looked around the room and when I didn't see

my fanny pack on any of the shelves, I started dumping the contents of each carton on the floor. Some of the pieces of fabric were twisted and bunched, but others fluttered to the floor like rainbow-colored flags. My fanny pack tumbled out of the third carton. I jerked open the zipper, pulled out my camera, and was soon downloading the pictures onto my computer.

After scrolling through the images from the quilt show, I selected two that clearly showed the knots on Claire's quilt and clicked on the print icon. If only I'd known what those knots really were, I would've taken more photos.

I found a place to start, positioned the ruler under the line of text, and began the slow process of writing the translation on my notepad one letter at a time.

ddy stay away.

I was pretty sure *ddy* meant Daddy. Was Claire saying her father was still forcing himself on her?

A help me stop

The text ended at the edge of the photo, thwarting any further attempt to translate the rest of the line. However, I was pretty sure *A* referred to Alexander Godwin, who helped Claire cut her father off. Didn't Will Terry say that happened about a year ago? This proved Will was telling the truth. I hurried on because goodness knows I didn't want such unwelcome pictures lingering in my head.

I laid out the second and only other readable photo, hoping for the best.

my new meds

The rest of the section was unreadable. Well, this only proved she was taking meds at some point, but she probably stopped taking them because of her pregnancy. If they were the same drugs used to kill her, how did the killer get her to take them?

There was more text at the bottom of the photo.

A my secret

The next letters were *lulr*. What in the heck was that? After wracking my brain for words that might fit and coming up with nothing, I decided to recheck the photo. Sure enough, I'd missed a knot. The word was actually *luvr*—probably shorthand for lover. By now I knew *A* stood for Alexander. Here was the proof Godwin was Claire's lover.

Big money 4 BCA. 4 r futur

This was the clearest string of text yet. Claire was going to give a large donation to BCA, Godwin's nonprofit. However, I didn't recall seeing a recent large donation in the BCA file in Claire's office. I wonder if she ever followed through?

The clock read eight. I thought about calling Detective Beavers and telling him what I'd just discovered, only I wasn't sure I was ready for another encounter. In fact, I was terrified. What if he kissed me again? I was so out of practice, I didn't know if I could handle an actual romance.

I let the animals out one more time and when

they came back in, I set the alarm. Then I got into my pajamas and made a pot of tea, preparing to read long into the night if necessary to get the answers I was after.

The next quilt I wanted to examine was the baby quilt, to find out why Alexander Godwin tried to get rid of it, although I was sure I knew— the message would confirm he was the father of Claire's unborn baby.

The pictures in Claire's files were so much clearer than the ones I took. I suspected Claire hired a professional photographer to take them. This crib-sized quilt featured yellow baskets with bright gold French knots on a white background. Almost every knot was clearly visible. I began with the photo of the upper left-hand corner of the quilt and laid a ruler on top to find the line of text.

4 my baby but A doesn't want.

So I was right. Godwin was the father of Claire's baby. I was starting to get used to Claire's short-hand.

not leave wife.

Claire must have been devastated when she didn't find her happy ending after all. Did she know about Godwin's wife also being pregnant?

I picked up the next photo in the series.

A 4 abort. My heart brokn. All re money.

A whole hour had passed while I deciphered that little bit, but I wasn't about to stop.

I say no more losing babies.

Poor Claire. Did Godwin panic and kill her because she was determined to keep their baby?

The final entry was the most shocking.

Cancel big money. Tell board. Baby name will b Godwin.

Oh my God. Claire signed her death warrant. If she really intended to expose Godwin, he stood to lose everything. The large donation Claire planned to give to BCA, his career, his reputation, and maybe even his marriage. No wonder he threw this quilt in the Dumpster—the message gave him a strong motive to kill her.

I knew I couldn't wait any longer to call Beavers.

He picked up on the second ring. "Beavers." There was a television in the background.

I realized I didn't know what to call him now that we'd kissed. Detective? Arlo? Honey? "Hey."

His voice was smiling. "Is this a social call?"

"No. I figured out who the murderer is."

He chuckled. "Who's the killer this time?"

I ignored the sarcasm. "It's still Alexander Godwin."

"Can't be. Godwin was with his wife the night of Claire's murder."

"Well, duh. Why wouldn't she lie for him? I have new evidence pointing straight to Godwin as the killer."

"What new evidence?"

"I read the quilts."

"What quilts? Are you saying the Terrys handed over the quilts to you?"

"No. I have photos of them."

The sarcasm left Beavers's voice. "Photos? What photos?"

"Don't ask. I just translated the baby quilt and part of the stolen quilt, and—"

"The stolen quilt? You have a part of the stolen quilt? Where'd you get *that*?"

"Not the quilt itself. I took pictures of it."

"Don't you ever listen, Martha? Didn't I ask you this afternoon to tell me if you knew anything more?"

"That's why I'm calling. I'm telling you now."

"Anyone else know?"

"Not yet."

"Have the photos and the notes ready for me. I'll be right over, and try your best this time to keep all this to yourself, just for now."

"Okay, but *no kissing*!"

Strange sounds came over the phone. Wheezing. Choking.

"Don't worry." He swallowed his laughter. "If you're right, I'll be too busy closing this case, and if you're wrong, I'll be too busy yelling at you."

CHAPTER 32

Before Beavers arrived, I made a copy of my translation and clipped it to a dozen photos of Claire's quilt to make a neat package, and as soon as he walked in the door, I handed him the package. He petted Arthur while he looked over the material. "This doesn't look good for Godwin. I'm going to go pick him up now." Then he looked at me. "You still have to explain where you got these photos and why you withheld them from the police."

"You've had the photos all along. They're in Claire's computer."

"Did you print those photos before Kaplan took Claire's computer away?"

I didn't want to tell him about Lucy downloading them on a flash drive, so I just shrugged my shoulders. He could think whatever he wanted.

Beavers just stared at me, wagged his head in resignation, and turned to go.

"What?"

"You're either really smart or really lucky, Martha."

"Give me some credit." I put my hand on my hip. "Luck didn't figure out the code was in Braille, and luck didn't translate the code."

"But luck has kept you alive so far. Until we know for sure Godwin is the killer, I want you to keep your alarm on and Arthur by your side."

I thought better of telling him Ray's semiautomatic pistol was in my bedside table.

That night I dreamt Alexander Godwin broke into my house, dissolved all my headache pills in a glass of wine, and forced me to drink them. When I started to lose consciousness, he carried me to my bed and stood over me with a knife, preparing to stab me. I tried to scream, but I was paralyzed. I woke up with my heart pounding. Arthur must have sensed my distress because he jumped up on the bed and lay down right next to me. Dogs really could read minds.

SUNDAY

CHAPTER 33

At nine the next morning, Lucy and Birdie arrived to help me put my sewing room back together. Lucy brought the rest of the pumpkin-walnut loaf, and I made a pot of coffee. Before we started working, I showed them my notepad with the translation of the quilts.

Birdie shook her head. "Looks can really be deceiving. When I saw him at the wake, Dr. Godwin appeared to be such a devoted husband, so respectable."

Lucy frowned. "What I can't figure out is how he had the nerve to show up at the wake of someone he killed. I mean, that's cold."

"No doubt he's been feeling a lot hotter since Detective Beavers picked him up last night."

We freshened our cups of coffee and carried them to my sewing room. Cardboard cartons full of jumbled-up cotton material were stacked against one wall, and in the middle of the floor, where I dumped them yesterday, were more piles of fabric, some of which I'd used in my Civil War quilt—a tiny print in double pink, black squares marching across a gold background, purple paisley, and a green leafy print.

Lucy picked up the fabrics from the floor, Birdie carefully folded them, and I stacked them on the shelves according to color. All the miscellaneous items like rulers, scissors, pins, and needles were collected in an empty cardboard box to be sorted through later.

When the floor was cleared, Lucy emptied the rest of the cartons and we sorted fabric. Half-yard cuts and under went to Birdie to fold, while Lucy managed to fold the larger cuts.

"Look what I found." Lucy pulled a crumpled sheet of paper from a twisted chunk of blue and tan shirting. The composite drawing of the quilt thief wearing a ski mask fluttered to the floor. The only distinguishable features were the odd little eyes and a physical description: *Caucasian, 5'5" to 5'8" stocky.*

I picked up the drawing. "This isn't much to go on, but there's enough to know Godwin must have gotten someone else to steal Claire's quilt from the quilt show. He is, after all, around six feet tall and slender." I put the paper next to my notepad in the kitchen.

By noon the three of us had cleaned and organized my sewing room. I stood back to admire our hard work. We'd sorted through all the sewing notions in the cardboard box. Scissors, rotary cutters, my collection of antique pin cushions, thimbles, needles, binding clips, and dozens of other sewing accessories had been put back in their proper drawers.

My reclaimed fabric sat neatly folded on floor to ceiling shelves along one wall. One whole shelf was filled with just the blues (I have a weakness for blue), from robin's egg polka dot to a deep indigo fish batik made in West Africa. The year before I painted the room a soft dove gray—a nice neutral background for the rainbow hues of my fabrics. The whole effect was calm but cheerful. "My sewing room has never been so neat." I smiled.

"What do you need to clean up next?" asked Lucy.

"I did my bedroom yesterday, so I guess the kitchen is the only big project left."

"Well, we might as well jump in as long as we're here."

Lucy put down the last piece of fabric. "Let's eat first. I'm hungry. Do you have anything, or shall we run down to the Sandwich Shoppe?"

"How about leftover barbeque?"

By three in the afternoon, my friends were gone, my house was restored, and I was relaxing in the living room with a can of Coke Zero, wondering how Beavers was doing with Godwin. Bumper jumped up on my lap purring, and settled down for a nap while Arthur put his chin on my knee, asking for some attention. I closed my eyes and smiled, thinking life couldn't get any better than this. Did I really need a man? Animals were much safer and, in my experience, a lot more loyal.

As I scratched Arthur behind the ears, I remembered Dixie was supposed to come over this evening to pick up the appliquéd flower basket wall hanging I promised to give to the charity auction for the Blind Children's Association. I really needed to get out of my work clothes and take a shower before she came, but I didn't have the energy to clean up right then. I figured she'd call at some point to get directions, at which time I'd freshen up. Then I fell asleep.

I woke to Arthur growling softly and somebody knocking on my front door. "Okay, Arthur, I'm awake now." I got up, turned on the porch lights and strained at the peephole to see who it was.

Dixie stood looking at the door and blinking rapidly. I'd never given her my address. How did she find me?

I turned off the alarm and opened the door. "Hi, Dixie. Come on in. I apologize for my appearance, but I thought you'd call first for directions. How did you know where I live?"

Dixie wore a long-sleeved blue shirt and polyester trousers. As she strode into the living room, she smiled. "Your check. Your address and phone number were on the check you gave me. All I had to do was look up your address on Google maps, *et voilà!* If you don't want anyone to know where you live, you shouldn't publish the information on your checks."

Her last remark struck me as a little short of friendly, if not downright snarky. I walked toward the kitchen. "Well, how about some tea?"

She followed me as far as the island. "Fine."

I put on a pot of water. "I'll just go and get the quilt." Arthur followed me down the hall to my sewing room and back to the kitchen, never moving more than two inches from my legs. I realized Arthur hadn't been out in the backyard since early afternoon, so I opened the back door for him, but he just sat at attention and looked at me.

"Go outside, Arthur, and be a good boy." Arthur didn't move. "Go on." I shoved him outside in the dark and closed the door.

While I made the tea, Dixie sat at the island and admired my quilt. Then she held up the composite drawing of the thief sitting on the counter. "Do you mind if I ask what this is? Looks pretty official."

I told her about the drawing, hoping she couldn't see my notepad sitting next to the picture with the translation of the quilts and my commentary. Poor Dixie. I didn't want to be the one to tell her Godwin was a murderer. His behavior had already caused Claire to withhold a huge gift of money to the Blind Children's Association. Who knew if BCA could survive the scandal of Godwin's arrest? If not, Dixie would be out of a job and in these difficult economic times and with her impaired vision, she might not easily find another.

When she put the drawing back, she glanced at my notepad. Before I could stop her, she brought it close to her face to read.

Dixie looked at me with a strange expression.

"I'm sorry, Dixie. I didn't want you to see those."

"Since when do you read Braille?"

"I don't really. I just downloaded a copy of the alphabet from Google and . . ."

Wait. Dixie was looking at snippets of whatever text I gleaned from Claire's baby quilt and my comments on the text. Nowhere on my notepad did I make any reference to Braille. So how did she know those short phrases were a translation of the Braille on the quilt?

Dixie squinted at me from behind her thick lenses, her eyes blinking wildly.

And suddenly I knew.

CHAPTER 34

Sometimes a quilter could get so focused on stitching together small pieces of fabric she'd need to take a step back and look at her composition as a whole. She would need to evaluate how each element came together to make the overall design. One way she could do this would be to look at her quilt through the wrong end of a pair of binoculars. The resulting image of the quilt was so reduced in size she could see her creation from an entirely new perspective. Flaws in the design just popped out and screamed to be fixed.

I'd been looking at Claire's murder too closely. Each element of the puzzle was like a small patch with its own unique color and details. I needed to take a step back and look instead at the overall design. I missed some obvious inconsistencies, starting with the composite drawing of the thief. Godwin wasn't a fit, but Dixie was. Like the wrong end of binoculars, the thick lenses of her glasses made her eyes appear to be smaller than normal—just like in the drawing.

I should have kept my big mouth shut and sent Dixie home, but the words flew out before I could stop them. "It was you. You stole the quilts."

Dixie stopped blinking and tilted her head, focusing on me with an unsettling stare. Chills tickled the hair on the back of my neck as she got up and came around to my side of the island.

I continued talking, figuring out the details as I went along. "You were the one who received the baby quilt from Claire for the auction. When you handled it, you must have realized the knots were Braille. So you read the quilt and discovered Claire was pregnant with Godwin's baby. Godwin wanted her to get an abortion, but she was going to keep the baby. She was also going to expose Godwin and cancel her bequest. You realized Godwin wasn't the only one who'd be ruined. If he went down, so would the Blind Children's Association."

Dixie licked her lips and slowly weaved her head from side to side. "No . . . ."

Like an idiot, I kept talking. "You couldn't let that happen, so you threw the baby quilt in the Dumpster. Then you learned one of Claire's quilts was displayed in the quilt show. You had to find out if that one also contained Braille."

Dixie's head was still moving from side to side. "You can't prove any of this."

If I were smarter, I would've stopped talking, but

my mouth got in the way of my better judgment. "Yes. I can. There was a woman at the quilt show who kept touching Claire's quilt. There are witnesses who will be able to identify you as that woman. You kept touching the quilt because you wanted to read the Braille. When you found out Claire wrote about her affair with Godwin in her quilt, you were compelled to get rid of it. So you came back the next day and stole it. You also grabbed a couple of other quilts to make it look like a random theft. You tried to disguise every feature that might identify you, but you couldn't disguise your eyes." I waved the composite drawing in front of her.

Dixie made a low, growling noise in her throat. "You think you're so clever."

Yes, I did. I was too impressed with my own cleverness to recognize the danger gathering all around me. "Did Godwin know about the Braille in the quilts? Did the two of you conspire to get rid of them?"

"Godwin didn't know anything, and he wouldn't have figured it out. He's not that smart."

"So you decided to steal the quilts all on your own?"

Dixie curled her lip and opened and closed her fingers. "Have you ever wanted something so much you'd do anything to protect it? I never told Godwin about the quilts because he would've fired me if he realized how much I knew about his personal life. I took a chance and told him I knew about Claire and the baby. I didn't tell him how I knew. I warned him if he ever tried to fire me, I'd go straight to his wife. It was job security."

"Godwin's been arrested, Dixie. There's nothing more to protect. He's going to go to jail for murdering Claire. You'll have to answer for stealing the quilts."

Dixie brushed past me and headed for the stove. I watched as she reached over to the drawer next to the stove and pulled out a Henckels with a seven-inch serrated blade. "You little witch. I tried to warn you to back off, but I guess you were just too dumb to take a hint."

I looked at her hand and remembered the knife in my pillow and the note. My mouth went dry. "My God, Dixie. You know where I keep my knives. This isn't the first time you've been in my house, is it? You're the one who broke in, trashed my house, and left the note in my pillow."

"I wanted *all* the quilts!"

I couldn't take my eyes off the knife. "You must have been frustrated when you broke in to Claire's house and didn't find them there."

"What're you talking about? I never broke into Claire's house. I didn't know about the other quilts until you told me they were here in your house."

"I told you?"

Dixie smiled triumphantly. "Yes, on the phone. When I offered to come get the baby quilt, you told me you were taking *all* of Claire's quilts back to the Terrys."

She was right! When would I learn to think before I spoke? It was a character flaw I'd have to work on if I ever got out of this alive.

"I wanted to find out what her other quilts revealed, to see if I needed to get rid of them, too, but once I got inside your house, I couldn't find them."

Dixie tightened her grip on the knife.

Arthur was barking outside and clawing at the door. From the time Dixie first appeared at my front door, Arthur had growled; then he resisted leaving my side, even refusing to go outside. Why hadn't I realized the guard dog was *guarding* me?

I tried to sprint to the back door to let him in, but she quickly stepped in front of me and pointed the knife. I threw up my hands in surrender and hastily backed up until my back hit the island. Then I slowly sidled toward the open space between the kitchen and the living area. My mind ricocheted between blind panic and reason.

If Dixie was the one who broke in to my house, then Godwin's alibi for that night could be solid after all. Acid burned the back of my throat. I reached the end of the island and put my hand on the counter to steady myself as the horrible truth exploded behind my eyes.

"Oh my God!" I clutched the edge of the counter. "Godwin didn't kill Claire—you did."

Dixie's mouth twisted open. "Godwin always got

what he wanted, but he made a huge mistake with Claire. When she canceled her big donation, he panicked. Told me to call to see if I could change her mind. After I read the baby quilt, I knew I could never change her mind. She was determined to expose Godwin, even if the exposure destroyed BCA. I couldn't let that happen."

"I don't understand. I thought you and Claire were friends. You said so yourself."

Dixie scoffed. "Life is so simple for people like you and Claire. You don't have to work like the rest of us. You just do your little bit for charity, pat yourself on the back, and move on. You don't care about those of us who can't just *move on*."

Now wasn't the time to point out to Dixie the only reason I wasn't still working as an administrator at UCLA was because of my disability, not because I was a member of the idle rich—which I wasn't. "Are you talking about the blind children who come to you? Surely there are other places where they can go for help, places where you could work if worse came to worst and BCA shut down."

"If a scandal shut down BCA, no one would want to hire me. I'd be tainted for life. There are few jobs for the visually impaired, even in an agency like mine. Besides, disabled people have no value in our society. It's a form of abuse that never gets talked about."

Dixie wasn't wrong. The same thing happened to aging women.

"I help the parents respect their kids, to really see them and listen to them. They learn to value my expertise because I've been there. They admire me and depend on me to rescue their children."

"And all of the admiration would stop if BCA folded?"

"Are you serious? I already told you nobody wants to hire a woman who's legally blind. Without my glasses, I can't read, I can't drive, I can't even cook. You can't begin to know what it's like, you with all your leisure time and your stupid quilting." Her eyes started to blink again. "I'm sick and tired of people like you and Claire—idle, useless people."

Arthur continued to bark and snarl at the door behind Dixie, but there was no way I could get to the door without getting sliced by the Henckels.

Shaking inside, I held up my hands again in an effort to keep her talking and buy some time. I needed to get to the gun in my bedroom. I started inching backward out of the kitchen toward the bedroom. Dixie came around the island and matched me step for step down the hallway.

"How did you get Claire to take all those drugs? I doubt she would have taken them voluntarily because, as you found out, she was pregnant."

Dixie smirked. "I went to her house to go over some details of the charity auction. I brought her a 'healthy treat' of hand-squeezed grapefruit juice from the trees in my yard. I figured the bitterness of the juice would disguise the flavor of the drugs dissolved in it."

As she spoke, I looked for some evidence of remorse, but Dixie's eyes glittered with some mad logic known only to her.

"Did it work?" I still inched backward.

"Not completely. She realized something was wrong when she started to get dizzy. She got scared and tried to get to the phone to call for help, but I was too strong for her. I forced the rest of the drugged juice down her throat until she passed out. Then I waited for her to stop breathing."

I never stopped moving, but my progress was slow. Every muscle in my body screamed for me to turn and flee, but I knew I'd never get to the bedroom if I made any sudden or rapid movements. Dixie was too close. I tried to stay calm and focused. "What was the blood on her hands from?"

Dixie pulled up one long sleeve, revealing healing scabs where something sharp had recently grated down her arm. "While I was shoving the drugs down her throat, the little whore scratched me with those hard acrylic fingernails she was so proud of."

"Are you secretly in love with Godwin? Is that it? You must love him an awful lot if you'd kill for him."

Dixie's eyes bulged behind her lenses and she thrust the knife once through the air for emphasis. "You don't know *jack*. I was in love with Claire, but I couldn't let her know. She wasn't into women.

Godwin I despise. I am the one who built BCA up from nothing. It's my life's work, my great achievement. I did all the hard work but Godwin took all the credit."

"How did you let that happen?"

"Unfortunately, I needed someone like him. He was the handsome, attractive face of the organization. He was the one who could pull in large donations. I didn't care who he slept with to get money. And believe me, he was always sleeping with somebody."

My backward progress was painfully slow. I estimated my bedroom was another twenty feet, at the far end of the hallway. I had to keep her talking. "I thought Claire was really devoted to BCA. Why would she want to destroy it?"

"Claire was naive enough to believe Godwin's lies. I guess when she found out what he was really like, she wanted to get even. I wouldn't have cared, but if she disgraced Godwin, BCA wouldn't survive. I wouldn't survive. In the end, it came down to choosing between Claire and my life's work. Claire lost."

I was now just about fifteen feet from my bedroom and the gun in the drawer. "I can imagine how you feel, Dixie. Men have been exploiting women throughout history. I'm surprised you let him manipulate you. You seem so smart and independent."

"Nice try, Martha." She took one large step forward.

Another large step and she'd be close enough to kill me. I turned and ran down the hall toward my bedroom. I had to get to the gun, or I was dead.

Dixie was right on my heels. She grabbed a handful of curls from behind and my head jerked back, knocking me off balance. I twisted my body and rolled toward her, shoving with all my might at her shins. The blade of the knife slashed the air just inches from my face as the two of us went down.

Dixie fell backward and landed on her butt, the knife skittering out of her hand. While she fumbled around for the Henckels, I scrambled to my feet and ran for my life.

Time seemed to stop and the air felt heavy and viscous as I ran in what seemed like slow motion to my bedroom. My heart boomed in my ears, each beat sounding deep and urgent. Dixie cursed as she got up off the floor. "You're dead!" she screamed.

I whipped through the doorway into my bedroom, diving toward the table beside my bed for the gun.

Dixie was only a few steps behind in the hallway screaming, "I'll kill you!"

I picked up my grandmother's blue and yellow Ohio Star quilt off the top of my bed. With a snap I unfurled it and threw it over Dixie's head just as she came through the bedroom door.

Her arms flailed inside the quilt. The knife slashed through the fabric of the precious eighty-year-old quilt as Dixie struggled to untangle herself.

Meanwhile, I yanked open the drawer, pulled out the gun, and fumbled to release the safety. Then I pulled back the slide to put a round in the chamber just the way Joey taught me.

Dixie threw the quilt on the ground and growled, "You're dead now, you bitch. . . ." She stopped and frowned when she saw the gun I pointed at her.

My tongue peeled off the dry roof of my mouth. "Drop the knife, Dixie, or I swear I'll shoot you dead." I wished the gun would stop shaking.

Dixie was only five feet in front of me, within easy striking distance. She smiled slowly at my jittering hands. "You're too scared to use that thing. You probably don't even know how."

Suddenly she raised the knife and took a step forward.

I shut my eyes and squeezed the trigger of the Browning semiautomatic .22 caliber pistol.

CHAPTER 35

A fine mist of warm blood sprayed on my face and arms. When I opened my eyes, Dixie was on the ground clutching her bloody right shoulder and moaning. The quilt lay next to her. The blue and yellow patches were turning scarlet, soaked through by Dixie's blood.

The knife clattered to the ground beside her. I stuck out my foot and vigorously kicked it under the bed, beyond her reach. Then I bent down and snatched off her glasses and put them in my pocket.

She moved her head from side to side, moaning, "Help me."

Still holding the gun in one hand, I bent down and shoved the quilt against her shoulder with my free hand. I hated to do that to my grandmother's lovely quilt, but it was already ruined. Even if I could repair the slashes from the knife, there wasn't enough spit in the world to dissolve all the blood that had stained it. "Don't move." I tried to staunch her bleeding. "I'm calling for help."

I stepped around her and ran to the back door to let the dog inside. My hand left bloody smears on the doorknob. Arthur looked at me as if I were a total idiot and hurried around me to the bedroom where he stood over Dixie. One thing Beavers hadn't included in the instruction manual for Arthur was the command for "Don't let her get up." I needn't have worried. Every time Dixie moved, Arthur growled and bared his fangs.

"Good boy." I wiped my bloody hands on my shirt. I ran back to the kitchen, put the gun on the counter, and grabbed the phone. My hands were shaking so badly I had to punch in Beavers's number twice before I got it right.

"I just shot the killer."

"You *what*? Where are you?"

"I'm home. She needs an ambulance. Arthur is guarding her right now."

"Her?"

"Dixie Barcelona. From the Blind Children's Association. She told me she killed Claire and then she chased me with a knife. She's crazy. I was forced to shoot her or she would have killed me, too."

"You *shot* her? With what?"

"Ray's gun."

"I thought I—"

"So sue me!" I was yelling now. "I need help!"

"Have you called nine-one-one?"

"*You* are nine-one-one!"

"Okay, okay. I'll take care of it. Stay put. I'm on my way."

"Please hurry."

Three minutes later I heard the blaring sirens coming closer and closer. A red EMT truck from the LAFD and two squad cars screeched to a halt in front of my house. I opened my door and the medics put down their gear when they saw the blood on me.

"You need to sit down, ma'am. Where have you been hurt?"

"Not me." I pointed them toward the bedroom. "Down there."

Two officers with their guns drawn looked down the hall and saw Arthur. "Call off your dog, ma'am."

"He's a trained police dog. He won't hurt you. Come here, Arthur. Everything's okay now." To my surprise he got up and trotted toward me.

"Be careful. I kicked her knife under the bed."

The policemen came back from the bedroom holstering their guns. "All clear." Then they motioned for the paramedics to go to Dixie.

Another cop sat me down in the kitchen, took out a metal clipboard, and inserted a blank report. "What happened here?"

I pointed to the Browning on the counter next to the phone. "I shot her with that."

"Start from the beginning."

After about ten minutes, the medics wheeled

Dixie out on a collapsible gurney. They'd cut away her clothing and draped a white sheet to cover her breasts. Her shoulder wound was wrapped with a thick pad of gauze that was already turning bright red. An oxygen mask covered her face and an IV line hung on a short pole above her head.

I stood and walked toward the medics. "Wait a minute." I pulled Dixie's glasses out of my pocket. "She'll need these."

Beavers walked in the front door as Dixie was wheeled outside. He took one look at me and his face turned ashen. "Are you hurt?"

At first I was confused, then I remembered the blood on my face, shirt, and hands. "No, no. I'm fine."

"Let's get you cleaned up." He took my elbow and gently guided me over to the kitchen sink. He grabbed the dish towel hanging there and turned on the hot water.

I took off my glasses and pressed the steaming wet towel to my face, welcoming the warmth. Then I dissolved into tears.

Without a word, Beavers wrapped his arms around me and held me while I leaned into him and sobbed. "It's all over." He stroked my head. "But this is your last crime scene, Martha Rose. From now on, you're grounded."

In spite of myself, I started laughing hysterically.

MONDAY

MONDAY

CHAPTER 36

I waited until the next morning to call Quincy because I wanted to be sure I was calm and confident when I told her about Claire's story and shooting Dixie. She wanted to fly back to LA, but I was able to convince her I was just fine. Then I drove over the hill to visit Uncle Isaac.

I arrived at our old house in the Pico-Robertson area of West Los Angeles around ten. Built before World War II, the unassuming little stucco bungalow with a red tile roof sat up from the sidewalk on a modest grassy knoll. I walked up the narrow cement walk and let myself in the front door. My uncle was in the kitchen making a pot of freshly ground coffee to go with a cinnamon *babka* he pulled straight from the oven—my bubbie's recipe. He stood about five feet six and kept his white curly hair cut short. When he saw me, his smile folded his face into delighted wrinkles, and his hazel eyes crinkled. He grabbed my face in his hands and kissed my forehead. "The little bird has flown back to the nest."

I sat down at the familiar kitchen table with a gray Formica top and chrome legs. This was where, as a little girl, I'd eaten my Rice Krispies, cut out paper dolls, and painted with a child's watercolor paint box purchased at Ralph's Five and Ten Cent Store.

Across the room, toward the back door, the pantry doors stood open. The shelves still sagged under the weight of the old Lodge cast iron pans. Time stood still in my bubbie's kitchen. Uncle Isaac cut a generous piece of babka hot from the pan. It filled the house with the aroma of yeast, cinnamon, butter, and caramelized sugar. I was silent for the first few bites, just enjoying the way the pastry filled my mouth with such good and powerful memories. When I was finally able to speak, I sipped at the steaming coffee and described to him the drama that occurred over the past couple of weeks.

Every once in a while he gasped, "Oy! What were you thinking?"

"I'm all right, Uncle. I want to be sure you know that. I wasn't hurt except for my pride when I spent a night in that nasty jail."

He bumped his forehead with the palm of his hand. 'This is what I sent you to college for? This is how you use that brain of yours? Tracking down killers and thieves? Traipsing around like a *meshuggenah*, getting thrown in jail and almost getting killed, God forbid?"

"I started out just wanting to help an old woman whose daughter died. I had no clue things would get so complicated and dangerous. I guess it's like playing poker. I got dealt some pretty interesting cards and wanted to stay in the game to see where those cards took me. The longer I stayed in, the more chips were at stake. In the end it was too late to pull out."

Uncle Isaac got out of his chair and kissed the top of my head. "Thank God you're all right. And, by the way, you'd make a terrible poker player."

I shifted in my seat and took a deep breath. "There was something else I came to discuss."

"What?"

I was hoping this conversation wouldn't end like all the others before it when I'd been lied to or manipulated into dropping the subject. I took another deep breath. "I want to have a serious conversation about my parents."

Uncle Isaac walked over to the kitchen sink, picked up a sponge, and wiped the counter in slow, tight circles. "What's to discuss?"

Here we go again. "Uncle, I'm not a child. I know you've been lying to me all these years. I don't think my parents were ever married, and I'm pretty certain the story of my father dying in a train wreck before I was born is a lie."

He pressed down harder on the sponge. "How did you decide that?"

"For one thing, I've never seen a marriage certificate."

"I told you a hundred times, it got lost when we moved to California."

"So why do I have the same last name as you, Bubbie, and everyone else? Why wasn't I given my father's last name?"

He refused to look at me. "You know why. Without your dead father to take care of you, it was easier to give you our family name."

"I know what you've told me, and I've always chosen to keep my doubts to myself. Not anymore. Now I want to know the truth."

"What's changed? What's the big deal after all these years?"

"During the last couple of weeks, while I was involved in solving the mystery of the quilts, I met a young man who inspired me to find out the truth about my parents—no matter how painful it might turn out to be."

The sponge stopped moving. He raised his head to look at me, and red crept up his cheeks. "I never wanted you to get hurt."

"And I never wanted to hurt you by calling you a liar, but it's time to be honest with each other. You can stop protecting me. I'm not leaving today until I have some answers."

He slowly turned from the sink to face me,

shoulders drooping in resignation. "Believe me, there's not much to tell. You have to understand that because of her condition, we always sheltered your mama."

"What condition?"

"You know how she was, may she rest in peace. Her head was always in the clouds. I don't know how else to describe it. From the time she was a little girl, she lived in another world. She was . . . childish."

I remembered all the times I tried and failed to get my mother's attention and her love. "So you're saying she'd always been remote? I thought she just didn't like *me*."

"No, No! God forbid! You had nothing to do with it. Your poor mama was born that way."

I wasn't sure that made me feel any better.

"Anyway, when she was young, about seventeen, she met a man. From what we were able to piece together later, he took her to his hotel room several times."

"If she was so sheltered, how could that happen? Didn't you ever notice she was gone?"

"Ours was a small town. We never thought anyone would harm her, so we didn't feel we had to watch her every minute. She was, after all, not retarded. Just naive."

I tried to imagine what life must have been like in the mid 1950s in a small midwestern town. Shady streets? Clean air? Lilac-scented breezes in the spring? Friendly neighbors looking out for one another?

"It wasn't unusual for your mama to go on long walks by herself, or sit for hours reading in the library. We just thought she was doing something like that. Anyway, the worst happened and she got pregnant. She was too innocent to understand what was happening to her. It was your bubbie who suspected something was wrong and took her to a doctor.

"Anyway, when your mama broke the news to him, the louse told her he was going out of town to visit his sick mother. He promised her they'd be together as soon as he returned."

My head spun. What kind of man would take advantage of someone like her? Although I knew the answer, I asked anyway. "Did he come back?"

"What do you think? She never saw him again. When your bubbie and I found out she was pregnant, we tried to track him down. Your mama called him Quinn, and the hotel registration confirmed his name was J. Quinn. He listed his permanent address as a post office box in Omaha. The box number turned out to be phony."

"Phony in what way? That there was no such number?"

"No. All the post office told us was that the box wasn't registered to any Quinn and they refused to tell us who it was really registered to."

I wracked my brain thinking of other ways he

could be found. "Do you know what he did for a living? Did my mother?"

"The hotel owner didn't really know. The man was a transient. Your mama said he painted pictures. That's all the information we had to go on, your bubbie and me. Unfortunately, it wasn't enough to find him."

You could have done better than that! "Did you think of hiring a detective agency to track him down?"

Uncle Isaac looked at me with great tenderness and sadness. "No, faigela. Your bubbie and I decided to bring your mother to California to make a fresh start. Two months after we arrived, you were born." He smiled and gestured toward me. "A real native Californian. We made up the story about the train wreck to protect your mama's reputation and to spare you the stigma of being . . ."

I spat bitterly, "A mamser? An illegitimate bastard of a child?"

"Don't say that! We never thought of you that way. You were our whole life."

By now, tears coursed down my cheeks. I covered my face with my hands and cried softly, emptying the tears bottled up inside me for so many years.

Uncle Isaac patted my shoulder. "No, no, faigela. Don't cry. Don't cry."

When I could speak, I wiped my eyes with the back of my wrists. Uncle Isaac handed me a paper napkin for my nose. "Did my mother ever describe him, ever talk about him?"

"We told her not to. We were afraid she'd let the truth slip out. She didn't have the *sechel* to judge what was safe to say and what wasn't, so we just told her not to talk about it anymore."

Well, in at least one respect, I was my mother's daughter. I'd done a lot of loose talking recently that almost got me killed.

The missing pieces of the story began to come together like the patches in a quilt. I now knew more about my parents and about how I came to be, but there was so much more to know. I cried some more for my poor mother, for the pain of Quinn's betrayal, and for the lie she was forced to live her whole life. I wept for my uncle and Bubbie, who devoted their lives to care for my mother and me. And I wept for myself. Born because of one lie and raised on another. Not likely to ever find out the full truth of who my father was or what happened to him.

My uncle patted my shoulder again. "This is why we never told you, faigela. We wanted to spare you. We just wanted you to have a normal life, to be happy. There was nothing we wouldn't do for you or for your mama."

"I know," I choked. So that was that. As far as anyone knew, my father could still be alive. A good detective agency might even be able to find him, but did I really want to go there? Maybe Uncle Isaac was right. Maybe it was wiser to just not talk about it and move on.

I got up and hugged my uncle in a long embrace. His bony old shoulders protruded through the blue sweater he wore. "Thank you for the truth. I hope you know you'll always be my real father, Uncle Isaac, and I hope you know how much I love you and appreciate what you did for me and my mother."

Those old shoulders shook as he hung on to me and wept.

TUESDAY

CHAPTER 37

The following day was Quilty Tuesday again, just two weeks after we discovered Claire's body. I sat with Lucy in Birdie's sewing room helping her cut out wedge-shaped pieces for her Grandmother's Fan quilt. Birdie was using lots of greens and yellows. Each block featured a fan with scalloped edges appliquéd to a background of unbleached muslin. She used a pencil to trace around the template for each ray of the fan while Lucy and I cut out the pieces with our Gingher scissors.

"So what happened after Dixie threw away the baby quilt in the Dumpster behind her building?" asked Lucy.

"Dixie realized she'd never get Claire to change her mind about exposing Godwin. So she went to Claire's house under the guise of working on the auction. She brought some fresh grapefruit juice spiked with drugs. When Claire realized she was being poisoned, she tried to run for help, but Dixie easily overpowered her and forced the rest of the drugs down her throat."

Birdie looked up. "Where did the blood on Claire's hands come from?"

"Claire got manicures every week to keep up her acrylic fingernails. They weren't long, but they were as strong as knives. When she fought back, she scratched Dixie's arms pretty deeply."

Birdie twisted her braid. "So, how did Dixie know about Claire's other quilts?"

"Like everyone else, she read about the upcoming quilt show in the *Daily News*. On opening day, Dixie scoped out the show and found Claire's newest quilt. She wanted to know if Claire wrote anything else damaging to BCA, so she attempted to read the Braille on the quilt but was stopped several times by the White Gloves. The next day she dressed up like a man and stole the quilt. She took ours as well, hoping to make it look like a random theft."

Lucy cut into a ditsy green print. "What happened to your quilts?"

I looked at Birdie, trying to think of the best way to break the news.

"Go on, I need to know."

"Dixie admitted she burned them in her fireplace. The police went through her trash, but the remains were already in the landfill."

Birdie pursed her lips and frowned hard. "They're sure?"

"Yes, Birdie. Forensics found some singed scraps of fabric in Dixie's fireplace. I was able to identify one of them as the double pink from my quilt."

"So then what happened?" asked Lucy.

I picked up a green and blue print featuring little flying swallows with forked tails. "Well, you remember the following Tuesday was when I visited BCA and stumbled upon the baby quilt the homeless woman, Hilda, had rescued from the Dumpster? The same evening, I got a call from Dixie offering to drive over and pick up the quilt. When I declined, she decided to come over anyway and take it from me. If I'd been there, she probably would have killed me rather than leave a witness behind."

Birdie looked up from her tracing. "How did she know where you live?"

"I gave her a donation earlier that day, and she got the information off my check. I also let slip Claire's other quilts were at my house, so I really made myself a sitting duck."

Lucy paused and raised her head. "Fortunately for you, you got arrested and spent the night in jail. Otherwise she would have killed you right then."

"Yeah. Fortunately." I had a hard time keeping the sarcasm out of my voice. "Anyway, on Thursday Dixie came to the wake to see if she could read any of the other quilts, but the guards wouldn't let her touch them."

"So when you offered to give a quilt to the auction, she saw a chance to go to your house and kill you?"

"Not exactly. I don't think Dixie came over with the intent to do me any harm. After all, I didn't have the quilts anymore. I left my translations of the quilts on the counter. Dixie saw them, made a comment, and I realized she was somehow involved. As the pieces of the puzzle started to fall into place I couldn't help myself. Stupidly, instead of keeping my mouth shut, I confronted her. Once she realized I knew what she'd done, she tried to kill me. Even so, I'm glad I only wounded her." I reached for a new piece of fabric.

Lucy shook her head. "I just can't accept that someone who'd devoted her life to helping handicapped children could murder Claire and her unborn baby."

Birdie nodded in agreement. "I know what you mean. Dixie seemed like such a nice person. She must have been crazy to do what she did."

"Yes, I was totally taken in by her, too. Dixie poured her life into BCA. Her work was her whole world. I found out from Arlo she had a rough time as a visually impaired child. She'd lost a significant amount of her vision by the time she was seven. When she grew up, she devoted her life to helping blind children.

"Then on Sunday night I saw another side of

Dixie, the same side Claire must've seen before being overpowered. Dixie thought her life's work was about to be ruined. She became enraged and willing to kill to protect the thing that mattered to her most."

Lucy nodded and pointed at me. "Remember, if it weren't for Ray's gun, you'd be dead, too."

I shuddered at the mention of the gun. "Thank God Joey taught me how to use it. By the way, the police will return the pistol when the case is concluded."

Lucy nodded. "What about the break-in at Claire's house? Why didn't Dixie look for the quilts and the list of quilts right after she killed Claire? Why wait and come back later?"

"Dixie didn't break in to Claire's house. Will Terry arranged that."

"You're kidding!"

"After I left Siobhan's house the first time, she told her husband I was going to find the stories in Claire's quilts. Naturally he didn't want anyone to know those stories, so he arranged for someone to stage a break-in at Claire's and steal the quilts. Unfortunately for him, I'd already removed them. All his hired goon managed to get was the list of quilts Claire kept in her files.

"When he found out his thug had been too late, Will called me and tried to talk me out of looking at the quilts. When that didn't work, he insisted on giving me only three days, hoping I wouldn't have enough time to decipher the stories—if there were any."

"What did he want with the list of her quilts?"

"In case there were stories in the quilts, he hoped to buy them all back under the guise of 'sentimental value.' It was all about damage control."

I started cutting a piece of yellow and green yarn-dyed plaid. "As for Godwin, the media is hot on the scent of a good story. Apparently that wasn't the first time Godwin seduced a patient, especially the pretty or the wealthy ones. Turns out Godwin's wife was a former patient of his, too. She had no idea he was being unfaithful with Claire."

"What a dog!"

Birdie handed over a new stack of marked fabric pieces to be cut. "I'll say. What did she do when he was arrested?"

"Well, when the police asked Mrs. Godwin to corroborate her husband's alibi, Kaplan made sure she knew all about Claire and her pregnancy. I think he hoped to shake the alibi, as they say."

"Poor thing. I imagine she was quite shocked."

"And angry. She threw her husband out."

"And here I thought she was just a 'pretty face.'" Lucy wiggled her fingers in the air. "That young woman gets major points for having the good sense to dump him."

"Well, the media will have a field day with Godwin. He's sure to be disgraced once all the facts of his involvement with Claire are revealed. He may even lose his medical license. Unfortunately, BCA is done for."

"At least there will be a little justice for poor Claire." That was Birdie again, the gentle optimist. "Some of the scoundrels in her life are getting their just desserts!"

Lucy asked, "So, what about Will Terry? How's Claire going to get justice where he's concerned? The statute of limitations must have run out on the incest years ago."

"Yes and no," I said. "The statute has expired on the childhood incest, but the recent incest is still considered a crime. Unfortunately, Claire's not alive to file a complaint. The good news is Siobhan kicked Will out of the Benedict Canyon house the night of the funeral—preventing him from destroying Claire's quilts."

Lucy finished cutting the piece she was working on and put her scissors in her lap. "Good for Siobhan. Unfortunately nothing will have a real impact on the man. He has more money than God and can live wherever he wants."

"It is a shame, but making Will Terry's crimes public would mean exposing Jerry Bell as a product of incest, and Siobhan won't do that to Jerry. She cares for him a lot."

"How do you know?"

"Jerry called me yesterday to thank me for

everything. Told me he has visited Siobhan every day since the funeral. Siobhan learned from the family attorney that Claire left everything to Jerry in her will. They all were completely surprised."

Lucy raised her eyebrows. "Lucky boy!"

"There's more. Siobhan informed Jerry she's revising her will. Jerry is now a very rich man and will become even richer. He told me he and Siobhan plan to set up a multimillion-dollar foundation in Claire's memory to provide psychological and medical care for kids who are underserved." My cheeks heated. "They want me to sit on the board."

Birdie smiled at me tenderly. "Martha, dear, you hardly knew Claire, yet you risked your life to get to the truth about her story and her murder. You turned out to be her best friend, poor thing. Wherever she is right now, thanks to you, Claire must be very happy to see her mother and son are finally together."

"Amen." Lucy smiled at me and picked up another piece of fabric. "So after they took Dixie away to the hospital, what happened?"

"Arlo told Detective Kaplan to take over and close things up. Then he helped me pack a few things and we left."

"The same Detective Kaplan who arrested you for stealing Claire's computer?" asked Birdie.

"Yeah, the same."

"He didn't try to arrest you again for attempted murder?"

I laughed. "He wouldn't dare. Besides, when Dixie's DNA is matched to the DNA found under Claire's fingernails and in the blood on her hands, he said a conviction would be a slam dunk, even if Dixie later denied what she confessed to me."

"So when can you get back into your house this time?"

"Actually, I can go back now, but Arlo advised me to hire a crime scene cleanup company to come in and get rid of the blood first because it's a bio-hazard. The cleanup will happen tomorrow." I looked down and gathered all the pieces I'd cut out and stacked them into a neat pile.

Each time I called Beavers by his first name, my friends stole a glance at each other and smiled.

Lucy put her scissors down again and looked at me. "So, aaah, do you have anything to tell us? You know, maybe about where you've been since Sunday night?"

Sunday night I didn't ask Arlo Beavers to take me back to Lucy's house, even though he told me he and Arthur would drive me and Bumper anywhere I wanted to go. I didn't bother to point out to him I was perfectly capable of driving myself, or that I didn't need to be taken care of. After all, hadn't I proved myself by sussing out the real killer and surviving an attempted murder?

Instead, I looked into his dark brown eyes and

told him to take me home. His home. Warm honey spread all over my insides at the memory of the last two nights. I leaned back in the chair and surrendered myself to the soft chenille upholstery. I couldn't remember the last time my body felt so relaxed and free of pain.

"So?" Lucy insisted. "Where have you been?"

It had been difficult to say good-bye to Arlo this morning. I still felt his moustache tickling my neck as he held me close and could still smell the clean scent of patchouli soap on his wet skin fresh from the shower. But Tuesdays with my friends were sacred. I looked at them with great affection and smiled slowly. "Let's just say Arthur and Bumper are cultivating a close friendship."

"How close?"

I grinned. "As close as you can get."

Please turn the page for an exciting sneak peek of
Mary Marks's next Quilting Mystery
Coming in November 2014
from Kensington Publishing!

CHAPTER 1

Yesterday I joined Weight Watchers for the eighth time. The lecturer Charlissa told me to get rid of all the bad food in my house and take a walk every day. So I did what she told me, confident *this time* I'd work the program successfully.

After a breakfast of egg whites scrambled in one teaspoon olive oil, I bent over to put on my new white athletic shoes. The top of my size-sixteen Liz Claiborne stretch denim jeans dug into my waist-line. No doubt about it. At the age of fifty-five I, Martha Rose, was outgrowing the largest clothes in my closet. I didn't think I could feel any worse today, but I was dead wrong.

I lived with my orange cat Bumper in a friendly residential area of the San Fernando Valley. Directly behind my house stood a fenced off baseball field. A ritzy private school, whose nearby campus had run out of room, had muscled their way in and built a large new stadium on parkland right behind our quiet street.

On the far side of the field, less than two hundred yards distant, the Los Angeles River flowed east through the San Fernando Valley crossing Glendale to downtown LA and out to sea at Long Beach. I planned to walk around the perimeter of the field to the bank of the river and back again. What a mistake.

In the summertime, the air can sizzle by noon. At eight o'clock this morning in late August, the temperature had already reached seventy-nine degrees. Gravel crunched under the rubber soles of my new shoes as I ambled along a dry path just outside the tall chain-link fence around the baseball field and onto the river bank. No bushes were allowed to grow on the near side, the private school side of the river. Only small weeds and grasses parched in the heat. But thick coyote brush, deer weed, and cottonwood trees topped the far side of the riverbank.

Concrete covered the bottom of the river, and the slopes were sprayed with stucco courtesy of the Army Corps of Engineers. In the wintertime, rainwater from the mountains transformed the LA River into a raging swift water death trap. Someone managed to drown in it every year. And after the rainy season ended, the river dried to just a trickle. This day in late August, only a thin thread of brown water inched downstream.

I heard something scuttle through the dense

brush on the far side of the river and looked up to
see the fluffy brindled tail of a coyote just before he
disappeared into the landscape. I also made out
bits of color hidden beneath the larger bushes,
flashes of metal and plastic. I could barely identify
a couple of sleeping bags and what looked like a
cooking pot. I knew those bushes sheltered the
homeless almost year round. I just couldn't detect
anyone there at the moment. The homeless knew
how to become invisible.

As I walked on I spotted a large heap of clothing
about ten yards ahead. At first I thought someone
used this isolated spot to dump their trash. But
when I walked closer I saw the body of a man tangled inside the dark jeans and maroon and gold
baseball jersey. The dark red ground underneath
his battered head crawled with ants and flies. His
jaw hung open at an unnatural angle and I didn't
need to check his pulse to know he didn't have one.

The shaking started somewhere in my knees, and
my stomach pushed up toward my throat. This was
the second time in four months I'd discovered a
dead body. My head started to float away—déjà vu
all over again.

The first time I'd been with my quilting friends,
Lucy Mondello and Birdie Watson, when we discovered the murdered body of another quilter. I was
the one who eventually figured out the identity of
the killer. The guy who worked the case was Arlo

Beavers, a tall, hunky LAPD homicide detective with a white mustache.

Beavers and I have been dating since then, which is kind of surprising since we started off on the wrong foot. He kept warning me to stop poking around the investigation. In the end he was right. Because I refused to stop searching for answers on my own I was thrown in jail and almost killed. After that, I promised myself and my friends I'd just quilt like a normal person and leave the policing to the pros.

And now, I would have to tell him I just stumbled on what was obviously another murder. I wondered how he would react. Still staring at the dead man, I pulled my cell phone out of my pocket with badly shaking hands. Thank goodness Beavers was on speed dial.

"Arlo, it's me. I just found a dead body."